Finding the Kingdom of the Centaurs

FRÉDÉRICK S. PARKER

To my family

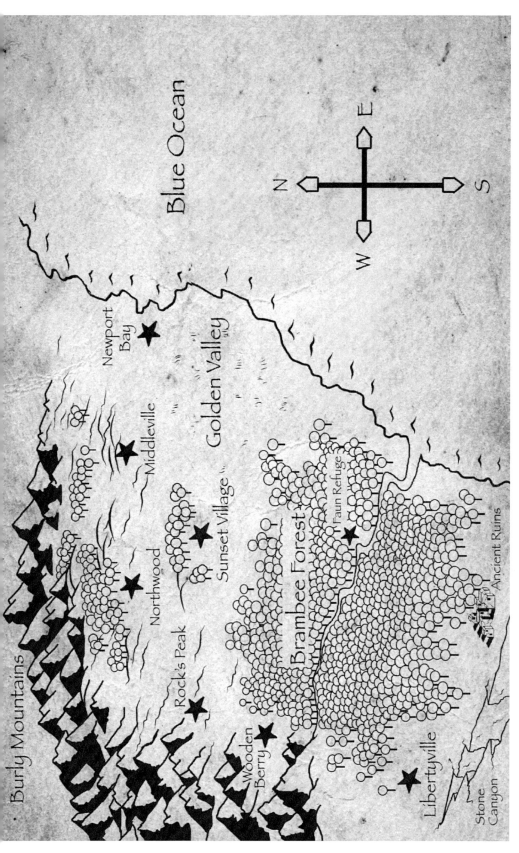

Chapter 1

OLIVER

"Oliver... *Oliver Hamilton,* are you listening to me?"

I didn't look away from the classroom window until I felt a sharp jab in the ribs. I was currently in English 11, sandwiched between my two best friends, Jason Garrett and Jessica Thomas. To my left, Jason sat slumped back in his desk, his right eyebrow raised as he fixed me with a perplexed gaze. To my right, Jessica stared fixedly ahead, a curly lock of hair twirling around her index finger.

"*Mrs. Waterberry is talking to you!*" she hissed when I gave her a puzzled look. *No way!* Slowly turning in my seat, I looked up. Sure enough. Our English teacher, a tall bony woman with equine features was glaring down at me from behind thick black-rimmed glasses.

"Uh, yeah?" Sitting up straight, I tried to look as if I'd been paying attention. That was impossible. It was clear that Mrs. Waterberry had just asked me a question and was now waiting for a response. "Uh..." I glanced around the room, my ears pounding. "Could you repeat that please?"

"I've already asked you twice to open your book to page 124 and read the first paragraph," the teacher informed me, her already thin lips forming a taut line. "But obviously you were too busy daydreaming. Perhaps some time in the principal's office will help you focus?"

"Uh, no," I stammered, my face growing hot as the whole class stared at me, unblinkingly. "I'm sure I can concentrate." I clumsily pulled my literature book toward me, almost ripping out a dozen pages in the process. "I just got a little carried away."

"Just make sure it doesn't happen again." Mrs. Waterberry returned to her desk, deep creases of confusion forming across her brow.

I nodded and started reading from the top of page 124. I could hardly believe I'd zoned out in her class. I was, and have always been, one of her best students. I've never skipped a day or come unprepared. I always pay her my utmost attention and never talk back. And I didn't just have good grades in English; my name has been at the top of the school's honor roll since the beginning of junior high school. But today things were different. Today my mind was consumed.

The moment the bell rang, I jumped out of my seat and headed to the door. Mainly I was trying to escape what had just happened. Joining the flock of students in the hall, my friends and I headed straight for the cafeteria. Due to high attendance at this school, lunch has been divided into three parts: A, B and C. For those who have A lunch, meal time comes immediately after four hour. Individuals who have B lunch go to fifth hour for twenty-five minutes, go to lunch then return to class for the remainder of the hour. And those with C lunch, like us, first attend fifth hour for the full fifty minutes, then head to the cafeteria.

Most students elect to dine at the many fast-food restaurants that surround the school. My friends and I tried eating out once, but unless you're one of the first to arrive, you're unlikely to get your food in a timely manner. Jessica was against the idea from the start based on the lack of restaurants with health-friendly menus, but she was quickly out voted. While Jason had been yearning to escape the stuffy cafeteria for sometime, I was simply feeding a rare salt craving. Long story short, we ended up having to scarf down our health-ambiguous meals on the way to sixth hour.

"What's the matter with you?" Jason asked as the three of us took our place in line. "Your mind never wanders in class." With sturdy eyebrows, thick lashes and a get-all smile, he is classically handsome. His eyes are a light hazel and his jet-black hair is combed back in a modern-day pompadour. In fact, everything about Jason is modern, from his stylish shirts to his name brand shoes. His clothes are formfitting, but not too tight. Just tight enough to show off his well-toned body. The one exception to Jason's modern style is his car. A 1983 Z28. But despite the vehicle's age, it still looks brand new.

I sighed, running my fingers through my hair. I wasn't sure I wanted to tell him what was going on. Jason isn't exactly the kind of guy you confide your innermost thoughts to. Besides, I knew how he felt about my writing. The truth is, ever since I was young I've wanted to be an author. So far, all I have are countless unfinished stories filed away somewhere on my computer, but I refuse to give up. If you asked my friends they'd say I have the world record for the most unfinished stories. And it wasn't even that my stories are incomplete. In my head, I know how they all end. The problem is completing each one before starting the next. Then, some months ago, while I was doing a routine inventory of my more obscure stories, I stumbled across one that I'd written in middle school. It started out as a class assignment focused on self-description from an external perspective. Basically we were supposed to create a third person version of ourselves. I ended up writing about a character named Legion. He was my secret self buried just beneath the surface. My other half. Though the assignment was only supposed to be a few pages long and that's all I'd typed up, in the back of my mind it felt like a much longer story. But scanning the piece, for the life of me, I couldn't remember what it was. This disturbed me.

Not wanting a similar incident with any if my other stories, I decided to finish them all. Since they were all connected one way or another, I'd decided to allow myself one last story. One that would tie them all together. All I had to do was start typing. Only I couldn't figure out where to begin. At first I thought it was a simple case of writer's block, so I spent a few hours each evening before bed brainstorming. But when nothing came to me after a few weeks, I started to worry. Before I knew it I was obsessed. I spent every waking hour trying to overcome this dilemma. But the more I thought about it the harder it became. Before long, I started having trouble concentrating in class. I did my best to hide my problem from my friends, my teachers, and the other students. For a while I think I succeeded. Inevitably, the other shoe finally dropped.

"I don't know," I replied, giving a noncommittal shrug. "I guess I was tired. I was up late last night working on the paper that's due on Friday."

Out of the corner of my eye I saw Jason and Jessica share a look. I should have known better. I couldn't fool them. Having been my two best friends for a long time, they know me better than anyone. I could tell they knew something was up and they wouldn't rest until they got to the bottom of it.

After we had made our way through the long winding lunch line and were seated at our usual table, Jason leaned forward, a determined look in his eyes. "So," he said, a casual air to his tone. "Are you planning on telling us what's going on or do we have to beat it out of you?"

"What are you talking about?" I innocently opened my carton of milk.

Meanwhile, Jessica was casually flipping through her latest science magazine. When she isn't attempting to analyze the thoughts and feelings of unsuspecting students, she is contemplating the cosmos. In her opinion, the better one's understanding of the universe, the more meaningful his or her life becomes. Her unyielding conviction that we are not alone in the universe is enough to intrigue and inspire any young author. Jason, on the other hand, lives in the moment. He doesn't think much of Jessica's views of the universe and he thinks writing is for historians. Sometimes I wondered how the three of us became friends.

"I'm talking about your little episode in class earlier," Jason clarified, redirecting my attention. "You're so serious about your class assignments. If the school burned down, you'd probably commit suicide."

"Not true," I insisted, unwrapping my sandwich. "I'd simply transfer to a different district."

Jason folded his arms on the table, completely ignoring his lunch. "Well, I know how much you hate missing class. Remember two years ago when you got the flu? You made me go to all your teachers and get detailed descriptions of your homework assignments for the whole week and a half you were absent."

"So?" Now I carefully cut my apple into thin slices. "I didn't want to miss any crucial points."

"Look!" Jason's voice elevated as I started peeling my orange. "I know how important school is to you! You don't miss it unless something's going on."

"Nothing's going on," I said calmly, pulling out my English literature book, intending to read the pages I'd missed in class.

"I rest my case." Jason gestured at the book that was now propped up against my backpack, which was sitting on the table beside me. "You can't help yourself. School is your life."

"Since when is that a crime?"

"Does this have anything to do with your little fantasy about being an author?" he asked, his expression suddenly becoming suspicious. "You always get distant when you're thinking up another one of your little fairy tales."

Jessica looked up from her magazine. "Are you starting another story? This is getting out of control."

I tore my eyes away from the pages of my book long enough to give her a curious look. Unlike Jason, when it comes to my passion, Jessica is very supportive. In fact, now days she's the only one I let read my stories. She always said I had a good thing going. Why she was suddenly siding with Jason is beyond me. They are usually at each other's throats.

"What's that supposed to mean?" I asked, setting down my milk carton. "I thought you liked my stories."

"I do," Jessica said, a certain hesitance to her voice as she twirled a strand of long, beige blonde hair around her index finger. "The only problem is that none of them are finished. Sure you have about a hundred good beginnings, but what about the ends? Publishers don't print half-stories. Besides, I just think there are more important things in life."

"Like what?"

"Oh, I don't know," she murmured wistfully, her Hydrangea blue eyes drifting casually to the science magazine in front of her. "The possibility of life on other planets."

"Not that again!" Jason grunted, making a face. "What makes you think there's anyone out there? Don't you think they would have contacted us by now if there were?"

"Just because they haven't made contact yet doesn't mean they don't exist," Jessica snapped. "Besides, what if we're the ones who are supposed to contact them? Ever think of that?"

"We don't have the technology to go searching the galaxy for potential life," Jason said, looking venomous. "And even if we did, why would we spend all our time and energy on something so futile?"

Seeing that things were back to normal between my friends, I blocked out their bickering and, once again, submerged myself in O'Connor's "Good Country People."

Outside the air was chilly and snow, like wisps of icy cotton, clung to every surface. But that did nothing to impede the sunlight that broke through the branches, swaying in a near-invisible breeze. However, all this was lost on me. As the three of us walked home after school, Jason and Jessica were still arguing about the universe, only now they were using phrases like, "spiritual enlightenment" and "just living in the here and now." I was a thousand miles away. All that mattered was continuing my brainstorming. I was sure that I was only inches away from finding a solution. As I ambled down the sidewalk, my heart pummeled my ribcage.

"Isn't that true?" The question came out of nowhere and it was accompanied by a blow to my bicep.

"What?" I was momentarily disorientated. Looking up, I was met with Jessica's inquiring gaze. "Isn't what true?"

"There are hundreds of billions of galaxies in our universe, right?" she reasoned matter-of-factly. "And within each one there are hundreds of billions of stars," Jessica continued without waiting for a response. "I refuse to believe that with those kinds of numbers, our star is the only one with a planet capable of supporting life. I mean, statistically it just doesn't make sense."

"Statistics are just a basis for determining results," Jason grumbled. "Like percentages. Just because the numbers are in favor of something happening, doesn't mean that it will. You could have a 99.9 percent chance of dying from some weird disease, but that doesn't mean you will."

"I understand how percentages work," Jessica said coldly, pushing her hair out of her face. "But there has to come a point when the numbers are so high there is no other alternative."

"Like?"

"Of this we are certain. The universe is made up of billions of galaxies, each one containing billions of stars, all of which are millions of light years apart. Who knows how many other planets there are out there? Seeing as our solar system alone has nine—"

"—Eight," Jason corrected.

"—The possibility of others doesn't seem so farfetched. Most people can't even wrap their minds around numbers like that, so how can anyone even think of questioning the existence of alternative life?"

Jason whistled sharply. "It's a wonder your head doesn't explode."

"There are millions of species on this planet," Jessica continued, ignoring him. "And new ones are being discovered all the time. Do people really believe that life is such an unusual phenomenon? Why can't there be at least one other intelligent species on just one other planet, somewhere out there?"

"Because," Jason stated, a slight glint in his eyes. "Chance would have it that we are alone in the universe."

Jessica's nostrils flared. "You know what? I don't know why I even bother talking to you. You are as intelligent as a television set."

"Oh, that reminds me!" Jason suddenly snapped his fingers, making both Jessica and I jump. "There's this really cool action film in theaters now and I thought the three of us could go see it after school!"

"You are one of a kind!" Jessica declared, her eyes as round as saucers. "The universe to movies in point sixty seconds. *You* are what scientists should be studying."

"Ha ha," Jason smirked, looking un-amused.

"No really," Jessica insisted, studying him with mild curiosity. "How do you do that? What goes on inside that brain of yours?"

It was a nice try on her part. She's been trying to analyze Jason for years now. But of all the people in this city, he is the most closed-off person I know. He refuses to let Jessica or anyone get too close. He lives under the firm belief that if people were meant to share their thoughts and feelings, humans would have the ability to read minds.

"Don't try going all shrink on me," Jason warned, shielding his face with his hand as if somehow Jessica might be able to gain insight by simply looking into his eyes. "I don't care how many other victims you've managed to ensnare, you're not getting in my head."

"Whatever." Jessica shrugged, attempting indifference. "I was just wondering what makes you think we'd go to the movies with you?"

"I got tickets!" Jason said, his voice rising several octaves. "I thought it'd be a good idea to get them before they were all sold out."

"Do you know us at all?" Jessica asked, arching an eyebrow. "Since when do Oliver and I watch movies? Today's television is one of the many reasons the human race is gradually becoming less intelligent."

Jason looked dumbstruck. "What are you talking about? You watch TV!"

"Only educational shows… in moderation. None of that reality nonsense."

"Besides," I added, absentmindedly. "Tomorrow is a school night. There's no way I'm missing class because I stayed out too late. Fridays are when you have the most guaranteed time for homework a part from holidays."

With any luck, a statement like that would convince my friends that I was back to my old self. I didn't need either of them bringing up what happened in English class again. Judging by the look on Jason's face it worked. His gaze shifted back and forth between me and Jessica as if he were struggling to figure out a particularly difficult math problem. After a moment, the look of confused concentration changed to extreme frustration as he continued down the sidewalk, his head down and his shoulders hunched.

"How in the world did I get stuck with you two as friends?" he muttered, a dark look in his eyes as he glared at the pavement. "I can't believe I actually convinced myself you'd be interested."

By then we'd reached Jason's house. He stalked up the front walk without another word to either of us, and, as Jessica and I continued down the sidewalk, we heard his front door slam shut. For a few minutes Jessica and I walked in silence. Then she suddenly turned to me, apprehension haunting her faintly freckled face.

"Oliver, do you think I'm too harsh with Jason? I mean, I'm just trying to get him to open his eyes for once in his life. Is that so wrong?"

The way she spoke made it sound like this was something we were in the middle of discussing and I'd just told her that I thought she was mean and had an evil way of getting through to people. I flinched at her accusatory tone and Jessica immediately apologized.

"I'm sorry, I didn't mean to sound so harsh, but there must be some way to get through to him."

I shrugged. "I don't know. I'm no good at talking to people. Maybe you haven't noticed, but I spend most of my time in books."

"What I'm trying to say is, do you think we should cut Jason a little slack? He's just an ordinary boy living in today's world, and let's face it, neither of us can honestly say we're normal. Jason has been trying to get us to go see a movie with him for ages. Maybe we could do it just this once… for his sake. Ever since his mom left, he's been more and more distant. I've tried so hard to keep him from going down the wrong path."

I knew Jessica was right. The reason the three of us are friends is because things haven't always been like this. Before Jason's mother walked out on him and his father five years ago, things were different. He was different. He has always been a skeptic, but since his mom left he's become increasingly bitter.

After thinking it over, I decided we should probably go. On the rare occasion that I watch movies, I restrict it to the weekends, but if this was just a once-in-a-lifetime thing, maybe it wouldn't be that big a deal. Especially if it meant keeping Jason from going on a killing spree sometime in the near future.

"I guess it couldn't hurt," I finally said. "I just hope we don't have too much homework tomorrow."

"Great!" Jessica looked relieved. "I can't stand the thought of letting him down. I keep seeing us when we were little. He was so light and carefree. Remember how he'd always try to get us to go with him to that power plant outside of town? The one with the high wire fence and the 'danger, high voltage' signs?"

"Yeah," I mused thoughtfully. "He was convinced he would get super powers if he touched one of those converters."

"I remember that," Jessica said with a shudder. "I was sure he was going to kill himself. I tried to convince him that the woods surrounding it were far more exciting."

"Really?"

"Yeah." she stopped as we arrived in front of her house. "I would pretend it was a jungle and tell him stories about the mysterious creatures that lived there."

Just then I had a light bulb moment. The feeling of blinding realization doused me like a bucket of ice cold water. "That's it!" I cried, slapping myself on the forehead. "I know how it begins!"

"How what begins? What are you talking about?" Jessica asked, looking shocked at my sudden outburst.

For a second I didn't answer, still recovering from my epiphany. "My story. I know how it begins!"

"What?" Jessica looked like she was struggling to keep up. "You started another story? Oliver…"

"No time to explain." I was now talking very fast, my mind racing with excitement. "I have to go. I'll see you later." With that I hurried down the sidewalk to my house, leaving Jessica standing on her front walk, looking bewildered.

When I arrived home, I took off my jacket in the entryway and hurried upstairs to my bedroom. My room, which is the first door on the left, could be best described as a parent's greatest dream. Being someone who likes to keep things neat and clean almost as much as schoolwork, everything on the shelves and in the drawers is pretty well organized; all my clothes were neatly folded and my books and music were in alphabetic order. Like Jessica said, we are not the most normal of kids, but what more can you expect from someone who was raised by a mother who has her own rigid views of how a child should be brought up? According to her, anyone who was anyone has a good education, thus a good job. Even though I am most parents' dream kid, even my mother thinks that I have flaws. For example, my desire to become a writer. I have to hide the notebooks I use to record my ideas because she doesn't think an author is a suitable profession. She'd much rather I became a lawyer like her. Then, I too could spend a million hours at work and never sleep.

After entering my bedroom, I set my backpack on the floor beside my bed, reached under the mattress and pulled out my story notebook. So far, I have about twenty pages of quickly scribbled ideas and the occasional doodle of some mystical creature; a many-winged butterfly or a giant but gentle serpent. Before typing any story, I develop as much background as I can. I like to make my imaginary worlds as realistic and detailed as possible. It helps build the illusion.

Picking up a pencil, I sat down on my bed and leaned up against the far wall. Looking over some of the stuff I'd already written down, I started chewing on the eraser. Then, flipping to a new page, I began jotting down notes. All I really needed were key words to insure that I wouldn't forget the main details of my revelation. Now that I had this information, I was finally ready to start the long-awaited story, the one I felt was necessary to tie all the others together.

A couple hours later, after I'd finished my homework, I called Jessica to tell her that I was planning on finally finishing all my half-tales. I promised that this would be the last one before completing the others. I felt that making this promise would make it easier to keep. If I failed to follow through, I wouldn't just be letting myself down, I'd be letting her down as well. I also told her that tomorrow I would have the beginning of my story for her to read.

"I look forward to it," Jessica said and I could hear the seniority in her voice. "Who knows," she added. "The universe is a vast and unpredictable place. You just might make history someday."

Chapter 2

MANDAYUS-CORPUS

I had been staring at the distant stars and galaxies in the vast empty space that surrounded the ship for so long they had started to look like little shiny blurs. The two dimensional screen before me created a perfect representation of the outside world. Those stars may have slipped from focus, but they were still more inviting than where I currently stood. The navigation room is small, agonizingly small and my computer console takes up most of the space. Standing upright, I have just enough room to turn around. The elasty belt around my middle, which is a near-tangible force field, is the only thing that keeps me from connecting repeatedly with the walls every time the ship makes a course correction. All my years at the academy hadn't prepared me for how boring being a navigation officer would be. But I wasn't going to complain. I have been waiting for this mission for too long. At the moment, the most exiting part of my job was every few minutes when I sent computerized messages to the captain, informing him that the stars and galaxies that showed up on his monitor were still millions of light years away. Soon all of that would change. After years and years of tedious data transfers, simulation and verification tests, I was lucky enough to get a place on this mission, the last one for several centuries.

Turning my attention away from the monitor, I decided to remedy my boredom. Using the Virtual Reality Software System, or VRSS, I idly entered the password to my latest daydream. One which involves me successfully navigating the fleet to our final destination, coming to the captain's aid when all the other crew members are indisposed, and saving the day. I was just getting to the part where, having heard of my heroic journey, Emus-Jacqueline proclaims her undying love for me, when the intercom's red light flashed on and I heard the voice of Walmus-Marcus as clearly as if he were standing right beside me.

"Are you going to send the latest coordinates or does the captain have to come up there and get them himself? You do realize we are preparing to engage the Ultra EM 50,000. We would not want to make the jump blind to our surroundings."

I opened communications. "Yes, I am sending them now. Give me a second."

"I know that your father has a high place in the Court," Marcus sneered. "That would explain how you managed to get into the Spacing Academy. How you managed to become a navigation officer is beyond me. With you as our eyes, we will be lucky to make it out of the local sector alive."

"Just a moment." Illuminating a 3D map of our currently position, I did some quick calculations. Acquiring the location of the stars in the closest galaxies, I hastily sent the results to the bridge. "Here are the coordinates." I then removed my finger from the intercom button so that Marcus wouldn't hear the insult I muttered under my breath.

According to him, I am a spoiled, high-class kid who gets everything easy. But my father's position in the High Court isn't what awarded me top marks in my class. I became a navigation officer because I worked hard. I earned my place aboard this ship. Maybe I do get lost in my own imagination sometimes, but I firmly believe I have what it takes to do something great. I was just waiting for my moment. Someday I would be a creator, the most exciting and honored position for any young pilot. The whole reason I joined the Spacing Program. I could just picture the moment when I was named a creator and given the authority to man the most powerful device our race has ever built, Magnum Opus, the machine with the power to create stars.

Save for the necessary measures to ensure perfection, we have developed a device with the ability to do our work faster and more efficiently with the single press of a button. But, just like in the construction of a building, all the necessary steps still have to be taken. First a group of highly trained individuals collaborate on the location and the structure of the new system, then architects lay out the blueprint. Finally computers turn that blueprint into digital information which is downloaded onto a chip. Subsequently a fleet takes the computer chip and the machine on location to finish the job.

A few minutes later, I heard the captain's voice over the intercom as he informed the crew that the ship would be engaging the Ultra EM 50,000 and my heart started racing as I heard the countdown begin; 10, 9, 8… I could hardly believe it, I was on my first mission! I had dreamed of this moment for so long…7, 6, 5… I was on my way to the top, nothing could stop me now… 4, 3, 2… I gripped the edge of the console… 1. The ship shuddered as the captain took it into mega drive. Looking at the 2D screen, I could see the very fabric of space fold in on itself as the Ultra EM 50,000 propelled us forward, taking us to another part of the universe. After a few seconds, the ship stopped vibrating and everything remained completely still. Gazing intently at the screen, I couldn't see anything, just an endless sea of black nothingness.

"It will take a minute or so for space to re-align itself around us in our new location," the captain's voice said over the intercom. "I want all personnel to be prepared for re-entry."

After a few seconds, distant stars began to pop into view outside the ship, and within seconds we were once again surrounded by space. I was just letting out a sigh of relief when the ship gave a sudden, violent jolt. All the emergency lights around the cockpit began flashing like the bio-luminescent spots on a lighting pod. I looked at the transparent image just in time to see the vast shape of a star materialize in front of us. Only this one was not millions of light years away, it was practically on top of us, its gravity slowly pulling us in. The ship began to rock like a boat on choppy seas as we were dragged forward. I started to feel sick to my stomach as the vessel gave another violent jolt. Squeezing my eyes shut I felt the heat in the cockpit begin to rise. It took me a moment to realize I could hear a multitude of voices over the intercom as the pilots and the captain attempted to maneuver the ship away from the G2 dwarf.

This is it, I thought desperately, my nails scrapping the smooth black surface of the computer console, *I am going to die!* Who would have thought my dreams would come to such a violent end? I shook my head. *This cannot be it. I am only 5,000! That is only 5 percent of my life! I still have another 95 percent to go!*

After a few more heart-stopping seconds, the rocking stopped and I opened my eyes. The star was no longer in my line of sight. According to my computer it was now behind us and we were pulling away with increasing speed. Straightening up, I wiped the sweat from my forehead and breathed a sigh of relief. Maybe I was too young to die, but I didn't have time to relax. A moment later, the captain's voice was calling all personnel to the bridge. Swiping a heat sensitive pad, the elasty belt slid from around my belly and its many translucent, web-like straps quickly retracted into the walls. Exiting the navigation room, I hurried down the corridor to the main level of the ship.

When I arrived on the bridge it looked like everyone else was already there. The two pilots and the communications officer were still positioned at their posts, but the rest of the crew was gathered in the middle of the room. Leading the herd was Walmus-Marcus. As I entered, every head turned and I felt my blood pressure rise. The level of animosity that emanated from everyone was so strong I could almost taste it. Furthermore, it all seemed to be directed at me.

"Way to go, Mandayus!" Marcus hissed and I noticed that he used my title name only. In some situations one will address the accused in this manner as a sign of disapproval or disgrace. "Are you the navigation officer or what? You almost got us all killed!"

"What?" I wasn't sure if I had heard him correctly.

"What coordinates did you send me before our jump?" the captain asked, his dark eyes ablaze as he clutched the digital file in his hand.

"Uh, coordinates 56732/24901," I said, my face burning as the entire crew continued to glare at me.

"Are you sure?" the captain handed me the digitally recorded note. "Because this says you typed in coordinates 56632/42901. That takes us to a completely different sector entirely."

I stared down at the 2D file in my hand. How could I have made such a mistake? I was so sure I had typed in the right numbers.

"This cannot be right," I breathed, still not taking my eyes off the translucent numbers. "I do not understand."

"This happened because you spend all your time daydreaming," Marcus said, his arms folded across his chest, a look of utmost loathing in his emerald eyes. "If you spent half the time you do in that artificial reality game of yours as you did actually working, this would not have happened. It is like I always say; respect does not breed brains. Your father might be a great man, but you are pathetic!"

"Angry words will not solve the problem at hand," the captain said calmly. "Obviously a mistake was made, but it will not do to belittle each other. The appropriate course of action is to ensure that this does not happen again."

"I think we should dump him on the nearest planet and be done with it," Marcus grunted. "That is the only way to ensure that he does not screw up again."

"Mandayus," the captain said, not looking at me, "Go to your chambers. We will collaborate on an appropriate course of action for your negligence."

An hour later, I found myself standing with my back to the doors of the conference room. My hands were clasped tightly and my palms were dripping with sweat. It was over. All my hopes of becoming a creator were finished and all because of a stupid daydream. The conference room was usually only used for important meetings or unforeseen disasters. Is that what I had become? A disaster? The captain sat at the head of the long black table. All the key members of the mission took up the rest of the chairs, including Walmas-Marcus. He was seated closest to me.

"Mandayus-Corpus." the captain spoke slowly and deliberately. "The other officers and I have decided that the best thing for this mission is to continue with as few interruptions as possible. We are on a tight schedule and the fiasco that took place a little over an hour ago, not only put the entire mission in danger, but also cost us a fair amount of time. We feel that the rest of this trip would be better off without the possibility of that sort of thing happening again. We scouted the area and there appears to be a planet at close proximity that has intelligent life. As a part of the Spacing Program, it is our duty to analyze and record this sort of phenomenon. You will be given all the essentials to carry out this job and we hope that you will consider it an honor."

"Yes, sir." I felt my heart sink. That's just what I need, to be stranded on some planet while the rest of the fleet went on. It's not often expeditions stumble across alternative life, but when they do, usually it's nothing interesting. At school they showed us 2D images of these galactic worms that were found some thousand years ago. Nobody has found anything really worth scrutinizing. No doubt I was going to be bored out of my mind waiting for the crew to return.

Standing up, Marcus used a 2D projector to flash random images in the air above the table. "One of the most intelligent species on this planet are called humans," he informed me stepping forward. "We picked up and recorded some of their radio and TV transmissions. After we drop you off you may study these transmissions at your leisure. It will make it easier for you to blend in."

"Blend in?" I repeated.

"Yes," Marcus said, giving me a hard look. "This race is far more intelligent than anything we have encountered in this universe. If they see you, who knows how they will react. That is why you must blend in." That's when I noticed the transmorpher. It was near the edge of the table, partly hidden from view. "But do not worry," he continued, picking up the device as I took a step back. "It will not hurt and we should only be gone for three days." Having said this, he aimed the transmorpher at me, passed his finger over the glowing image of a meta-flower and a golden beam of light shot out, hitting me square in the chest.

To my disbelief I started shrinking smaller and smaller. Within a few seconds I wasn't much more than four feet tall. My hands were chubby and long pale yellow hair hung down around my face. After briefly studying my new body, I looked up at Marcus who now towered over me.

"Why am I so small?" I demanded, brushing my hair away from my face. "The humans in those images were much bigger than this."

"Humans do not live as long as we do," Marcus said simply. "If I matched your age to that of a human, you would be a corpse. Instead I did a ratio; your emotional development would make you roughly equal to a 7 or 8-year-old human."

"Why not do an intelligence ratio? Surely I am more intelligent than a human child."

"As a matter of fact you are," Marcus said, scratching his chin with a false air of contemplation. "You are smarter than a human child. Your intelligence equals that if a 30 to 35-year-old, but I thought it would be more fun to do it maturity-wise."

"That is not funny!" I protested, my temperature rising. "How can I walk around looking like this?"

"That is enough," the captain interjected. "We do not have a lot of time. Mandayus-Corpus, we will drop you off in a secluded area not far from a human town. We will give you the basics in case of an emergency and you may pack whatever you need to complete your research. Now we must go."

My eyes shifted to the transmorpher, but Marcus shook his head, a malicious smile spreading across his face.

"Guess again." The glee that radiated from him was sickening. "I think you can stay like that for a few days. It might humble you."

Ten minutes later, I entered the Emergency & Supply Unit with a travel pouch disguised as something called a duffle bag. Illuminating the translucent monitor with a quick sweep of my index finger, I started requesting the items I would most likely require during my time on the minuscule planet below. As I tapped the icon to each gadget, a powerful robotic arm swung into action, plucking said item from its respective shelf. Among the things I packed were a pair of ocular-scopes, a cerebral scrutinizer, and a bio-scanner. In case of an emergency I also retrieved some skin repair gel and, for internal damage, an internal restoration device also known as an IRD. Last of all, I packed one of the ship's emergency nourishment tubes and a few books to keep me occupied while I was away.

Suddenly the door to the Emergency & Supply Unit swung open. I might not have noticed if it hadn't been for the motion in the corner of my eye. Seeing that it was Marcus I immediately looked away. "You know it is customary to announce yourself."

"I just wanted to see how you were doing."

"Leave me alone," I said in my agonizingly young human voice as Marcus closed the door behind him. "I think you have humiliated me enough."

"Hey, I did not make you give the captain the wrong coordinates," he said defensively as he moved to a new location, forcing me to look at him. "I just wanted to wish you good luck. I think you are taking this very well."

I gazed mournfully at the tube of nourishment before shoving it into my bag. "What choice do I have? I really have messed things up."

"I know," Marcus said, his hands behind his back. "But it was no more than what could be expected."

"I know what you are doing," I hissed, narrowing my eyes. "You are always saying what a spoiled kid I am and how I would not be where I am if it were not for my father. If that were true, why are you trying so hard to get rid of me? Obviously I have something otherwise you would not be threatened by me."

"Believe whatever makes you happiest," Marcus said calmly, his hands still behind his back. He was emitting so much joy it was suffocating. "But the only reason I want you out of here is so that you do not get us all killed. It is only a matter of time before you make your biggest mistake yet. With any luck it will have you kicked out of the Spacing Program so I never have to face my own mortality again."

I folded my arms, trying to ignore his euphoria. "What happened earlier was a fluke. It could have happened to anyone."

"I think the sooner you admit that you are a bad navigation officer, the happier you and the rest of us will be." Now Marcus sounded bored. "Not everyone has what it takes. I know this is your first mission, so I think that if you quit now, at least you will not have to live with the shame of actually killing someone on your conscience."

"What do you want?" I demanded, my stomach clenching into a fist. "I know you did not come here to wish me luck, so I would really appreciate it if you would kindly leave me alone!"

"The captain wishes to speak with you before you go," Marcus said, his tone expressing blatant indifference. "With any luck he is planning to make your stay with the humans permanent."

Without another word I turned and marched out of the Emergency & Supply Unit and down the corridor to the captain's quarters. On the way there, I passed the Security Level of the ship. Somewhere down there, Magnum Opus was being kept safe. As I climbed the steps passed the Security Level, I eagerly looked down the corridor in hopes of seeing something interesting, but the passageway was empty except for two large steel crates halfway down the hall.

I don't care what Marcus says, I thought grudgingly as I continued up to the captain's deck. I was a good navigation officer and I was convinced that some day I would be an even better creator. If he hadn't hassled me for the coordinates earlier, I wouldn't have made those mistakes in my haste to get them delivered. If anyone was to blame it should be him.

When I arrived at the captain's quarters, I announced myself and waited for his response. I have never been in his room before and, I must say, on entering I saw that it was far nicer than what I had to live in. Most of the crew's rooms only had enough space for a bed, which we almost never used. In my newly acquired human form if I were to stand in the middle of my chambers with my arms straight out at either side, my fingertips would brush all four walls. But this place was impressive with additional gadgets, books, and curious glass jars, and enough space to accommodate the entire crew. It was everything I could do to keep my mouth from falling open.

"Hello, Corpus," the captain said as I closed the door behind me and I felt a flutter of hope rush through me. Addressing one with only his or her second name is as gracious as just the title name is offensive. In most circumstances it is a gesture of friendship or familiarity. Maybe there was still hope in getting back into the captain's good graces.

"Hello, sir," I said, standing in front of the door, my hands behind my back. "You wished to see me?"

"Yes, do sit down." the captain gestured to the chair on the other side of the desk opposite him.

It took me a few seconds to get situated, but when I was finally seated the captain spoke as if there was no pause.

"I wanted to apologize for the way we are dealing with this situation," he said, staring fixedly at one of his curious glass jars. "I must admit it was not my first choice, but given the severity of the situation, Walmus-Marcus, as my commanding officer, did not give me much of a choice. And the rest of the crew felt it would be safer all around if you were elsewhere while we completed this mission. You do understand, do you not?"

"Yes, sir."

"We are all aware of your father's position in the High Court and hope that this will not affect your feelings toward the Spacing Program. I just want to do what is best for the fleet."

"Yes, sir," I repeated, my shoulders sagging. "I understand."

"Good." As the captain stood up I could sense his relief. "I am glad that you are okay with this whole messy business. I think you have the makings of a fine navigation officer, you just need a little more focus." And he held out his hand for me to shake.

"Yes, sir," I replied, wincing as he squeezed my tiny hand in his massive fist. "Of course."

"Great," the captain said, cheerfully patting me on the back. "Then we should see you in a few days. Good luck!"

Chapter 3

JESSICA

It was Thursday, a few weeks into February. The weather was still cold, but the sun hadn't stopped shining. I got up at seven, just like I did every morning, took a shower, got dressed, and joined my parents at the kitchen table for breakfast. If everything went to plan, I usually had at least twenty minutes with my mom and dad before they left for work. Today's breakfast comprised of soggy French bread and stringy bacon and eggs. My mother isn't the best cook in the world, but she tries. When our plates were clean and I'd kissed my mom goodbye, my parents pulled out of the driveway, leaving me to clean the table. Once all the dishes were in the sink, I grabbed my backpack and met Oliver Hamilton out front. As I fell into step beside him, he handed me a stack of papers that had been stapled together at the top left corner.

"This is what I have so far," he said, looking adorably vulnerable. "I started it before I went to bed last night. I hope you like it."

"You know I will," I assured him, slipping the packet into my backpack. Oliver is always writing stories for me to read and, unlike Jason I actually enjoy his talent. True, he has a tendency to start stories and never finish them, but that doesn't really bother me. I believe in unconditional love and support. Also I noticed that a lot of Oliver's stories suggest that he is still puzzling over his own origins. Most of his characters' fathers are either scarce or nonexistent.

It just so happens Oliver never knew his dad. He left when Oliver was just a baby. As a child, he would ask his mother countless questions about him, but she refused to talk about it and after a while Oliver learned not to bring it up. Jason, of course, has about a million theories about who Oliver's father is, but none of them are very realistic or nice. Personally, I don't think it matters. I'd liked to believe that deciding to abandon one's child is the hardest decision a parent has to make. Whoever Oliver's father is, I hope he had a good reason for leaving.

A couple minutes later, we arrived at Jason Garrett's house. He was waiting for us on the sidewalk out front, a big grin on his face. Last night after Oliver called me, he called Jason and told him we would go to the movies with him. I don't think I've ever seen him this happy before; he didn't seem to be able to keep his feet on the ground. As the three of us walked to school, he kept going on and on about how much we were going to love this film.

"It's going to blow your minds!" Jason declared, clearly oblivious to the fact that neither Oliver nor I were listening. "I mean, if it's anything like the trailer… God, just you wait! Imagine the perfect storm of cinema all in one place! I'm telling you, Jess. This movie will trump that documentary crap you watch."

I might have said something to that, but I didn't want to rain on Jason's parade. He may be shallow and his priorities are completely off base, but at least he is passionate. Still, even I had to admit he was getting a little obnoxious.

"Have you started that assignment that's due in world history?" I was using so much energy to tune Jason out, I almost didn't catch Oliver's question. Looking up, I saw him watching me, his intense eyes searching my face.

"Uh, yes." For a second I almost forgot how to speak. "I think I'm at number seven."

The thing I like most about Oliver is how different he is from other people. If he isn't submerged in some assignment, than he's off in his own world, daydreaming. For whatever reason he seem so secretive, so different. Part of that, of course, is the fact that he hardly ever speaks… unless it is school related, which makes analyzing him difficult. I'd ask him what he thinks about (unlike Jason he probably wouldn't shy away), but when I look into his eyes I get lost in the mystery that resides within. And it isn't just his eyes. Saying that Oliver has medium-length sandy blond hair and almond-shaped, light aluminum grey eyes might sound simple, but words don't come close to describing him. There is something about his entire face that is captivating. It's hard to explain, but he has a sort of natural beauty. I suppose Jason is good looking too, but in a different way. He has the more classic good looks whereas Oliver's are more gentle and down-to-earth.

"If you need any help, just let me know."

"Absolutely."

With a sparkle in his eye, Oliver's gaze returned to the sidewalk. His expression seldom gives anything away, but there was definitely something in his eyes. I wanted to say more, a desperate attempt to maintain the connection, but Jason's voice bursting in my ear caused me to lose my train of thought.

"…And don't get me started on the lead roles. Sure the guy's okay, but his co-star? Man, that chick is hot!"

By the time we arrived on school grounds, I was sure Jason had covered the entire cast and crew. I was getting ready to tell him any more detail and there'd be no point in seeing the movie when he spotted a group of senior girls chatting merrily by the flagpole. The look on Jason's face suggested that he'd like to cast them in his own private film. I was just turning my attention back to Oliver when the first bell rang.

"Come on, let's go," I said, nudging Jason disapprovingly as he continued to ogle the senior girls. "We don't want to be late."

The three of us have most of our classes together; English 11, French II, Science, etc. In fact, the only class we didn't share is fourth hour. I had study hall while Jason and Oliver had art. I decided I'd read his story there. I didn't have any homework, plus the teacher doesn't mind what his students do so long as they're occupied. After saying goodbye to my friends after world history, I headed off to Room 107. I took my usual seat beside Aaron Applegate, pulled out the beginning of Oliver's story, and began to read:

The Kingdom of the Centaurs

The Kingdom of the Centaurs stretched from the foot of the Burly Mountains to the sandy shores of the Blue Ocean. Here, the most rich and prosperous lands were concealed within; shimmering water lapped miles of coast line, a vast valley of golden blades swayed in gentle winds and villages sprinkled the terrain where families went about their daily lives. But the most impressive thing about this land wasn't the castle, with its many towers and beautiful tapestries, or the snow-capped mountains in the distance. Some would say the most impressive part of this region was the Brambee Forest. With vegetation clustered tightly together, the vast jungle was the most lush and fertile place for hundreds of miles. From giant trees reaching as high as two hundred feet to small shrubs, bushes and ferns, the dense woodland was a very beautiful and diverse place. Sunlight was almost completely blocked out except for random patches strewn here and there across the forest floor. Places where golden rays had somehow managed to find a small window in the vast canopy. Apart from the sound of birds singing softly in the branches, the forest was completely silent.

Suddenly the most beautiful creature imaginable stepped out into a small clearing. Standing roughly eight feet tall, the handsome young centaur surveyed his surroundings with sharp, yet affectionate eyes. He knew these woods like the back of his hand and for that reason understood them like no one else could. This is because he was Quaymius, great-grandson to Artayus the Great, and this beautiful forest is his home.

At that moment the youthful lad was hunting silver-tailed deer, a stealthy creature that is very hard to find; only the very lucky manage to get a glimpse of its silver tail before it vanishes from sight.

Quaymius listened intently to the surrounding forest for the slightest rustle of leaves or the faint snap of a twig. In his left hand, hanging loosely at his side, he held a magnificently honey-wood bow. Around his waist he wore a leather belt with a silver, elongated octagon over the middle of his equine chest. His smooth, shiny palomino fur seemed to glow in the surrounding darkness. His hair, which is long and sandy blond, hung over his shoulders and down the middle of his back. His almond-shaped eyes are a light clear grey. Around his forehead he wore a bandana to keep his bangs out of his eyes and a quiver of arrows rested comfortably at his left shoulder. But this young boy's most defining feature wasn't the sword, whose hilt was visible from within its sheath at his side, or his small dark green vest or fingerless gloves. This gorgeous creature's most defining characteristic is the curious white pattern of a flower on his right upper thigh. The tattoo is a symbol of the Flower of Peace, the mark some centaurs imprinted upon themselves to show their allegiance, not to the king, but to the forest and the creatures who live there.

As Quaymius gazed at his surroundings, quite suddenly, breaking the calm air that drifted lazily through the jungle, came the distant sound of hooves pounding the mossy earth. Somewhere within the thick undergrowth, terrified screams could be heard disrupting the once tranquil atmosphere. And, though it was impossible to make out the words, it was clear that someone was in danger.

Out of the corner of his eye, the young Rebel saw a flash of silver as the deer, who had been hiding nearby, took flight at the disturbance. But Quaymius did not go after it, knowing there would be another time to hunt wild deer. Right now there was someone who needed his help. The Rebel slowly drew an arrow from over his shoulder and notched it on his bow. After scanning the trees for a moment, listening intently to the distant cries, he stepped out of the clearing toward the sound of hooves. The farther he moved through the forest the less dense the vegetation became until the trees were well spaced, allowing him to see farther. Now Quaymius could make out what appeared to be a small family of centaurs galloping through the trees. They were being chased by three others. Their pursuers wore green, silver-rimmed capes that bore the black silhouette of a centaur holding a bow and arrow; the symbol of the royal palace. These were King Mytus's men, making their routine search of the forest for any outsiders, also known as Rebels. To those who dwelled within the woods they were known as Followers because of their devotion to the king.

Hot anger bubbled up within Quaymius's chest as he watched the faithful servants slowly closing in on the helpless family. The youngest was falling behind. If he was captured, he would be sent to the palace to join the hundreds of others the Lord of all the Centaurs had locked in the deep, cold dungeon. Quaymius knew that somewhere up there his mother and father were being held captive, all because they did not agree with the king's mad lust for power. The Rebel had been separated from his parents when he was only seven years old and he hasn't seen them since.

Just then the young child, who had now fallen desperately behind the others, tripped and fell. Knowing there was no time to lose, Quaymius charged forward. As he did so, he shot arrows one after another at the Followers. The arrows flew swiftly through the air and pierced, not the Followers' flesh, but their cloaks, imbedding themselves into the nearest tree, pinning them in place.

As Quaymius approached the three royal servants, making sure they were well secured, another Rebel came galloping out of the thick interior of the forest and stopped beside him, her bow also aimed at the intruders. She had long fiery red hair that fell around her ivory face. Her almond-shaped eyes, as green as the surrounding trees, watched the Followers with unwavering disdain. With her high cheekbones and flawless skin, Avril was an incredible sight to behold. But Quaymius was not impressed. The moment she stopped beside him, his grey eyes narrowed and he looked away.

"*You are free to go*," he whispered in Polytaurus to the young child. By now he had gotten to his feet and was staring in awe at his savior. Everyone knew the common tongue, however, for most Rebels it is the only language they spoke. "*These things—*" Quaymius jerked his head dismissively at the Followers who had begun to shift uneasily in their restraints. "*—will not bother you anymore. Go, be with your family.*"

"*Thank you!*" the youngster replied with great relish. "*Oh, thank you, Quaymius,*" and he turned and cantered off into the depths of the jungle.

As soon as the colt was out of sight, the boy Rebel turned to look at the Followers, who were now trying in vain to pull the arrows from the tree in an attempt to free their cloaks.

"*Identify yourselves!*" he declared.

"*Kobalt son of Klem,*" the white guard said at once.

"*Almaeon son of Odessa,*" replied the grey one.

"*And you?*" Quaymius prompted, staring at the last Follower.

"*Arsenic son of Atlas,*" the chocolate centaur grunted reluctantly, a fierce look on his face.

"You will not return to these woods if I release you?" Quaymius inquired, no longer speaking in Polytaurus although his accent was heavy. "You would not want something like this to happen again."

"You think you are so strong," the bravest of the three said, glaring at the young Rebel. "But someday you will be stopped. Just like your great-grandfather." He too spoke in English, but unlike Quaymius, he did not possess a Polytaurian accent. In the Kingdom of the Centaur the quality of one's English determined his level in society. Everyone knew Polytaurus, but if you truly considered yourself superior, you only spoke it in the privacy of your own home. Being a born Rebel, Quaymius's knowledge of the English language is not extensive, but he did understand what the Follower had said. His only use of the language was to show the upper class that he too was intelligent. English-users were usually considered educated and he wanted them to know he was not a mindless savage. Raising his head defiantly, he lowered his bow and took a step forward so that their faces were only inches apart.

"I am simply trying to live my life in this world," he hissed. "I cannot choose who my ancestors are, but by the mighty gods I would sooner die defending these people than follow a king whose laws are corrupt. He is not a man worthy of honor; he kills and imprisons the innocent. For that reason I will allow you to walk from these woods. Not because I am in sympathy with you, but because we do not kill just to prove we are right."

Arsenic glared at Quaymius, but didn't say a word. Then the female Rebel spoke for the first time, her bow still aimed menacingly at the three captives.

"So what will it be?" she demanded. Her accent wasn't as heavy as her companion's, but her voice itself was unusually strong, causing the Followers to blink in surprise. "Will you leave this forest and never to return, or become relics of our most recent victory? I know the king would not be pleased with that."

"We promise to leave and never return," Kobalt and Almeaon replied, both bowing their heads. "You have our word."

"And you?" Quaymius asked, eyeing Arsenic.

For several seconds the brave guard did not speak, he just stared at the two Rebels with cold hateful eyes. Finally he nodded. "Yes, I promise never to return."

"Good man." Avril lowered her bow as the other Rebel drew his sword and cut the strong material of the Followers' cloaks, releasing them.

As soon as the Followers were free, they took off at full speed to the edge of the forest, their tattered and torn cloaks billowing behind them.

"Well, that was fun," Avril said, returning the arrow to the quiver on her back. "We should do this more often."

"*Why have you come?*" Quaymius asked in Polytaurus, not looking at her as he returned his sword to its case at his side.

"I thought you could use some help," Avril replied, watching him with obvious disappointment. "You are always trying to do everything by yourself, but you don't have to. We are all in this together."

"This is not some contest to be won," Quaymius said, switching back to English, his voice sharp. "This is my life and I don't need your help. When my great-grandfather turned his back on the kingdom he turned his back on me. Now I must live in his shadow."

"But you believe in his cause," Avril said, narrowing her eyes. "If it weren't for Artayus the Great, the fauns might have been wiped out."

"I don't disagree with what he did! But because of it, my mother and father are in prison and my grandfather died there."

Avril's green eyes flashing with determination. "If it weren't for Artayus none of you would be here. He made all of this possible by giving us a voice, by giving you a voice. Now we no longer have to sit back and watch as the king breaches whatever boundaries he desires, we have the power to say no."

"In the houses of the young and the innocent my family is a source of shame and ridicule." Quaymius spoke softly, his voice barely above a whisper. "Because of him, I can only enter the seven villages in secret, under cover of darkness. Yes, my great-grand father was a great man. He gave me this life, but in doing so he also took away my choice."

"So you wouldn't have become a Rebel if given the choice?"

"No, if I had been given the choice, I would have *chosen* to become a Rebel."

"Is that it?" Avril fought back the tears in her eyes. "You wish to spend your life in solitude, hidden away from the rest of the world?"

"If I must."

"What about me? What about all the other Rebels? We bear the same burden as you, we face the same consequences if we are caught."

"I have to go," Quaymius suddenly said, breaking eye contact.

"Where are you going?"

He hesitated. If he told her, would she want to come?

"Please," Avril begged, touching his arm. "I swear I will not interfere."

"I've been thinking it over. It is clear that all the misfortune that my family has suffered leads back to the cave."

"So?" she frowned, not sure what he was getting at.

"Aren't there legends about that cave? Haven't there been stories about individuals who have entered it and come out claiming to have seen a world beyond our own?"

"Yes." Avril nodded. "But those are only children's tales."

"My whole life I've lived according to my great-grandfather's beliefs," Quaymius said, folding his arms across his chest. "I have followed in my father's footsteps before me, but all this time I never wondered if there was something more."

"How do you mean?"

"Before, I just listened to what other people said, never questioning any of the stories; this is who I am and this is what I must do. But it recently occurred to me how few Rebels actually believe my great-grandfather ever encountered another world. For many of them it's just another part of the fascinating tale of who he was and what he's done for the fauns. Nobody actually believes he ever saw a human."

"Why would they? The king and many others over the centuries have examined that cave and it has yet to show any passageways to another world. Why would it open up to Artayus the Great and not to anyone else?"

"That's what I intend to find out," Quaymius replied as the two of them headed back into the safety of the jungle. "I think that if I see some of the other stories that have been told about that cave, there might be an answer. The Old Library has thousands of ancient documents. I'm sure I will find something there."

"As a child, a lot of those tales were read to me," Avril said as they arrived at Quaymius's den, a low leaf structure that blended in with the surrounding shrubs. A place that most Rebels used only to sleep and hide. "And I assure you there is nothing out of the ordinary about the way those people entered the cave."

"Maybe," her friend said, pulling only a cloak out of his refuge and tossing it over himself. Now he looked like the beggars who were often seen prowling the streets. "But I want to be sure. There might be something small, too trivial for anyone to notice."

"I don't know." Avril looked uncertain. "The stories all seemed pretty straightforward to me."

"I have to do this." Quaymius pulled a small clear bottle out of a pouch in his cloak and carefully unscrewed the cap. "It's the only way to bring back my family's honor. The only way to free my parents once and for all."

"Here, let me help you." His confidant took the bottle and poured a small portion of the cream-colored dust into the palm of her hand. "You need to be careful, you're running low." Circling around to Quaymius's right side, she gently started rubbing the powder over the pearly white tattoo on his upper thigh. The beggar's cloak covered the boy Rebel's head and torso, but it wasn't quite long enough to conceal his entire body. The powder would ensure that no unwanted eyes would fall upon the symbol.

"When will you be back?" Avril asked as Quaymius carefully arranged the material of the cloak over his upper body to make sure it hid his hair, his bow and arrows, and his sword. "It's not safe to leave the forest for too long at a time."

"I should be back before nightfall," he replied, taking the bottle from her and returning it to its pouch. "But if I'm not, don't come looking for me. It's too dangerous."

"Promise me you will come by my shelter when you get back," Avril said, moving closer to him, her green eyes looking deep into his light grey ones. "I just want to know that you're safe."

"I'll be fine." Quaymius gazed calmly back at her for a moment before taking off through the forest.

Of the seven villages, the young Rebel was heading for the capital. Positioned in the center of the region atop a grassy hill, it is the largest and busiest of the towns. Quaymius had been there many times, but it never got any easier. One mistake and he, too, could be locked in the king's dungeon. If that happened, the last heir of Artayus the Great would be silenced for good. Still, there was no guarantee that the king would imprison him. He had been the rock in Lord Mytus's hoof for a very long time. It wouldn't be that surprising if the king had him executed. It was a wonder he hadn't killed the Rebel's parents. Quaymius assumed this was because the king was trying to lure him out using them as bait. But he didn't care. The only thing that mattered was that his parents were still alive. So long as they were prisoners, he would do what ever it took to free them.

A few houses in, a large wooden sign hung over the stone street. It read: "Welcome to Sunset Village." Quaymius saw this message every time he came here, but he knew it wasn't meant for him. So long as King Mytus was lord of the centaurs, he would not be welcome. Ignoring the sign, the Rebel carefully made his way through the village to the Old Library, one of the few places in town that he had never been. Built into the rocky hillside, the Old Library was very easy to discern amid all the other buildings because it was the tallest and the oldest. Dating back to the dawn of written history, the library was thousands of years old. The entrance was made of white marble that had been repaired and replaced time and time again over the centuries. The two stone statues of the centaurs that guarded the entrance were so worn and crumbling it was a wonder they were still standing.

On entering the Old Library, his cloak pulled tightly around him, Quaymius was once again amazed at the signs of time. On shelves for as far as the eye could see were stacked hundreds upon thousands of books draped in thick cobwebs. Most of them looked like they hadn't been read in years, their contents outdated. Even the guardian who welcomed Quaymius at the door looked like he might fall to dust.

"Is there anything I can help you with?" he asked in a voice that was tired and worn with age.

"Yes," the Rebel replied in a low, but firm voice. "I would like to see all the documents you have regarding the cave at the center of the forest."

"Many have come with that request," the old guardian sighed, giving the youth a knowing smile. "Many have searched for answers."

Taking one last look at the world behind him, Quaymius followed the guardian into the shadowy depths of the library. "So, can you help me?"

"Of course," the guardian replied, leading the way down a long corridor lined with rows and rows of books. "The Old Library has everything. Leave no book unturned and you shall know more than any living soul. The knowledge within these wall could make you very powerful."

"That's a lot of reading. It would take a lifetime."

"If you want anything worth having, you must make sacrifices."

"Have you read all the books in here?" Quaymius arched a skeptical eyebrow.

"No, but then I've never been one for power."

By this time they'd gone so deep into the library, the young Rebel wouldn't have been surprised if they'd reached the center of the hill the king's palace rested upon. Right when he was starting to wonder if they would come out the other side, the old centaur stopped in front of a door leading into a small room whose walls were also lined with books.

"This room contains all the myths, fairy tales, and legends of our people," the guardian said softly. "It also contains stories whose origins are unknown."

Quaymius nodded, gazing solemnly around the room. He felt overwhelmed by all the books that surrounded him.

"Will you be needing anything else?" the ancient librarian asked when the young Rebel didn't move a muscle.

"No," the boy replied, taking a deep breath and letting it out. "This will do. Thank you."

"By the way," the guardian said, observing him thoughtfully. "There are many kinds of powers in this world. The kind that traps people and the kind that sets them free. What kind do you seek?" And in the blink of an eye he was gone.

"Wait!" Quaymius hurried to the doorway, but on looking up and down the hall, the old guardian was nowhere to be seen. Bemused, the Rebel returned to the center of the room and gazed at the books that surrounded him. It appeared that the room was divided in two; English on one side, Polytaurus on the other.

Wow, Quaymius thought, making his way over to one of the shelves, *I hope this isn't all about the cave. It will take me forever to read all of this.* After staring at the many titles for a moment, he saw an old worn-out book entitled *The Tale of the Centaur and the Cave*. He pulled the book off the shelf and flipped it open. There was an oddly new-looking futon in the corner of the room. Quaymius went over and lay down, his side against the wall as he started to read:

The Tale of the Centaur and the Cave

In the Ancient Kingdom of the Centaurs, in a time too distant to remember, there once lived a young boy who loved to sneak out of the village and go on little adventures. No one is really sure of his name. Over time it has been lost to a tide of new titles, but for the sake of this story, he shall be called the Great One, for in his youth he made a lot of fascinating discoveries, including the Land of Mist beyond the Burly Mountains, and the Lake of Dreams. One day, he decided to explore the cave at the center of the Brambee Forest. The young boy set out on his journey early in the morning and was not seen again for fifteen years. When the world had all but forgotten him, he re-emerged, telling tales of a strange new land where a race of beings lived. He went into great detail about how he had just been going on another one of his adventures when he was attacked by a herd of angry griffin and took refuge in the cave. Time and time again villagers examined the cave, but there was nothing to suggest it had supernatural powers of any kind. The Great One spent the rest of his life in exile, refusing to change his story even though no one would believe him.

The End

Quaymius stared at the story for a moment, then flipped to the next page; *Gone But Not Forgotten.* The next story was about a beloved young child who wandered into the Brambee Forest late one night against his mother's wishes and was never heard from again. The gist of the tale was do as your mother says. The last story Quaymius read was a lengthy anecdote about a man living during the Centaur-Leviathan Wars. He managed to avoid enslavement by escaping into the jungle and entering the cave. He also was never seen again. When the Rebel finished the story it occurred to him that he had no idea what time it was. In the heart of the Old Library there could have been a hurricane outside and he wouldn't have known. Frustrated that he had spent what could only have been hours reading countless fairy tales, and still had nothing to show for it, the Rebel got to his feet and re-shelved the books.

It seemed to him that his journey had been pointless. A lot of those stories stated that they were based on other stories, which were probably based on yet earlier ones. It was hard to tell which tales were genuine and which weren't. It would take Quaymius forever to find the originals. He didn't even know where to look. But as far as he could tell, the cave's powers, assuming that it had any, were truly mysterious and unpredictable. Obviously the cave wouldn't reveal its secret to just anyone. The key was figuring out who it would open up to. In his youth, Quaymius, with his best friends, Duke and Naomi, had visited the cave many times, but it had appeared as nothing more than an empty cavern. The Rebel had long since given up hope of ever entering it.

So, with a heavy heart, he left the library. Just as he'd feared, night had fallen. The king always had his guards patrolling the streets at night, on the lookout for anything unusual. Getting back to the forest would be difficult, but not impossible.

Quaymius moved quietly through the shadows of the small shops and boutiques that lined the streets. Whenever a guard came into view, he would press himself flat against the side of the nearest building, hoping that they wouldn't see his pearly white tail amid the shadows. After an hour of weaving between and around buildings, Quaymius finally made it to the edge of town and took off down the hill and across the valley toward the forest. At night the tall trees looked eerie and foreboding, but the young Rebel knew it was the only place where he was safe. When he finally returned to his shelter he was so overcome with exhaustion, frustration, and disappointment any thought of seeing Avril had completely slipped his mind.

The next morning, Quaymius woke up bright and early as usual to go meet his friends at the riverbank and catch them up on everything that happened the previous night. He knew that Duke and Naomi would be eager to find out what he knew. Unfortunately he didn't have anything interesting to tell them. But he set out to the river anyway, in need of something to lift his spirits.

Of all the inhabitants of the Brambee Forest, Quaymius spent the most time with Duke and Naomi. The Rebel had known the faun since they were little. Except for his mother, Duke's entire family had been captured by the king's men. Thanks to Quaymius, they, like so many other forest dwellers, owed him their freedom. Naomi, on the other hand, was one of the few sea folk to owe the centaur her life. The Realm of the Mermaids and the Kingdom of the Centaurs had very little communication. But seeing Naomi under attack by an angry sea demon, Quaymius plunged into the Blue Ocean and saved her. Now the three of them haven't been apart for more than a week.

The young Rebel was somewhat of a hero in the eyes of many, but whatever services he provided didn't change him in the slightest. He was never pompous or proud. Sure his adventures changed him. After his parents were captured he was forced to grow up pretty fast, but in most respects he was just as modest as ever.

When Quaymius finally arrived at the riverbank, Duke and Naomi were already waiting for him. The faun was seated on his usual perch atop the large black rock that stood near the edge of the water and Naomi was sitting on the grassy bank, her powerful orange tail swishing back and forth in the rushing water.

"We were beginning to think they'd finally got you," Duke said, looking up as Quaymius stepped into the clearing. "We were getting ready to send out a search party."

"They'll never take me alive," the Rebel replied, but only half-heartedly. He still couldn't get his mind off the dead-end road of the previous night.

"What's wrong?" Naomi asked, seeing the troubled look in his eyes. As she spoke, she twirled a long golden lock of hair around her finger. It was a rather intriguing habit she had developed in the five years that Quaymius had known her. "You look down," the mermaid continued, surveying the centaur with concerned blue eyes. "You did find something interesting last night, didn't you?"

"Not really," Quaymius said wearily. "I spent hours in that library, but nothing seemed to add up. There are hundreds of stories about the cave. Some of the individuals came out of it a few years later, while others were never heard from again. The only pattern I saw was all who entered seemed to be young. But even we couldn't get in so that can't be the key."

"Maybe you're just thinking about it the wrong way," Naomi said thoughtfully. "Maybe it's something more subtle than age, something symbolic."

"Like what?" Duke demanded, a sarcastic air to his tone as he swept his shiny black hair straight back. "The color of their fur? What could possibly be symbolic about entering a cave?"

"Maybe if you thought about it for two seconds you could figure it out," Naomi said, narrowing her eyes. "Instead of always finding something to ridicule or sneer."

"Well, it's easy to sneer when every word that comes out of your mouth is gibberish," Duke shot back, his usually good looks twisted into an ugly smirk. "But I don't know why I'm surprised. You're always speaking gibberish."

"It only sounds like gibberish to those who don't know anything," Naomi said hotly, folding her long pale arms and sticking out her chin. "People like you."

Duke opened his mouth to retaliate, but Quaymius stepped forward, intervening. "Guys, I think we're getting off point. We're supposed to be thinking of a way to enter the cave. If we could somehow bring back some evidence that humans exist, the king would have no choice but to admit he was wrong and free us once and for all."

Duke arched a skeptical eyebrow. "Quaymius, there has never been any proof that humans even exist. They are just another part of the fairy tales that have been circulating through centaur history for thousands of years."

"I don't know," Naomi mused. "In every story I've heard, each person who returns from his or her adventure tells of strange, two-legged creatures. That sounds pretty consistent."

"Yeah, but less than half the people who wander into the cave actually get a chance to tell their story," Duke reminded her. "The majority of them disappear without a trace."

"Which is also consistent," Naomi pointed out. "I know there's some kind of pattern here, if only we could all go up to the library together."

Quaymius shook his head. "It's too risky. The king's guards know you guys are my friends. If they see a centaur, a faun, and a mermaid all heading into the Old Library together, they're sure to get suspicious."

"So what do we do?" Duke asked. "It sounds to me like stalemate."

"I don't know." Quaymius thought it over. "Some of those stories have to be true. There has to be a specific way to enter the cave. I just can't figured it out. I think the key is finding someone who can."

When I finished the story, I folded it up and returned it to my backpack. Over the years I've read a number of Oliver's tales, and though he usually has a pretty large variety of subject matter, I couldn't help noticing that most of them circle around centaurs. That didn't bother me. I enjoy reading all his stories, I just hope someday I get to finish one. My favorite story is called *Lord of the Centaurs,* which is about a young prince named Arcron. From what I got to read, he was on his way to becoming one of the greatest rulers in history. I don't know why, but something about centaurs seemed to fascinate Oliver. Hopefully, whatever his obsession, this story would be the last before he finished the others. I can't wait to see what happens with Prince Arcron.

As for this new story, *The Kingdom of the Centaurs,* it was really good. I was eager to tell Oliver what I thought. When the bell rang ending fourth hour, I gathered my stuff together and headed to English 11. Like our teachers, I knew Oliver doesn't like disruptions, so I just gave him the thumbs up as I took my seat. I would wait until lunch before giving him any in depth opinions.

"Okay," Mrs. Waterberry said as the final bell rang and everyone was seated. "Now that we've finished 'Good Country People,' I would like some healthy discussion before we continue on to our next short story. And, no, you do not get to choose your own groups." Her gaze momentarily rested on Jason. "The last time that happened there was more conversation than deliberation. When I call your name get with your groups as quickly as possible. Goodwin, Charleston, Bentley, and Freely." Desks squeaked as the four hastily united. "Thomas, Hamilton, Summers, and Waterhouse." Giving Jason a goodbye wave, I turned my desk to face Oliver's while Leslie Summers and Wendy Waterhouse came over to join us. Meanwhile, Mrs. Waterberry continued calling groups. "Garrett, Masters, Jackson, and Mills." Out of the corner of my eye I saw Jason make a face as he was paired with the only other student in this class who was as driven as Oliver. George Masters. I like him because he shares my views on the existence of alien life. Jason doesn't because George is convinced that he was abducted. Furthermore, he isn't shy about it and will tell anyone willing to listen.

"Okay," Oliver said, taking charge as he cracked open his literature textbook. "Let's start with characterization."

*   *   *

When the bell rang, signaling C lunch, Oliver and I waited outside the classroom while Jason assured Mrs. Waterberry that his paper would be ready to turn in on Friday.

"So you liked it?" he asked, glancing in the doorway to make sure our friend was still occupied. "You thought it was okay?" He didn't let on, but I knew he was referring to his story.

"I thought it was great!" I said enthusiastically. "It was really something."

"Really?" From his expression it was clear he wasn't sure if I was just telling him what he wanted to hear. "Do you really mean that?"

I looked him straight in the eye. "Oliver, you know I like your stories. You don't need to second-guess yourself."

"So everything flowed smoothly?"

"Yes. I only have one question and it's regarding name pronunciation. This Avril character, is that Avril like Avril Lavigne?"

A faint smile fluttered across his lips. "Actually, I was thinking more along the lines of the French word for April. I thought it sounded nice."

"What sounds nice?" Jason asked, stepping out of the English classroom to join us.

"Nothing." Oliver shifted his backpack on his shoulder. "Come on, let's go to lunch."

On the way to the cafeteria, Jason grumbled irritably about George. Apparently their discussion session didn't go well. "Can you believe that guy?! He accused me of being crazy. Me! I'm not the one telling everyone I was abducted."

"You were supposed to be discussion the short stories," Oliver pointed out.

"Yeah, well, we got a little sidetracked."

"You know, he could be telling the truth." I noted. "Just because something sounds insane, doesn't mean it is."

"Yeah, right," Jason snorted. "If aliens were real and they did decide to come here, why would they abduct George of all people? Perhaps they find severe acne fascinating."

I shook my head despairingly. "Jason…"

Oliver brushed my arm, signaling that I should fall back, allowing our self-absorbed friend to drift ahead. "He's beyond our aid."

"You may be right."

"Tell me more of what you think… about my story."

"I think it's incredible how much detail you put into everything," I said under my breath as the three of us made our way through the lunch line. "It's clear you've put a lot of thought into it."

"Yeah," Oliver sighed, glancing at Jason who was trying to score an extra corn-dog from one of the lunch ladies. "I've been working on the background information. At home I have this old notebook full of ideas."

"Wow," I breathed. "You're really making this into a whole other world. When I read it, it was almost like I was there."

After we got our lunch, we went to our usual table and sat down.

"She likes me," Jason said out of the blue as he stared passed me at something on the other side of the room.

"Who?" I asked skeptically. "Not the group of seniors you were ogling this morning?"

"No. Well, yes, but I was talking about that lunch lady."

"Tabitha?" Oliver raised an eyebrow.

"No." Jason looked put-off as he picked up his extra corn-dog and waved it in our friend's face. "Amanda. I'm pretty sure she's got the hots for me."

"You're a good-looking guy," Oliver said absentmindedly, squeezing dressing onto his salad.

"You know it," Jason said with a wink.

I dipped my corn-dog in a pool of ketchup. "I think the main reason you have trouble finding a girl—"

"—Who says I have trouble finding girls?" A crooked grin spread across Jason's face as he gestured around the room.

"That's *willing* to go out with you," I continued. "Is because of your attitude."

"What attitude?" A suggestive smile spread across his face as I licked the ketchup off the end of my corn-dog.

"That's what I'm talking about," I sighed, setting my corn-dog back on my tray and folding my hands on my lap.

"What?" Jason asked with false innocence. "I don't know what you're talking about."

"Not only are you vain and degrading, when it comes to sex you have the IQ of a male goat."

"Not so," Jason said, running a hand over his slick black hair. "I have lots of charm."

"Yeah, right," I scoffed, twirling a lock of hair around my index finger. "I can see it simply oozing off you."

"Speak for yourself," Jason grunted. "Why do you always do that with your hair? That's not attractive."

"You know what?" I snapped heatedly. "People like you are too quick to point out the flaws in others, failing to acknowledge the flaws within yourself. Why do you have to be so insensitive?"

"What are you talking about?" Jason demanded, looking taken aback. "You just said I was an egotistic, sex maniac with no charm and an attitude problem."

"No, I didn't," I hissed, glaring daggers at him as I scooped up my tray. "I would never stoop to that level! I was simply stating that there are aspects of your personality that could use improvement. Besides, even if I had said what you think I said, *which I didn't*, there's a difference between saying something to help someone as opposed to saying it just to be mean. I can't believe I actually felt sorry for you! You should consider yourself lucky that Oliver and I decided to go see that movie with you. Just because your mother walked out on you, doesn't mean you have to condemn the whole world!" With that I turned and stalked away.

I threw my untouched lunch into the nearest trash bin and hurried from the cafeteria. My heart was pounding hard as I stopped outside the doors, trying to catch my breath. Jason and I argued all the time, but it has been a long time since I've been that angry at him. Sometimes I wish he would accept that his mother is gone and not let the anger turn him into something ugly. There was a time when Jason was friendly and I enjoyed being around him. Not anymore. But no matter how aggravating he could be, I knew I had no excuse for yelling at him like that. Sooner or later I would have to apologize. Until then we would act as if nothing had happened. That's the way it always was.

Chapter 4

I watched grudgingly from under a tree whose bare branches wound like the tentacles of a Plexian as the ship took off, leaving me behind. This had to be the worst thing that has ever happened to me. I couldn't believe that after years of preparation I'd managed to botch things up so badly. Why do I always get so lost in my own imagination? Why do I make it so easy for Marcus to find ingenious ways of making my life worse? *Well, we will see about that*, I thought bitterly to myself as I swung my duffle bag over my shoulder. The next time I saw Marcus, he was going to be sorry. I was going to do something so amazing and wonderful there was no way the captain or any of the crew would remember my mistakes. I couldn't wait to see the look of shock on Marcus's face when the Academy named me a creator. Brimming with newfound confidence, I turned and started down the road toward the lights on the horizon.

It was almost nightfall when I reached the outskirts of town. Because of my temper, I decided to hold off my research until morning. After all, according to my studies, the dominant species on this planet slept during the night. I'd have much better results if I waited until daylight. In the meantime, I would go over my *Space Navigation* book and see if I could find anything on boredom since that's what got me into trouble in the first place.

When I was a good ways into town, I found a dark secluded place between two buildings to read my book. After I passed a few hours touching up on my navigation information guide, I pulled out the recorded information about humans and started going over it again. The recorded data told me a lot about the race. There were details about their different languages and cultures, their views and belief systems, what they liked to eat and their sources of entertainment. It was almost morning before I got to the end of the recording. When the 2D projector shut down I put it back in my bag. The yellow light source was starting to rise. If I wanted to make an amazing discovery about this planet, time was of the essence.

Walking down the street, the first thing I noticed were the various modes of transportation. Vehicles of all shapes and sizes crowded the streets. Back home I have seem very similar, self-propelled machines in virtual museums. Like everything else on this planet, public and private transportation were very primitive. Restricted to the ground, they were large, slow, and didn't maneuver easily. Based on the fumes that wafted from the back, I deduced that they operated on some kind of combustible substance. Doing a quick analysis, I discovered that these vehicles ran on refined petroleum. Despite pressure form neighboring civilizations, there were species within my universe who also used combustible elements as a source of fuel. From what I understood, such substances could be very unstable.

Next, I turned my attention to the environment. The oxygen levels on this world were far lower than my home planet. Surviving here in my true form would be possible, but highly impractical. However, despite less oxygen, there was a far higher plant life to human settlement ratio. Within city limits there were a number of locations sectioned off specifically for the growth of vegetation. Trees could be found everywhere and grass grew in large rectangular patches in front of business and residential homes. At the moment everything looked lifeless; the trees stood bare while the grass was dry and depleted. According to my data, this region was currently experiencing winter: a curious cycle of death and rebirth. One of its symptoms was fluffy white flakes that fell from the sky. I have visited many ice worlds in my time, but they were nothing like this.

Turning my attention away from the environment, I started focusing on the governing species of this planet. Humans. Everything about these creatures was different; the color of their eyes and hair. Their small stature, the complexity and brightness of their clothing as well as the roughness of their skin. I noticed that a large majority of humans suffered from a wide range of blemishes. Some of their faces were speckled while others had constellations of red bumps. The bumps were more common in the juveniles, however, the occasional adult did suffer from the same affliction. But all of this was secondary. It only took a few hours of observation for me to learn that this species had a number of odd behaviors, most of which they would partake in when encountering each other. Given their similarity to my kind, I was surprised at the level of physical contact they made with each other. In fact, a large part of their interactions involved some form of touch. Some of these behaviors included, but were not limited to, pressing their mouths together for varying amounts of time, wrapping their arms around each other or walking down the street hand in hand. Of all the strange behaviors I witnessed, the only one I recognized was the hand shake, which was used at almost every encounter and appeared to have an insurmountable number of complex variations. The most elaborate arising among the youth.

After several hours of research, watching the humans started feeling less like a chore. As the yellow light source passed its highest point, I started enjoying myself. Walking down the streets, I watched the local inhabitants in everything they did. I discovered that depending on where I want their clothes and behaviors changed. Outside tall reflective buildings they wore greys and midnight blues while speaking on crude communicators. Downtown, flocking around various drinking establishments, they dressed in black, ranting angrily and playing loud music, a spectrum of images spiraling up and down their arms. Near the schools they sported a range of colors, their voices lighthearted and joyful as they moved in corresponding clusters. I really wanted to try talking to one of them, but the Spacing Program strongly discourages direct contact with alien life forms with high levels of intelligence. So far, I was impressed. This was not at all the burden I'd expected. When they saw my report, the Spacing Program would definitely want to do further research on this species.

After spending all day studying the humans, I decided to take a break and document the other inhabitants of this planet. It was amazing how different these beings were from each other. As the day came to an end, I found myself standing at the edge of a large parking lot, trying to get a better look at some sort of insect on the bark of a tree. I was just increasing the power on the ocular-scopes, when someone spoke to me.

"Hey! Whatcha doing?"

Turning around, I found myself face to face with three young humans. In my new form they were taller than me, however, they were still juveniles. The female had long curly hair that hung passed her shoulders. There were two males, one standing on either side of her. One had hair as black as the night sky, the other was tall and slim. Unlike his friends he wasn't looking at me. Instead he stared off into the darkness, a distant look in his eyes. Using deductive reasoning, I concluded that the shorter of the two males had addressed me. *Oh no*, I thought, my heart beating faster as the girl took a step toward me, concern dominating her lightly speckled face. *If the crew finds out I communicated with this species, I will be in even bigger trouble.* Ignoring her, I picked up my bag and turned to go.

"Should you be out here all alone?" the girl inquired, determined to get my attention. Meanwhile the boy with black hair stepped forward to pick something up off the ground. "Where are your parents?"

I turned to look at her. She was standing roughly six feet away. Even in the dimming light I noticed that her eyes match the color of the sky during the day. I knew I should go, but I couldn't fight the curiosity. I have traveled to the four corners of my home galaxy and encounter beings of all shapes and sizes, but it never got old. I was still wrapping my mind around human's amazing intellect. It was nothing compared to that of my own kind, but it was still very impressive. I wanted a first-hand account of this race's intelligence.

"My parents are not here," I replied, remembering that to them I looked like a much younger version of their kind.

"You mean your mother lets you walk alone at night?" the human girl's eyebrows shot up illustrating her disbelief. "That's incredibly dangerous!"

I stared at her, not sure what to say. Apparently young humans did not wander around on their own. I needed to think of something fast. I may have spent the last twelve hours analyzing these people, but I still had a lot to learn. By now I was familiar with the way they spoke, but their vernacular was very odd. Looking up at this girl, I could tell she was awaiting a response. So far I had nothing. I didn't know much about humans in their private lives. If I tried to fake it, I could inadvertently arouse suspicion.

"I guess you are right," I said after a brief pause. "It is dangerous to walk around at night. My mother should know better."

I decided it was best if I got out of there as soon as possible. At this rate, it would not be long before they discovered my secret. I turned to leave when the black-haired boy called out to me.

"Wait! You dropped something."

I turned to look at him and saw, to my horror, that he was holding Magnum Opus in the palm of his hand.

Chapter 5

JASON

It was Thursday, the 22nd of February. I told my friends to meet me at my house at 7:45. They had agreed to come, but I wasn't sure if they'd show. For years I've been trying to get Oliver Hamilton and Jessica Thomas to go to the movies with me. Until now, they've always declined. Finally the impossible has happened! Sitting alone on my front porch I waited. Right when I was starting to think I'd blown it with all that movie talk, I saw my two best friends meandering down the sidewalk toward my house. Breathing a sigh of relief, I jumped up and came down to meet them. From afar, it might seem like talking a couple of normal high school students into going to see a film would be an easy task, but the truth is, it wasn't. First of all, Oliver and Jessica are not normal; they are the opposite of normal. Me, I like to do what every 16-year-old likes to do; watch movies, hang out and just basically have fun. The usual.

"You guys are not gonna regret this," I said, probably for the hundredth time as I joined them beside my car.

"So you keep saying," Jessica sighed, glancing at Oliver. "Come on, let's get this over with."

"Hold on." I held up a hand as she reached for the passenger's side door. "First things first. When was the last time either of you've seen a movie?"

"We watch them in school all the time," Oliver said with a shrug.

"I mean at the theater."

"That field trip in third grade!" Jessica blurted out as if this were a contest.

"Wow! That was eons ago." I turned my attention to Oliver. "And you?"

"My grandmother took my to see a movie when I was eleven. I guess it's been five years."

"You guys have a lot of catching up to do," I mused, opening the driver's side door.

Once we were all strapped in and I was pulling the car out of the driveway, I took an easy breath. Until last night I thought I'd purchased those tickets for nothing. Sure I could easily find someone else willing to accompany me, but I really wanted it to be my two best friends. Lately they were the only people I felt like hanging out with. As we pulled into the theater parking lot, I felt the need to document this occasion. As far as I knew, it would never happen again. My hands shook with excitement as my friends and I climbed out of the car and headed across the parking lot toward the theater. As we approached the front entrance, bypassing the long line to the ticket booth, Oliver looked warily at the poster for our show before wordlessly sliding his hands into his coat pockets and following me inside.

"Wow!" Jessica gasped as we entered the lobby, gazing over her shoulder at the people outside. "We're lucky you got those tickets in advance, otherwise we'd be here all night." I'm not sure where to start with her. She is a paradox wrapped inside a vortex cramped into an anomaly. The way Jessica probes people's minds makes me think she'll make an excellent therapist someday. She talks about the universe the way popular girls talk about fashion. In truth, I didn't know how her mind works. Describing Jessica's physical appearance is much easier. In a nut shell, she has long blond hair and blue eyes, but she is far from your average Barbie doll. For starters, her hair is a light beige blond. Not platinum. Very reminiscent of Meg Ryan in *Prelude to a Kiss*. Her eyes are lagoon blue and she has a few freckles sprinkled across her nose. Believe me there is nothing plastic about her. Unlike most of the girls who go to our school, Jessica makes absolutely no attempt to blend in; her clothes speak for themselves. She wears scarves, regardless of the weather. Dull colors mostly. Like greys and browns, but she has been known to sport a bright turtle green, or a bubble gum pink. She's never worn make-up a day in her life. The only thing I've ever seen her put on her lips is Chapstick. And the only jewelry she wears is a single silver star in each ear. When it comes to clothes, nothing Jessica wears seems to match, but somehow she pulls it off. Today she had a dark-grey wool scarf wrapped around her neck and she was wearing a beige long-sleeved suede jacket over a bright orange tank top and dark blue jeans.

"It's got nothing to do with luck," I said coolly, running my fingers through my hair. "Years of experience has taught me exactly how the cinema world operates."

As much as I would have liked to see this film on opening night, I'd decided to wait a week or so before coming. Not being traditional moviegoers, I didn't want Oliver and Jessica to get overwhelmed. It being Thursday would also help tone things down. In my opinion, going to the movies is like learning to swim; if you jump in too deep you may drown.

"Do you guys want anything to eat or drink?" I asked, turning to the others to make sure they were doing okay.

"No thanks, I'm fine," Jessica replied, looking around. "Oliver?" But he didn't answer. He was gazing at an undefined point on the far wall, once again lost in thought. Sometimes when I look at him I forget he's just a kid. He always looks so serious. Very Buster Keaton-esque. People are surprised to learn that Oliver has a wild imagination. But like Jessica, he also teeters on the edge of bizarre. With high cheek bones and pale grey eyes contrasting against light caramel skin, he has a look for the ages. But even more weird, Oliver is a school fanatic. He brings home the kind of report cards most parents kill for. If he's ever received an A- or less, I must have blinked and missed it. When he isn't acing an algebra test or completing a seven-page research paper in one night, he's lost in his own fantasy world, dreaming up some crazy fairy tale.

"So what time does the movie start?" Jessica asked, looking away from him.

"Uh, nine o'clock," I replied, glancing at my watch.

"What?!" Jessica looked up at the big clock that hung over the lobby entrance. "But, that's forty minutes from now!"

"What's forty minutes from now?" Oliver asked, momentarily coming out of his stupor.

"Jason brought us to the theater forty minutes before the movie even starts," Jessica said, looking irritated. "Why did we have to come so early?"

"Yeah," Oliver agreed, though he didn't look annoyed. "The arrow that indicates our show is now seating hasn't even lit up yet."

"What are we supposed to do for forty minutes?" Jessica demanded.

"First of all, let's move over here," I said, guiding my friends to the left of the concession stand. Now we stood at the hall entrance that lead to the individual screens. It was currently blocked off by a thick velvety rope that passed between two sliver stanchions. "Then I'll be happy to answer any and all of your questions." Now that we were stationed directly in front of the rope barrier, I turned to my friends, who were watching me quizzically. "Okay, what time would you have preferred to get here?"

"Well," Jessica said thoughtfully. "If the movie doesn't start 'til nine, then about eight forty-five, I guess. Why?"

"Did you see how many people were in line for tickets?"

"Yes."

"If we arrived fifteen minutes before the film started, twice that many people would have already passed through and would now be seated."

"So?" Oliver asked, looking back at the ticket line again. "You already paid for our tickets, they don't sell more tickets than there are seats available, do they?"

"No," I replied, trying to keep a straight face. "But if you're the last ones here you have to take whatever seats are left."

"So what?" Jessica still looked confused.

"Watching a movie in the theater is pointless unless you get a good seat," I explained. "That's why it's necessary to come early."

"Which seats are the best?" Jessica asked and I laughed, forgetting that this was her first time to the movies in almost a decade. However, I quickly broke off when she shot me a venomous look.

"Sorry," I muttered, covering my mouth. "Back row seats are the best."

"I always thought people liked the front row," Oliver mused. "Isn't the term 'front row seats?'"

"Lot's of people do like the front row, but I prefer the back."

"Why?" Jessica asked.

"Being that close to the screen makes me dizzy."

"Dizzy?"

"Yeah, the images moving at that proximity to my face makes me sick. It's sort of like a roller-coaster ride. Besides, from the back row, you can see the entire screen without turning your head."

"This is all very fascinating," Jessica said and she did, in fact, look intrigued. "But how does getting here forty minutes early prevent people from getting the best seats? Can't they just take whatever seat they want when the usher lets us in?"

For a moment I didn't answer. Then very slowly, trying hard not to smile, I said, "Jessica, see that black rope? We're the first in line."

*　　　*　　　*

"Wow!" I breathed as the theater screen faded to black and the lights came on. "That was truly amazing!" While everyone else bustled to leave the moment the credits appeared, I remained seated for a moment, still recovering from the aftermath of the film. It's been a long time since I've gotten that kind of adrenaline rush. I have never seen a movie with that much action before. My heart was still racing with excitement. Meanwhile, the screen room was emptying as everyone else headed along the aisle toward the exit.

"*Come on, Jason*," Jessica hissed under her breath, giving my sleeve a little tug. "The movie is over."

I blinked, looking up at her. For a glorious two hours I had forgotten where I was. Jessica was standing in the aisle, her arms crossed, Oliver by her side the usual far-off look in his eyes. Obviously neither of them had been as swept away as I had. *It doesn't matter*, I thought as I got to my feet and followed my friends out of the theater. I had had the experience of my life!

Jessica hadn't mentioned the argument in the cafeteria. I, too, was acting as if nothing had happened, but I knew sooner or later she would apologize. She hates leaving things unresolved. It's no secret that I avoid my feelings, but I couldn't ignore what Jessica had said. After my mother walked out on me and my father, everything changed. I changed. She left when I was eleven. Eleven! Before long I was hanging out with the wrong crowd. The misfits. It was just a matter of time before things went too far. Jessica dragged me back. Literally. She doesn't know it, but I owe her everything. Not that I'd ever tell her that. But there was one addiction she couldn't save me from. Girls. According to Jessica, my attitude keeps them away. What she doesn't know is that school is like the ocean and I don't fish in our waters. I merely browse. To avoid conflict, I pick up girls from other schools. That also reduces the drama; if they can't find me, they can't start trouble. I prefer to keep my love connections short and sweet. I don't bother with romance and certainly not with relationships. Promiscuous and insecure girls are the easiest target. They don't require a lot of time or work. I simply tell them what they want to hear and they are mine. For one night anyway. Of course, Oliver and Jessica don't know about this. I didn't let anyone see that part of me. This is how I've done things for the last year or so, but lately my heart hasn't been in it. In a manner of speaking.

"I must admit," Jessica was saying to Oliver, who looked like he was only half listening. "That was definitely one of the better films I've seen."

"Yeah," he murmured vaguely, staring at his shoes. "It was pretty good."

"See, I told you!" I said, catching up to the two of them and slapping Oliver on the back as the three of us exited the building. "Didn't I tell you guys it would be good?"

"Yeah, you did," Jessica sighed, twirling a lock of her blond hair around her index finger. "You wouldn't stop talking about it. I was kind of forced to tune you out."

"So," I said excitedly as we stepped out into the parking lot. "What do you guys say we do this again some time?"

"No can do," Oliver replied, snapping out of his dreamy haze and looking at his watch. "This is a once-in-a-lifetime thing. It's passed eleven. We have to get up early for school tomorrow. There's no way I'm missing class on a Friday."

"You guys are no fun," I muttered, shoving my hands in my jean pockets. "Where's your sense of adventure?"

"It's not about adventure," Jessica said, squinting at me in the fading light from the theater. "At least not the adventure portrayed on a television screen. Life itself is an adventure. Why waste it sitting on your butt?"

"Life, an adventure?" I snorted. "Yeah, right. Nothing exciting ever happens in real life. That's why I prefer movies. Do you see us facing the prospect of death every other second? No, I didn't think so. Nothing is an adventure without the heart-pounding, mind-numbing feeling of anticipation."

Jessica rolled her eyes. "Whatever. Only those who are truly connected with themselves could possible understand the thrills life has to offer."

There were about a hundred things I could have said to that, but right as I was opening my mouth I noticed a small kid standing next to my car near the edge of the parking lot. He was studying something in a nearby tree through what looked like binoculars. But why he was observing things at this time of night was beyond me. He also looked awfully young to be wandering around alone.

"Hey," I called, stopping a few feet away from him. "Whatcha doing?"

The boy looked up. When he saw me he quickly stuffed his binoculars into a large duffle bag that was sitting on the ground beside him and, with some difficulty, swung it over his shoulder and turned to leave. As he did so, an object fell out of the bag and hit the ground with an oddly loud thunk.

"Should you be out here all alone?" Jessica asked, stepping forward to get a better look at the kid while I bent down to pick up the square object. "Where are your parents?"

The little boy turned to look at Jessica, a look of mild curiosity on his face.

"My parents are not here," he said, his white-blond hair shining in the streetlights surrounding the parking lot.

"You mean your mother lets you walk alone at night?" Jessica asked incredulously. "But that's incredibly dangerous!"

The boy looked at her for a moment. It was odd the way he studied her like she was some kind of mildly interesting specimen.

"I guess you are right," he said after a second. "It is dangerous to walk around at night. My mother should know better." With that he turn to leave.

"Wait," I said, stepping forward. "You dropped something." I held up the smooth black cube. "What is this anyway?" It was like nothing I'd ever seen before. About the size of a Rubix Cube, the object was solid black. As I turned it over, a faint glow passed over the surface as if it were responding to my touch.

The little boy turned to look at me and when he saw what I was holding, all the blood seemed to drain from his face. "How did you get that?" he demanded, his Alice blue eyes as round as saucers.

"It fell out of your bag," I said with a shrug.

"It could not have!" the boy started to look scared.

"Well, it did." I turned my attention back to the cube just in time to see the words, Magnum Opus appear just under the surface. Below that was the shimmering red icon of a star. "What does this thing do?"

"Give me that!" the boy cried, rushing forward. "That is a highly advanced piece of technology!"

"Yeah, right." I chuckled, turning the thing over in my hands. "What would you know about advanced technology? What are you seven, eight tops?"

"I am not seven!" the boy snapped, his cheeks flushed and his eyes ablaze. "Give me that!" And he made a grab for the cube.

"Not so fast," I said, lifting it out of his reach. "First tell me what it is, then I'll give it to you."

"You could not possibly understand what that thing is capable of!" the boy tried to get the object away from me again, but was unable to reach. "It is beyond anything you have ever encountered."

"Jason!" Jessica snapped. "Give it back to him. Stop being such a bully!"

"I'm not being a bully," I shot back, still holding the device out of the boy's reach. "I just want to know how some kid, who's probably still in elementary school, thinks he knows something I don't."

"That is none of your business!" the blond-headed boy declared. "Now give me that!"

"Give it to him!" Jessica yelled.

"Fine!" I shoved the instrument at the child. "If you guys are going to whine like babies."

The boy snatched the cube from me and, in his haste, his small index finger passed over the red icon. A bright blue beam of light shot out of the side and hit Oliver square in the forehead. For a moment he just stood there, looking bewildered, then he crumpled to the ground. I dropped to my knees and managed to grab him under the arms just before his head hit the pavement.

"Oh, my god!" Jessica screamed, rushing over to kneel on the ground beside me. "Oliver, are you okay?"

He didn't respond, he just lay there limply, his head resting against my chest, his eyes shut. Jessica leaned forward so her ear was only centimeters from his face.

"What are you doing?" I asked as she grabbed one of his wrists and held it in her hand. For a moment she didn't answer, then she leaned back, a look of relief on her face.

"He's still breathing and he has a pulse. He's alive."

"What the hell did you do?" I demanded, glaring up at the boy, who was standing glued to the spot, a bewildered look on his young face. "What happened?"

The kid looked down at the device in his hands then back at Oliver, who looked like he was fast asleep, his eyes still shut, his face blank.

"I do not know what happened," the boy said, coming over and kneeling down across from Jessica. Using his thumb he pulled back one of Oliver's eyelids. His iris hadn't rolled back in his head. Instead it stared straight ahead, yet showed no signs of consciousness. The boy pulled his hand away and our friend's eye slid shut.

"Maybe if we…" Jessica's voice trailed off as she took Oliver's hand and began to bend his thumb back.

"What are you doing?" I asked.

"Sometimes when someone passes out, they'll wake up if pain is inflicted," Jessica said, her voice strained.

"So you're going to break his finger?!"

"I'm not breaking his finger," she grunted, now sounding annoyed. "I'm just inflicting pain to see of he wakes up. Besides, technically the thumb isn't a finger."

"Whatever," I muttered as she slowly bent Oliver's thumb farther and farther back. "It's an extremity."

After a moment, when he still didn't respond, Jessica let go of his hand, allowing it to fall back onto his middle.

"Maybe he just needs a few firm smacks in the face," I said, raising my hand.

"No!" Jessica grabbed my arm. "We need a strong scent to waft under his nose. That's sure to wake him up."

Now we both turned to look at the young boy, who was still kneeling on the ground staring at Oliver as if he was already dead.

"If you have any additional ideas, feel free to shout them out," I said as Jessica opened the side door of the car. "After all, it was your gizmo that put our friend in this state. The least you can do is help sort him out."

"I cannot believe this!" the boy murmured, staring at the ground as if he hadn't heard me. "I am in such big trouble. When the others reach the final destination and realize this thing is missing, I am dead!"

"Who are you?" Jessica asked, eyeing the black cube in the boy's hand after she and I had finished strapping Oliver into the back seat of the car. "And what did that thing do to him?"

The boy looked up at her, his mouth open slightly, but he didn't say anything.

"Well?" she prompted.

For a second he remained silent, looking as if he didn't know what to say, then after a moment his shoulders sagged and he slowly got to his feet.

"The truth is, I do not know what happened to your friend. This thing is not supposed to work when it does not have its core programming chip. If said chip actually had been in the system on the time of detonation, we would all be dead. But I have never heard of a situation where an unloaded machine has been used on another being. I do not know what the effect is, but it cannot be anything good. This is a very powerful device."

"Oh, my god!" Jessica whispered, her hand going to her mouth. "What are you?"

"What do you mean what is he?" I demanded. "He's a crazy-talking seven-year-old kid who's somehow gotten hold of a very dangerous machine. Come on, Jessica, let's go."

But she didn't move. she was still staring at the kid, a mingled look of fear and excitement on her face.

"Who are you?" she breathed. "Why are you here?"

"My name is Mandayus-Corpus," the boy said. "I was part of a mission to what you humans call the Andromeda Galaxy when…" he paused for a moment, his face turning red. "When there were some complications and the rest of the crew thought it best that I stay here while they went on."

"And what was this mission supposed to be for?" I asked skeptically.

Mandayus-Corpus looked at me, his light blue eyes impassive.

"We were on a mission to create a new system of stars with this." he held up the black cube. "Magnum Opus is the most powerful piece of technology my race has ever developed, and it can be very dangerous in the hands of," he paused, looking me up and down, "less intelligent beings. I just do not understand how it got into my bag. Usually they keep this kind of thing in the security room aboard the ship under lock and key."

"Oh, my god! I knew it!" Jessica exclaimed, looking at the so-called alien in awe. "I knew there was life out there!"

"Wait a minute," I said, holding up a hand. "If you're really an alien race, with lots of advanced technology, why is it that to us you just look like a little kid? Wouldn't such an intellectually superior being want a more... I don't know, advanced form?"

"It seems that our two races think a lot alike," Mandayus-Corpus replied. "The crew was impressed with the human's level of intelligence and independent thought. On this planet many of you seem to possess the desire to humiliate and shame those who displease you. This is a characteristic some of my own kind have as well. The one I speak of in particular is, I guess you could say, my adversary. We were always competing with one another, trying to be the best. When it was decided that I would remain here, I guess he decided he would further heighten my degradation and make me appear unreasonably young. You see, my race lives for thousands of years and the older you are the more honored and respected you are. To be stuck like this is extremely disenchanting."

"So you can't show us your true form?" Jessica asked disappointed.

"Sorry. No," the boy replied sadly. "Without the transmorpher, I am trapped."

"Well," Jessica said, putting her hands on her hips and casting me a sidelong glance. "This fellow crew member of yours sounds like a real nasty piece of work. I've always said that people are too quick to point out the flaws in each other, failing to acknowledge the flaws within themselves."

"Yeah, whatever you say," I muttered, then turning to the boy said. "So if you're an alien, how come you speak English? Is it like an intergalactic language or something?"

"I learned a great deal about your languages on landing here," he replied. "I studied the dialects appropriate for this region. I am not only fluent in English, but French and Spanish as well."

"A real genius, aren't you?" I grunted.

"I spent the last several hours learning everything I could about your race, but I still have a lot to learn. My instructions were to stay incognito."

"Well, Mr. Alien—"

"—My name is Mandayus-Corpus."

"Whatever. If you're so smart, can you help us?"

"I can try," the boy said shortly.

"It's decided then," Jessica said, her face shining once again. "You'll come with us... uh, Mandayus?"

"Please, call me Corpus," the boy said, a look of anxiety on his young face.

With that, we all got into my car and I drove us back to my house. After we got Oliver out of the back seat, still as unresponsive as ever, we carried him into the living room and laid him out on the couch. Since it was nearly midnight all the lights in the house were out. Hoping not to wake my father, I turned on the overhead light as Jessica went to the spice cupboard and pulled out an assortment of potential candidates. She returned from the kitchen a moment later, her arms full. One by one she twisted the cap off each bottle and swirled it back and forth under Oliver's nose, but when she finally got to the last one, he still hadn't moved a muscle.

"I had better link him to the cerebral scrutinizer," Corpus said. "It will give us a vague idea of what is going on." And he started rummaging through his duffle bag. After a moment or two he pulled out a small black cube that was similar to the Magnum Opus machine. When he touched it the same glow passed over the surface, only this time no words appeared. Just the brilliant purple image of a brain. The alien set the object down on the arm of the couch just above Oliver's head and sat back. Within seconds, a one foot by two foot screen materialized above the device. It displayed several jagged lines of varying colors that danced from one side to the other. Some of them changed constantly while others remained stagnant.

Corpus silently studied the screen, his eyes drifting from top to bottom. I could only assume he understood what the cerebral scrutinizer was telling him because after a moment he turned to Jessica and me.

"According to the computer, your companion's brain is showing an unusually high level of activity. Since we are dealing with something that has never happened before, I cannot say whether that is good or bad. It is only reasonable to assume the fact that there is any activity at all is a good sign. The only thing we can do now is wait until he wakes up."

"And if he doesn't?" I asked.

"We will have to try a different approach."

Jessica leaned forward and gently folded Oliver's hands on his chest, tears in her eyes.

"For now all we can do is wait," Corpus said, looking miserable. "Hopefully by tomorrow he will have regained consciousness. Now I know that you sleep during the night so I will keep an eye on him while you two rest."

"Don't worry," I murmured, patting Jessica on the back. "I'm sure Oliver will be okay. He'd sooner die than miss school."

Jessica gave a weak laugh and leaned against me, laying her head on my chest.

"I'm sorry about what I said earlier today," she said, interlacing her fingers in mine. "I can get a little carried away sometimes."

"It was nothing." I gently brushed a lock of her hair out of my face. "I said some things I shouldn't have."

"Life is too short to stay angry," Jessica whispered, looking at Oliver. "You never know what's going to happen."

"Don't worry about him. He'll be fine."

"I hope so."

"So, Mandayus," I said to the alien after a few minutes of silence. "What exactly are you guys?"

"I told you to call me Corpus," he said, a slight edge to his voice. "And I thought we already went over this? I am an extraterrestrial."

"I know, but what kind of extraterrestrial are you? You said you created the universe. Are you guys like gods or something?"

"We are not the creators of life," Corpus said bluntly. "Magnum Opus can only create non-living matter. We are not responsible for living things. Not even the mass on which they live. We build stars and only in this universe."

"There are other universes out there?" Jessica asked excitedly. "Is that where you came from?"

"Yes," Corpus replied. "My home world is within another universe."

"How did you get here?"

"There are many ways to travel between universes," the alien said matter-of-factly. "The fastest way is to journey through black holes. But that is not always the easiest route."

"Why didn't you just dimension jump?" I asked sarcastically. "I hear it's a lot faster."

"You are speaking about a completely different matter entirely," Corpus said, giving me a hard look. "There is an infinite amount of ignorance and misunderstanding when it comes to the subject of multiple universes. I could hardly expect someone like you to understand our planes of existence."

"What do you mean?" Jessica asked, leaning forward slightly with interest.

"We not only live in a world with multiple universes, there are also countless planes of existence; other dimensions, alternate or multiple realities and so on. To 'dimension jump' as your friend put it, would take us to a different plane of existence, not another universe. For example, we could wind up in a two-dimensional world. Being three-dimensional objects we could not survive; the consequences would be catastrophic."

"Wait. Back up a second," Jessica said, holding up her hand. "What's this about alternate realities?"

"In the most basic sense, an alternate reality, also known as an alternative reality, is one where an individual goes down another path from the one he or she is on in this reality. Each choice you make creates another reality so that every possibility is played out."

"Sounds like *Red Dwarf*," I murmured.

"Is it possible to cross over into one of these alternate realities?" Jessica asked, ignoring me completely.

"Theoretically it is," Corpus said thoughtfully. "But, from what I have heard, it is very difficult. I am not aware of any race with that capability."

"So why are you creating this universe?" Jessica asked, going back to the original topic. "What is its purpose?"

"We are not creating this universe. That is not within our power. We just create stars. They are our source of energy. Without them we cannot survive. At the center of every galaxy there is a black hole, this black hole transfers the star's energy from your universe to ours."

"Why don't you just create the stars in your own universe?" I asked.

"Our universe is very different from yours," Corpus said, studying me thoughtfully. "Our world cannot sustain the full power of these stars. The black holes act as filters. They not only slow down the passage of the star's energy to our universe, they also sift out all the elements that are harmful to our race."

"Of course it doesn't matter how these harmful elements affect us," I muttered.

"You are still here, are you not? Clearly you were meant to live in these conditions."

"So what about the planets?" I asked, changing the subject. "Where did they come from?"

"I do not know," the alien sighed. "I am neither an architect nor an engineer. I cannot pretend to know exactly how Magnum Opus works."

"There's purpose for you," I muttered sarcastically. "According to him we're just fragments of debris, floating aimlessly in space."

"That is not what I said," Corpus said indignantly.

"Yeah, but it's what you meant," I shot back. "You said Magnum Opus only creates non-living mass, right? But you also said you're not creating the universe, just the stars. So logically anything else is extra, anything else is debris. Unless, of course, planets were here before you guys came along."

"I was not there at the beginning," Corpus said darkly. "I would not know."

"Yeah, right," I snorted. "You've been Little Miss Know-It-All since you got here. Now you're pulling blanks?"

"I cannot know things that are beyond my understanding," the alien replied, a muscle working in his jaw. "For example, I do not know what has happened to your friend. But that does not mean I will not do everything in my power to help him."

"Well, you kinda have to. It's your fault he got this way."

"I believe that we are all here for a reason, good or bad," Corpus said in a low voice and his blue eyes seemed to darken, as if a shadow had passed behind them, making him look different, inhuman. "We occupy a mysterious and dangerous existence and I will not pretend for a second to understand why things happen the way they do. But here we are and I do not believe it was by mistake. Personally, I think the reason for our existence is as strange and mysterious as it was intended to be. Now you can hold me responsible for what happened to your friend if you want, but that will not do him any good. So I would appreciate it if you stopped blaming me for something I cannot change!"

"I, I'm sorry," I mumbled, not sure what to say. "I didn't mean to—"

"Hey," Jessica suddenly cut me off. "Besides us humans, is there any intelligent life in our universe?" It didn't look like Corpus's little outburst had fazed her in the slightest.

"Maybe," the alien said, suddenly looking like the innocent little boy he once had. "We would not know. We do not go out of our way to find out. What little life we have discovered in the past was by chance."

"How can that be?" Jessica asked incredulously. "Aren't you curious?"

"My species is much too advanced to care about something as insignificant as organic life forms. It is like humans compared to ants; so long as they are not in your way you could not care less."

"Nice comparison," I muttered, now embarrassed for allowing Corpus to intimidate me. "We're ants to you?"

"I did not mean it like that," he said. "I am just saying that your universe is a very big place and we do not have time to comb through it for potential life. We have important work to do."

"Well, you must not be so great if your crew didn't want you on the ship," I remarked. "What did you do to get kicked out anyway?"

"I did not get kicked out," Corpus said, his face turning red. "I am just staying here to do research."

I shook my head. "I'm not convinced. If alternative life is so insignificant to your race, then why would you bother checking us out? What about your mission?"

"I said we do not go out of our *way* to examine alternative life forms," the alien said impatiently. "But if we happen to stumble across something, then it is our duty to analyze and record it."

"You know what?" I tapped my chin thoughtfully. "I think that's all just a cover up to hide the real reason you're here. After all the damage you've caused since your arrival, I wouldn't be surprised if you nearly killed the whole crew aboard your ship!"

Corpus didn't say anything. Instead he folded his arms and turned his back on me, a ruthless look on his young face.

"Jason," Jessica sighed, sounding annoyed. "Stop that. Why do you always have to be such a jerk? Corpus, he didn't mean it. We're grateful for what you're doing for us, really."

"Yeah, whatever," he muttered. "You two should be sleeping, anyway. It is getting late."

No one said a word after that and sometime later I fell asleep. The last thing I saw was Corpus kneeling beside the couch, watching the cerebral scrutinizer as the jagged lines continued to dance across the transparent screen, a sad lost look in his eyes.

Chapter 6

MANDAMUS-CORPUS

It was interesting to learn that humans sleep lying down. For my people, this is only done in emergencies or if one is ill. Nonetheless, I was not unfamiliar with this phenomenon. There are a number of alien races in my universe who do the same thing. While the two humans rejuvenated, I sat silently watching the cerebral scrutinizer and wondering how Magnum Opus got in my bag. Given the security measures used to protect it, I found it hard to believe it got there by accident. And as I sat there in the dark with the only light coming from the 2D screen, I remembered that Marcus had come into the Emergency & Supply Unit while I was in there packing. Could he have put the creation machine in my bag while I was with the captain? But how? Only authorized personnel are given access to the security room. But it didn't matter. If Marcus had somehow gotten passed the guards and into the security room, there was no way I could prove it. I didn't have a shred of evidence. All I could do was try and fix the mess down here, and I knew that wasn't going to be easy with the human called Jason constantly challenging me. But it wasn't like I had a choice. If the crew found out everything that had happened since my arrival on Earth, I'd be out of the Spacing Program faster than I could say Magnum Opus, and all my hopes of becoming a creator would be ruined.

So, I sat silently in the dark, trying to think of ways to fix the problem. But it wasn't easy coming up with solutions to a problem that, until a few hours ago, I didn't think possible. Something was clearly going on, but I didn't know what. I considered using mind tricks to try and find out what was wrong with the human named Oliver, but I knew those were complicated and risky and probably shouldn't be used until I was more familiar with the situation. Furthermore, mind control and mind penetration are illegal and I didn't want to do anything that could get me reprimanded. Besides, I've heard that extensive mind manipulation can be unhealthy to the inexperienced. But if worse came to worst, I would probably have to take some drastic measures. I only hoped it wouldn't come to that. Hopefully, Oliver would wake up in a few hours and I could get back to doing my research for the Spacing Program and forget this whole messy business.

Chapter 7

Oliver

During the film all I could think about was my story. That's another reason I don't watch movies very often. Sampling other people's work only sparks my own imagination. Books are fine, but the graphic nature of the screen overpowers me. Usually I can't get more than five minutes into a movie without plunging into a world of my own creation. And now that Jessica had shown interest in what I had so far, I was eager to continue. It wasn't until everyone started heading toward the exits that I realized I'd daydreamed through the entire movie. As I quickly got to my feet to stand beside her, I could only hope that Jason didn't quiz me. I had no clue what the plot had been about. Luckily he was too blown away to notice. As we left the theater and headed toward his car, which was a good distance from the entrance, he and Jessica discussed the film. This, of course, gave me plenty of time to slip back into the imaginary world I had created. But after we arrived at Jason's car, things started getting a little confusing. I remember hearing my friends yelling. That was normal. But then I saw a flash of blue light and everything went black. The next thing I knew, I was face down on the ground, only it wasn't the hard pavement of the parking lot, it was soft and mossy like a forest. Pressing my palms flat on the ground, I pushed myself up into a kneeling position. Looking around I realized to my amazement that I was in what appeared to be a jungle.

Getting to my feet, I stared in awe at the sight before my eyes. I have seen pictures of jungles in books, I have viewed them on postcards, but never in my life have I seen a jungle quite like this. The trees, huge as they were, grew close together, their long branches and umbrella-like leaves blocking out most, but not all of the sunlight. The air was moist and warm against my skin. It was definitely an Amazon-like atmosphere. Somewhere in the distance I could hear birds singing softly in the trees and dancing from flower to flower were the most fascinating butterflies I'd ever seen. I walked in a small circle, taking in the incredible sight, and though I knew I must be dreaming I couldn't help thinking; *this forest looks just like I always imagined it!*

Determined to find out more about this mysterious place, I started making my way through the thick undergrowth. As I walked, I kept pinching myself, sure that any minute I would wake up and this beautiful place would be gone. But I didn't wake up. I kept walking and as I moved, the brush became thinner and thinner until I found myself at the edge of the trees looking out across a beautiful sunlit valley, the golden blades of grass gently swaying in the wind. In the distance, I could see a magnificent castle on top of a hill and halfway up the hill was a village.

How is this possible? I thought, dazed as my eyes moved to the mountains in the distance, looking impressive in the sun's evening light. *This can't be real, it just can't be.*

"Who are you?" a voice suddenly said and, turning around, I saw a tall female centaur standing about fifteen feet away. She slowly approached me, her hair like red hot magma flowing down her shoulders, her leaf-green eyes surveying me with mild curiosity. Close up I saw that she had high cheekbones, giving her a strong sturdy look.

"Are you some sort of faun?" she asked when I didn't respond. "It is not safe for fauns to be this far from the wood's inner protection."

"Avril?" I whispered, finally finding my voice as I stared dumbfounded at this gorgeous creature.

"How do you know my name?" she asked, narrowing her almond-shaped eyes. "What are you doing this close to the edge of the forest? If the king's men find you here, you will be captured."

"The king?" I breathed. "Lord Mytus?"

Avril nodded then looked out at the distant village. "We should go back in. It's not safe here." With that she turned and galloped off into the forest.

For a moment I just stood there, completely baffled. Then, not knowing what else to do, I followed her. She ran for a ways and, right when I was about to tell her I couldn't go any farther, she stopped and turned to face me. Here the trees were pretty close together so I had spent the last ten minutes fighting my way through them. Now I bent over, my hands on my knees, trying to catch my breath.

"What is your name?" Avril asked, studying me.

"Oliver," I wheezed, sweat trickling down my temples.

"And why do you wear these things?" she asked, pulling at my collar, her eyes traveling over my attire.

"They're clothes,." I said, slowly straightening up.

"I know what clothes are," Avril stated. "Why do you wear so many? And what has happened to your horns?"

"I'm not a faun," I muttered, brushing my hair out of my face and as I did so, a shocked look swept across her face. "What?" I asked, feeling somewhat self-conscious.

"You look…" Avril's voice trailed off.

"I look what?"

She blinked. "If you are not a faun then what are you?"

"I'm a…" I hesitated. I didn't know how I got here, but I wasn't sure telling her I was a human was the brightest idea. In the Kingdom of the Centaurs many believe that humans are just a myth. How would Avril react if I told her what I was? But then again, she was a friend of Quaymius. Maybe it wouldn't be such a big deal.

"Where's Quaymius?" I inquired, sliding my hands into my pockets, hoping I wasn't on the verge of upsetting the delicate balance of this world.

"How do you know Quaymius?" Avril asked, now sounding thoroughly confused then, quite suddenly, she grabbed me by the collar, lifted me about three feet off the ground and slammed me up against the nearest tree. "In the name of the gods who are you and what are you doing here?" she demanded, then she started speaking in a language I didn't understand, her grip getting tighter and tighter around my neck.

"No, please!" I gasped, panic gripping me. "I'm not a spy or anything like that. I'm a human. I know Quaymius is looking for a way to bring back the honor that his family once held. I can help. Please, don't kill me!"

Avril's grip loosened and after a moment she slowly let me slide down the trunk of the tree and back on solid ground.

"You are human?" she asked, staring hard at me. "How did you get here?"

"Uh, I'm not sure," I confessed. "But I know I can help you. Where's Quaymius?"

"He is not here," Avril said, looking sad. "He has gone to the Old Library. He said he wouldn't be back 'til nightfall."

"The Old Library?" My mind was working fast. "What is he doing there?"

"He wanted to find some stories about the cave. There are myths telling about a gateway from this world to yours, but nobody has ever been able to get it to work." Avril then looked at me her eyes hopeful. "Do you know how the cave works?"

I opened my mouth to say yes, then realized that I didn't know. *That can't be right*, I thought, *I've always known how the cave works. Why can't I remember?* I racked my brain, thinking about all the notes I'd made about this world and realized I had never once written down exactly how the cave worked. It had always been in the back of my mind, but I never felt the need to include it in any of my notes.

"I can't remember," I murmured. "But I do know that the cave works in strange and mysterious ways."

"You seem to know a lot about this place," Avril remarked. "Are you the human boy Artayus claimed to meet on his journey to your world?"

"No, that was fifty years ago," I said, then turned away and sneezed. "Excuse me."

Avril looked crestfallen. "That's a shame. I really would have loved to hear stories about Artayus the Great. After that adventure of his, things for his family didn't go that great."

"Yeah," I agreed, then sneezed again. "I guess that's right."

"Are you ill?" Avril asked, eyeing me uncertainly.

"No." I wiped my nose on the back of my hand. "I'm fine."

The centaur looked at me more closely. "Are you sure? You look a little pale."

"I think it's just that spicy smell," I muttered, sneezing yet a third time. "It's getting really strong."

Avril arched an eyebrow. "What spicy smell? I don't smell anything."

"You don't?" I groaned, covering my nose as I started to feel light-headed. "It's like I'm trapped in someone's spice cupboard."

"I don't smell anything," the centaur insisted, looking around, a puzzled expression on her face. "Are you sure you smell spice?"

I didn't respond. Instead, my eyes rolled back and everything went black. The next thing I knew I was lying on a pile of soft leaves in the corner of a low den-like structure. It was mainly made up of branches and leaves all hanging close to the ground. Avril was lying next to me, her fingers running through my hair.

"Where am I?" I asked, feeling a little disorientated.

"In my shelter," the centaur replied, withdrawing her hand. "You started acting kind of funny, then you fainted."

"Yeah." I remembered the dreadfully strong scent of spice and discovered to my relief that it was gone. "Sorry."

"No apologies necessary," Avril said, studying me with curiosity.

"What's wrong?" I asked when she continued to gaze at me.

"You look like him," she said fondly.

"What… who?"

"Quaymius. You look like Quaymius."

"Oh." I wasn't sure what to say to that. "That's nice."

"I brought you some food," Avril said in a rushed tone, gesturing to the ground. "A lack of nourishment can cause some people to lose consciousness."

Cradled in a leaf was an assortment of different kinds of fruit and vegetables. Though I was hesitant at first, once I got the nerve to try some, I found them to be quite delicious. When night started to fall, Avril expressed her certainty that Quaymius would come, but I had a feeling he wouldn't and when it was completely dark, Avril seemed to give in. We lay side by side on the soft bed of leaves and I stared up at the ceiling of vegetation, wondering how long I would be here and if I'd ever get back home. Sometime later I think I drifted off to sleep.

55

Chapter 8

JESSICA

It felt as if I was just getting to sleep when someone nudged me awake. Opening my eyes, I was looking into the young human face of Mandayus-Corpus. Despite the fact that he had stayed awake all night, he didn't look the least bit tired.

"It is seven in the morning," he said, now shaking Jason who was lying on the floor beside me. "I do not know if you want to go to school after everything that has happened, but I thought I would wake you anyway."

"So Oliver hasn't changed?" I asked, sitting up and rubbing my eyes.

"No," the alien replied, looking sad. "He has not regained consciousness, but his brain activity has remained level so we can only hope that he is not getting any worse."

"I should have gone to my room last night," Jason groaned, sitting up and massaging his right shoulder. "The floor is murder. Thank god I'm still young."

"Speaking of which, I met your father this morning," Corpus said, casting Jason an inquisitive gaze. "He was on his way to work. He said you guys are out of cereal. What does that mean?"

"It means someone needs to go shopping."

Ignoring the pain from sleeping on the floor, I got up and went over to the couch where Oliver was lying, just as still as ever. I could see his chest steadily rising and falling as he slept, or whatever he was doing.

"Come on," I whispered, resting my forehead on his shoulder. "You have to wake up. School starts in an hour. You can't miss class, you have a paper due, remember? You've worked on it all week and you know Mrs. Waterberry doesn't accept late work."

I slowly lifted my head and took Oliver's hand in mine. As I pressed it to the side of my face, Jason knelt down beside me and put his arm around my shoulder.

"She's right," he said to our friend's unconscious form. "You have to wake up, man. We need you."

After a moment's silence I got to my feet, letting Oliver's hand slide back down onto his middle.

"We'd better start getting ready for school," I said, trying to fight back the tears that threatened to run down my face. "I know he wouldn't want us to miss class on his account."

Jason sighed and got to his feet.

"Do not worry," Corpus said, his arms folded on the side of the couch. "I will watch him."

I was just turning to leave the living room with Jason when I saw something move out of the corner of my eye.

"Oliver?" I gasped, hurrying back to kneel on the floor beside the couch.

"What did you see?" Jason asked, close on my heels.

"I saw his eyes flutter!" I was now watching Oliver like a hawk. The room was still, all eyes focused on him. But after a few seconds, Jason took a step back.

"Maybe you just imagined it. Maybe you wanted to see him move."

"No," I insisted, shaking my head. "I'm sure I saw him move. I know I did."

But after a minute still nothing happened.

"Come on, Jessica. He's not waking up." Just as the words were out of Jason's mouth Oliver let out a soft groan and rolled onto his side.

"Oliver!" I practically yelled with excitement. "Oliver, can you hear me?"

"Yeah," he groaned, his eyes still shut and now Jason was kneeling beside me also watching him with excitement.

"Say something!" I urged, my heart pounding.

"Where am I?" he whispered, still not opening his eyes. "What happened?"

"You're at my house!" Jason said eagerly. "Come on, wake up!"

For a moment, Oliver didn't move, then his eyelids fluttered. It seemed to take some effort, but after a couple seconds he opened his eyes completely. After sweeping the room, his gaze landed on me.

"What happened?" he asked, confusion creeping onto his face as he glanced at Jason. "Where was I?"

"You were unconscious," I replied. "But now you're back."

Oliver gingerly pushed himself into a sitting position, the look of confusion getting more pronounced by the second.

"I wasn't unconscious," he said, running his fingers through his sandy blond hair. "It all seemed so real."

"What seemed so real?" Jason asked, but Oliver didn't respond. He had just noticed Corpus, who was sitting on the floor a few feet away.

"Who's that?" he asked, staring at the alien.

"That's Mandayus-Corpus," I explained, leaning forward to examine Oliver more closely. "The extraterrestrial."

"Mandy the what?"

"The one who got us into this mess," Jason muttered, standing up. "Him and his Magnum Opus."

"If I recall correctly," Corpus said, getting to his feet as well. "It was you meddling in my affairs that caused the machine to go off."

"It was your finger that hit the icon."

"It was you that took it away from me when I tried to warn you of its danger."

Jason opened his mouth to retaliate, but I stood up. "Listen, arguing won't get us anywhere. Whatever happened, it's in the past, okay? All that matters now is making sure Oliver is okay so we can go to school."

"I feel fine," Oliver said, eyeing Corpus uncertainly. "I just don't get all this alien business."

So we went over the story about Mandayus-Corpus, how he came to be here, and what had happened in the parking lot outside the theater. Oliver seemed unusually calm and relaxed as we explain everything to him and when we were done he nodded and said, "That explains a lot."

"What do you mean?" I asked.

"This Magnum Opus thing. You say it only creates stars? Well, it must have got an upgrade because I just spent the last several hours in a jungle."

"How is that possible?" Jason asked. "You've been with us the whole time. You never moved a muscle."

"I don't know how it's possible. All I know is that I was in the Brambee Forest with Avril."

"You were where?"

"The Brambee Forest?" I murmured, staring at Oliver. "That's not possible. You made that place up. It's a part of your story."

"I know," he said. "But after that beam of light hit me, I opened my eyes and there I was."

"You must have been dreaming," I concluded. "That's the only logical explanation."

"Well, it doesn't matter now," Jason said, looking at his watch. "School starts in about half an hour."

Oliver blinked in surprise and looked at his own watch. Seeing that Jason was right, he immediately started to get up, but I pushed him back down.

"Not so fast. I want to make sure you're okay."

"I said I feel fine," he sighed, looking impatient. "I don't want to be late for school."

"You might feel fine, but I think we should check just to be sure. Corpus, do you have anything that would tell us if Oliver's body is still functioning normally?"

"Yes." Going through his duffle bag, the alien pulled out an interesting looking device that had about ten long wires coming out of the front that spiraled at the ends. Aiming it at Jason, he passed his thumb over the glowing yellow image of a tree.

"Hey!" Jason yelled, pulling away as a beam of white light passed over him. "What are you doing?"

"This is a bio-scanner. It is used to get structural analysis on organic life forms." Almost instantly, a glowing web of data spiraled above the machine. "It should be able to tell us if anything is wrong." Corpus swept his finger through the translucent map, causing it to scroll downward in a rotating fashion. This revealed different angles as well as additional information. "The best way to determine whether or not Oliver's system is functioning normally is to compare it with one that is." Corpus deactivated the image with a quick flick of his fingers. "Assuming that you are alive and well, you are the ideal choice."

"What about Jessica?" Jason asked, eyeing the gadget with growing uncertainty.

The alien proceeded to run the bio-scanner over Oliver. "There are enough differences between the male and female form that the machine would notice and claim that Oliver was not functioning properly."

Jason opened his mouth to say something, a crooked grin spreading across his face, but quickly shut it when he caught my eye.

"Well, this claims that everything is okay." the alien said after a moment, studying the two scans side by side.

"How can you tell?" I inquired, momentarily forgetting my concerns. "There's tons of information in there. You didn't review it all."

"In most cases, the bio-scanner operates in milliseconds. Taking into account the usual differences between two organisms of the same species, it makes a comparison. If the two scans didn't match, the irregular data would turn red."

"What about his brain activity?" I asked, shifting my attention back to Oliver. "Has that changed at all?"

"No," Corpus said warily, turning off the machine. "But everything else is fine."

"Maybe you shouldn't go to school today," I suggested, looking from one of Oliver's eyes to the other. "This could be serious."

"Are you kidding?" he laughed, standing up. "We have a paper due in English 11. I can't miss class."

"What if something bad happens? Who knows what the extent of this is. You could be dying as we speak."

"Come on, Jess," Jason groaned, also looking irritated. "He said he's fine and the bio-scanner proves it. If he was dying, something would be out of sorts."

Clearly I was out numbered. "Fine, but I think you should take it easy."

"First I have to run home and get my backpack," Oliver said. "Then I'll take it easy."

Before I could say anything he took off out the front door.

Ten minutes later, the four of us were walking down the sidewalk toward school. When Oliver had returned from his house he looked a little paler that usual, but when I asked how he was feeling, he insisted that he was fine. Arriving on school grounds, Corpus said he would wait for us outside and my friends and I entered the building. Not completely convinced that Oliver was okay, I continued to watch him throughout the day. At first he really did seem fine, but as each class passed, it became clear that something was wrong.

When the teachers talk, Oliver always sits up straight in his seat, giving them his utmost attention. But today, after third hour, I noticed he had begun to slump in his desk. He appeared to be having increasing difficulty concentrating on the lesson at hand and his skin just kept getting paler and paler. Every now and then I saw him run his hands over his face, a pained look in his eyes. By fifth hour even Jason noticed something was up when, instead of getting his book out like he usually did, Oliver slumped down in his seat, hiding his face from view.

"Are you okay, man?" Jason whispered, giving him a little nudge.

Oliver slowly sat up and nodded. "Yeah, I'm fine."

"Are you sure? You look kinda pale."

"I just have a small headache," Oliver replied, closing his eyes for a moment before staring hard at the floor. "It's no big deal."

"I think you should go see the school nurse," I hissed from his right. "This could be really serious."

"No," Oliver stated firmly. "I am not leaving class."

"Okay, everyone, let's get started," Mrs. Waterberry called, standing up as soon as the bell rang. "First, I'd like the papers that are due today. Come on, don't be shy."

The room rustled as students sent their homework to the front of the class.

"That's very good," the teacher said, examining the crisp stack in her arms once she'd collected them all. "Much better than last time. I'm glad to see that some of you are catching on." She looked at Jason when she said this. "Does anyone have anything they would like to say about this assignment before we continue?"

"Yeah," Jason said, twirling his pencil back and forth between his index and middle finger. "I still don't get how we're supposed to know what authors who lived in the eighteen hundreds had in mind when they wrote this stuff. As far as I can tell, none of the short stories we're reading make any sense."

"Is there a point to this?" Mrs. Waterberry asked, looking impatient.

"Yeah," Jason said, leaning back in his desk. "When you get to my paper, don't be surprised if there's a lot of guesswork involved."

"Charming," Mrs. Waterberry muttered, placing the papers on her desk. "All right," she continued, turning to face us once again. "Resuming our reading, I believe we're on Chopin's 'The Story of an Hour,' which is on page 172. Unlike the others, this one is fairly short. Can I get a volunteer to read it?"

As usual no one volunteered.

"Okay," the teacher said. "Oliver, why don't you start us off?"

For the second time in his life, Oliver didn't immediately respond when addressed by a teacher. For a moment he just sat there staring at the floor, then very slowly he raised his eyes and, apparently with some difficulty, focused on Mrs. Waterberry.

"Read?" he said as if he'd never heard the word before.

"Yes," she said, looking alarmed. "You can do just the first two paragraphs if you don't want to read the whole thing."

His brow was furrowed with pained concentration. It seemed to take Oliver forever to grasp what the teacher was asking him to do.

"Uh, yeah," he said after a moment. "Yeah, I will." Unzipping his backpack, he tried to find his literature book, but after a few seconds he gave up. Slumping back in his seat he closed his eyes. Staying awake appeared to take every ounce of his energy. "I'm sorry," Oliver finally said, opening his eyes and looking up at the teacher. "I can't find my book."

"Here, use mine." Jason quickly slid his textbook onto our friend's desk. Meanwhile, I glanced down at his backpack, which was sitting open on the floor, his literature book in plain sight.

Oliver bowed his head, staring hard at the page he was supposed to read. After soundlessly moving his lips for a moment, he began to read, only it was nothing like his usual reading voice. Now his voice was so soft it was almost incoherent, he kept stopping to sound out easy words, and he seemed to be having difficulty concentrating on what he was doing. His eyes kept wandering and every now and then he'd squeeze them shut as if trying to overcome some sort of pain.

"Maybe you should go see the nurse," Mrs. Waterberry suggested, cutting over Oliver as the rest of the class started to mutter their confusion. "Obviously you are not feeling well."

As if that was his cue, Oliver slumped forward, his head hitting the desk with a thump, his whole body going limp.

"We'll give him a hand," Jason said as the two of us quickly got to our feet. "Come on, Oliver, let's go."

When our friend didn't move, Jason gave him a little nudge.

"Maybe you should call 911!" Wendy Waterhouse squealed, her dark brown eyes looking bigger still behind her thick lenses. "He could be coding."

"That's probably a good idea," Mrs. Waterberry agreed, but just as she reached to pick up her telephone, Oliver suddenly sat straight up in his seat.

"No, don't call 911," he said, grabbing his backpack and standing up, suddenly looking sharp and alert. "I think I just need to lie down for a moment." Nodding for Jason and me to follow him, he strode calmly out of the room.

"What the hell happened?" Jason demanded when we were a safe distance from the classroom. "Oliver, are you okay?"

"I'm not Oliver," he replied, casting a quick glance around. "Come on." And he started walking briskly toward the exit.

"Then who are you?" Jason asked, looking bewildered.

"It's me, Corpus," Oliver said. "Your friend is currently unavailable. I saw what was happening through the classroom window. Jessica is right, we do not know the extent of your friend's condition. By the way, you humans do an unhealthy amount of sitting down; public dining, office buildings, classrooms…"

"What?" I couldn't help expressing my surprise at these last words, regardless of who was in control.

"You sit down too much."

Despite my reaction, Jason was already in full gear, eagerly staring into Oliver's eyes, as if looking for some sign of the alien. "Are you possessing him?"

"*Of course not*," Corpus hissed, narrowing Oliver's eyes indignantly. "Possessing a person is taking control of his or her body merely for one's own personal gain. I am simply commandeering him. I think he passed out."

"So if you're now in control of him, where are you?"

"I'm waiting for you outside by the flagpole," Corpus in our friend's body said. "We have to return him to your house and get to the bottom of this. It's getting worse."

"What's getting worse?" I asked, hurrying to keep up.

"The pain," the alien replied. "That is one of the drawbacks in commandeering an individual's body. Their pain becomes yours."

We pushed through the double front doors of the school and hurried down the steps. In the middle of the grassy area out front, Corpus was standing beside the flagpole waiting for us. When we reached him he turned and headed down the sidewalk along side us.

"Is that hard? Controlling two bodies at once?" Jason asked, his eyes switching from Corpus to Oliver with mixed amazement.

"No," the alien said. "It's like walking and talking at the same time."

Meanwhile, Oliver walked silently beside us, his face expressionless, his eyes staring straight ahead. All the life he had possessed in the hallway a moment ago seemed to have vanished.

"What happened?" Jason asked, staring at his now vacant gaze. "Why does he look like a zombie all of a sudden?"

"Only Mind-Control Masters can make their victims appear realistically life-like for long periods of time," Corpus said matter-of-factly. "It takes years of skill to completely bend the mind to your will. Unfortunately, a lot of people who specialize in mind-control are criminals."

"Why?" I asked.

"Because mind-control is illegal," Corpus replied. "Only trained professionals are allowed to take control of an individual's body without his or her permission."

"Are you a trained professional?" Jason asked skeptically.

"No," the alien admitted. "But I understand the basic concepts."

"Where is Oliver right now?" I inquired nervously as he continued to walk silently beside me. "Is he aware of what's going on?"

"No. Like I said before, he is unconscious. His mind is crumpling under the strain of whatever is going on."

"So can you take over anyone you feel like?" Jason asked as if his stream of questions hadn't been interrupted. "For example, could you take control of me, or do your subjects have to be unconscious?"

"Technically I could take control of your body," Corpus said, sounding impatient. "However, I would have to release Oliver before doing so. But I wouldn't. As I have already told you, mind-control is illegal on my home planet. I don't take control of people's bodies whenever I feel like it. This was an emergency situation; I had to make a decision. Only Mind-Control Masters and criminal masterminds commandeer bodies, and I am neither. Besides," Corpus added, sounding slightly calmer. "Mind-control is a difficult practice. I wouldn't try it on someone who was conscious. I haven't had the proper training. Something could go wrong."

"Like what?" I asked, worry seeping into the outskirts of my mind.

"Like their brainwaves could get scrambled."

"How do you know that hasn't already happened?" Jason demanded, his sharp hazel eyes taking in every square inch of Oliver's face.

"I don't know for sure," the alien said. "But it's highly unlikely. Besides, Oliver needed our help. I didn't have a choice."

Jason looked like he might have an aneurism. "You mean his brain could be scrambled right now? Are you crazy?!"

"His brain is not scrambled," Corpus responded calmly. "The odds of that happening are thousands to one."

"But there's still a possibility?" I interjected, taking Oliver's hand. "What if he isn't all right?"

"Then I guess I will have one more problem to worry about," the alien said as Oliver gave me a deadpan stare. "All we can do is try our best."

I let go of his hand. It was creepy seeing my friend's eyes look so lifeless. At least when he's daydreaming he appears to be someplace nice. This was just weird.

When we arrived at Jason's house, we entered the living room. Oliver went over and sat down on the couch while Jason, Corpus, and I remained standing, facing him.

"What now?" Jason asked as our friend stared blankly at the opposite wall.

"You should get him something to eat," Corpus said, sitting cross-legged on the floor. "He's hungry."

"How do you know?"

"I told you. I feel what he feels."

"But he's unconscious."

"Yeah, however, his body is still functioning," Corpus said impatiently as he started rummaging through his bag.

"I'm hungry," Oliver stated flatly while the alien pulled the cap off a grey tube with his teeth.

"He sounds like a robot," Jason muttered, eyeing him distastefully. "I think I liked him better before."

"Come on," I sighed. "Just get him something to eat."

"Fine." After casting Oliver an unsavory look, Jason left the room.

"What's that?" I asked as the alien squeezed a minute amount of the dark gluey substance out of the tube into his mouth.

"Nourishment," he replied, making a face as he swallowed the sticky goo. "It's not as good as regular food, but the crew didn't want to waste quality sustenance on me."

"What exactly happened?" I asked, sitting down beside him. "Why did the rest of the ship want to finish the mission without you?"

Corpus's shoulders sagged. "I had the opportunity of a lifetime and I messed it up. Jason was right, I did nearly get the whole crew killed, all because I couldn't focus on my job for two seconds. Maybe Marcus was right, maybe I don't belong in space."

"You're just a kid, aren't you?" I murmured, staring at him closely. "In human standards you're very smart, but you're still very young?"

"Yeah," he sighed. "Maybe this body does suit me. Emotionally, I am just a seven-year-old kid."

"Well, I think it's great what you're doing." I placed a hand on his shoulder to comfort him. "We'd be nowhere without you."

"If it weren't for me, you wouldn't be in this mess," Corpus pointed out, a nervous smile creeping across his face. "I was the one who set off the creation machine."

"What's one human to your race? You stuck around and that's what matters."

Corpus didn't respond.

"What?" I asked, noticing that he was giving me a penetrating look.

"I want to know what you feel, but I cannot get a read on your emotions."

"What do you mean get a read?"

"Where I come from, our emotions radiate from us like an aroma emanates from a flower. We can sense each other's feelings. I assumed it would be the same here, but I cannot pick up anything. From what I've witnessed, you humans relay entirely on facial expressions."

I wasn't sure I followed. "I've seen you use facial expressions… Perhaps your people don't use them as much as we do, but still…"

"We do use them on occasion, but we don't relay on them to interpret each other's emotional state. Expressions can be faked, feelings cannot."

"What exactly…?" I started when Jason suddenly entered.

"This is all I could find," he said, holding up a container of glazed doughnuts. "Someone really needs to go shopping around here."

"Are they edible?" Corpus asked.

"Yes."

"Then they will do," the alien said and Oliver snatched the box away from Jason, opened it and started devouring the doughnuts.

"Okay," Jason grunted, looking peeved as he slumped down in the armchair. "What do we do now?"

"Well," Corpus said, returning the tube of nourishment to his duffle bag. "After he's done eating, we should try waking him up. I have a theory about what's going on. But first we need to find out more about this jungle. I think it's the key."

After that, the room was silent. Well, semi-silent. The only sound came from Oliver as Corpus had him wolf down one glazed doughnut after another. While he ate, Jason stared him down. I could only guess what he was thinking. Meanwhile, the alien sat cross-legged on the floor, his head bowed and his hands folded in his lap. So much had happened since last night, I felt like I was just starting to catch my breath. To be honest, I was still coming to grips with the fact that we had an extraterrestrial in our midst. There were so many questions I wanted to ask. So far I'd only scratched the surface. Not knowing where to start, I decided to continue the conversation from earlier.

"So you guys can sense each others emotions? Relationships must be pretty straightforward." As I said this I couldn't help glancing at Oliver.

"Not really," Corpus replied, raising his head, a thoughtful look coming across his face. "We can only sense certain things; happiness, sadness, anger…" As if he could read my mind, he added. "We cannot sense love."

"Oh." I was about to comment on that when Jason overrode me.

"I just had a thought." His hazel eyes were still glued to Oliver. "How do we know you're not here to invade our planet? For all we know your people are hovering just overhead, waiting to enslave us all."

"I am not here to enslave your race," Corpus murmured, his voice almost inaudible.

"We don't know that," Jason stated flatly, sitting up as he finally tore his eyes away from our alien-inhabited friend to look directly at the alien himself. "If I've learned anything, it's that aliens come to conquer. Our cinema is full of examples: *Independence Day, War of the Worlds… The Host!* For all we know you're the scout, verifying that we don't have the technology to resist."

"Jason," I signed, hoping to keep things civil. "If that were true, why would he be helping us?"

"How should I know? He's not human. Come to think of it, we don't know what he is. His intentions could be anything. And with that mind-control thing, we are powerless to stop him. Once he sends word to his people, we'll all end up like him," Jason gestured at Oliver. "Mindless and obedient. Who knows how many civilizations they've overthrown."

"We are not the bad guys!" Corpus hissed through gritted teeth. "We help people! You have no idea how many races we've saved! Before we came along the Hyzorians were being harvested like… like…" it looked as if he was searching for the right word. "Like cattle! Without us the Antomolites would be extinct, destroyed by their own planet! Thanks to my people, the Zizithora—"

"—Corpus, calm down," I cut in, desperate to defuse the situation. "Jason isn't trying to upset you. He's just… stressed. We all are. This whole ordeal has us pretty rattled."

I don't know if the alien believed me, but it didn't matter. By now Oliver had finished the last doughnut. Now that the box was empty, Corpus relinquished his hold on our friend and he slumped down onto the couch, motionless once more.

Chapter 9

OLIVER

After leaving Jason's house for school that morning, things got a little hazy. All I really remember is the mind-numbing pain in my head that was steadily getting worse. I wasn't completely aware of my surroundings until I heard someone saying my name over and over again. My head still ached, but the pain had died down some. When I opened my eyes I was lying on Jason's couch again and he, Jessica, and Corpus were all staring at me with looks of concern in their eyes.

"Did you go back to the jungle?" Jason asked after I'd pushed myself into a sitting position.

"No," I said, looking at each of them in turn. Jessica was standing with her arms folded, her index finger tapping her arm. The alien was a couple feet back, ringing the hem of his shirt. What had I missed? Maybe it was just me, but the atmosphere seemed a little tense. "What's going on? I thought we were in school."

"We were 'til you passed out," Jason said, a muscle working in his jaw. "Obviously you're not okay, man."

I held up a hand, sure I must have misheard him. "Wait a minute. We left school before seventh hour?"

"We kinda had to."

"Guys, we have to go back!" I started to get up, but to my surprise Jason pushed me back down.

"You're not going anywhere," he said, folding his arms across his chest. "According to our little alien friend, you might be in more trouble than we thought."

"But I can't miss class!" I gasped, my breath quickening. "I've never missed school without a written excuse!"

"There's a first for everything."

"This can't be happening." I ran my fingers through my hair as my head started to spin. It felt like all the air was being sucked from the room.

"Try and stay calm," Jessica said, a worried look on her face. "There's a reason you passed out."

"Yeah, because I didn't have breakfast this morning," I said, grasping at straws. "It's no big deal."

"I wish it were that simple."

"You guys can't keep me here." I made another attempt to get up, but once again Jason forced me back down. He might not have been as tall as me, but he was definitely stronger.

"Sure we can," he said confidently. "Especially if it means keeping you alive."

"Come on!" I protested, starting to feel desperate. "If we hurry we can still make it back before sixth hour."

"You're not going anywhere," Corpus said, stepping forward. "If my theory is correct, your condition could be very serious."

For a moment I just sat there, staring at my friends in shocked silence. I couldn't believe they were actually keeping me from going to school. But seeing that I was out-numbered I sat back on the couch, my teeth clenched. I didn't know what was going on, but it must have been pretty severe if Jason and Jessica were willing to forcibly keep me here.

"Did I at least get my English paper turned in?" I asked, grateful that there wasn't any homework due in any of my afternoon classes. "I can't remember."

"Yes," Jessica replied, sitting down next to me. "But now we need to talk about what's wrong with you. What can you tell us about the jungle?"

I didn't answer immediately. It was only now that I noticed an ill feeling bubbling up inside. My hand drifted to my stomach as I started to feel nauseous.

"What's the matter?" Jason asked.

"I feel sick. Like I overate, but I don't remember eating anything today."

"Never mind that. The jungle, tell us about it."

"Well, all I know is that it was like I was really there," I said thoughtfully, massaging my middle. "I kept pinching myself to see if it was just a dream, but I wouldn't wake up."

"When you finally did wake up, what was the last thing you remember?" Corpus asked.

"It was dark and I was in Avril's den. I thought I'd fallen asleep, but the next thing I knew Jessica was screaming in my ear."

"I see," the alien said, sounding unnerved. "I am going to do a little test. It might hurt a little, but it is necessary to understand what is going on."

My heart skipped a beat. "What are you going to do?"

Corpus went over to the arm of the couch where a small black cube sat and picked it up.

"I need to increase the power on the cerebral scrutinizer," he said, his finger drifting over the surface of the cube. "That might give us a better idea of what is happening."

"What's going on here?" I asked, getting more nervous by the second. "What's this about?"

"I have a theory about what caused you to enter that jungle last night and what's causing the headaches now," Corpus said. "But I need to test my theory before we take any drastic measures."

"Drastic measures?! I think we passed that when you mentioned pain."

"Everything will be okay, Oliver," Jessica assured me, taking my hand. "It's going to be all right."

"Just get it over with," I sighed wearily, sitting back on the couch. "If I die, I want you all to know how much I love you."

"Don't be so dramatic," Jason said, folding his arms. "You'll be fine."

"All right, here we go." Corpus gently stroked the exterior of the cube. The transparent screen went into static and I gritted my teeth as a bolt of pain shot through my head. The static began to clear and an image appeared. It was no longer the different colored lines, but an actual picture. Looking closer, I realized I was looking at myself lying on the bed of leaves in Avril's den, the two of us side by side. The centaur's head was resting on my chest and, though Avril's lips were curled in a slight smile as she slept, my face was completely void of expression. The only sign of life was my chest which steadily rose and fell to the rhythm of my breathing.

"Oh, my god," Jessica whispered, staring at the screen. "This can't be possible."

"Who's the pretty girl?" Jason asked, also gaping at the image. "She really seems to like you."

"She's a centaur and her name is Avril," I muttered, not taking my eyes off the two of us. Every now and then the Rebel would shift in her sleep while I lay unnaturally still. "She told me I looked like Quaymius."

"Who's Quaymius?" Jason inquired.

"Avril's wannabe lover," Jessica said, also not taking her eyes off the screen.

"Why does she think you look like Quaymius?" Jason asked.

I shrugged. "I don't know. We have the same color hair?"

"What does all this mean?" Jessica asked Corpus, her fearful eyes still fixed on the screen. "Is this a dream, are we watching Oliver's dreams?"

"How many people dream about being asleep?" Jason asked, arching a skeptical eyebrow. "I can imagine dreaming about a beautiful centaur maiden, but this seems a little farfetched. Besides, how can Oliver be dreaming if he's awake?"

"He's right," the alien said. "This isn't a dream. Nothing like this has ever happened before, but it seems to me that some other plane of existence has somehow been planted in Oliver's mind."

"You mean we're looking at another world inside his head?" Jason asked, his eyebrows raised.

"Not a world as we know it," Corpus said, thinking hard. "If a real world had been created we would all be dead. This world is much smaller. According to the cerebral scrutinizer, Oliver's brain activity is way beyond the normal level for a human being. Obviously the creation machine did something to him when it went off. I'd like to see this story that you wrote. It might have something to do with what's going on," Corpus added turning to me.

"Here, it's in my backpack," Jessica said, grabbing her bag and pulling it over. After a few seconds of rummaging she pulled out the packet and handed it to Corpus. He looked over the first few pages, his eyebrows becoming more narrowed as he went.

"How long have you been working on this story?" the alien asked after a moment, looking up.

"How long did it take me to type that? A couple hours."

"No, I mean how long have you been developing this? How much background information do you have?"

"Uh, tons," I said, scratching my head. "I've been putting it together for months."

"I see." Corpus looked more troubled by the minute.

"Why? What's wrong?" I asked, panic gripping me. To make matters worse, the queasy feeling inside was gradually intensifying. Something was definitely wrong.

"I think that somehow the creation machine has recreated this world in your mind," he said, looking disheartened. "I can only guess how, but for now that seems like the only explanation."

"Are you trying to tell us *The Kingdom of the Centaurs* is real?" Jessica asked. "You think it exists in Oliver's mind?"

"Yes," the alien said plainly.

"But you said there had to be a programming chip in the machine before it could do anything," she said nervously, twirling a strand of hair around her index finger. "Didn't you say it wasn't fully functional until it had that chip?"

"That's right," Corpus replied, turning to face her. "But apparently your friend has a very vivid imagination. Because this has never happened before, it's only reasonable to assume that a strong enough mind would have the same effect as the chip."

"But what about life?" Jessica said, now sounding desperate. "You said Magnum Opus couldn't create life. How do you explain the centaur and the vegetation?"

"Taking a wild guess, I would have to say Oliver's imagination, combined with the power of the machine, has recreated this world exactly the way he saw it in his mind; the landscape and the people."

Jason slumped down on the floor. "So what does all this mean? Is Oliver going to die?"

"Not if I can help it," Corpus said, staring at the transparent image. "Obviously the human mind isn't designed for this kind of pressure. That would explain the headaches. We can only assume that they will become much worse over time. The only alternative is to somehow try and separate this world from his mind."

"And how do you do that?" Jessica asked.

"I don't know," Corpus admitted, looking glum. "If I could enter this world, maybe I could extract Oliver from it, but it's a very risky process. They don't teach us mind penetration in the Spacing Academy."

"Well, can you try?" Jason inquired.

"I could, but if something goes wrong, the damage would be insurmountable."

"And if you don't?" Jessica asked.

"Uh, Oliver's mind would undoubtedly begin to collapse under the pressure of sustaining this world," Corpus said, looking as if it took every ounce of his energy just to say each word. "At first it would just be the headaches, but over time, his brain would begin to shut down."

"So either way, it doesn't look good for me," I muttered, staring at the floor.

"I'm afraid not."

"Then I want you to do it," I said as Avril changed position once again in her sleep. "I want you to enter my mind and try and separate me from that place."

"Oliver, are you sure?" Jessica asked, looking at me, her blue eyes full of fear.

"Yes," I said firmly, although my heart was pounding a mile a minute. "If I don't, sooner or later, my mind will cave in. At least this way I have a chance."

"Okay," Corpus said, sitting cross-legged on the floor in front of me. "I will try."

"So how will this work exactly?" I asked as the alien folded his hands in his lap.

"Under normal circumstances, mind penetration is used to observe people's memories as well as get a detailed map of their emotions," Corpus informed me. "However, given the irregularity of this situation, it is unlikely to function in that manner. Instead I am hoping I will be able to use it to enter into this world, aka your mind. If I am successful, I will appear on that screen with you and the centaur." With that, Corpus closed his eyes.

For a moment I didn't feel anything, then a blinding knife of pain pierced my mind. It felt as if someone was trying to force his way into my scull. I squeezed my eyes shut as a gasp escaped my lips. In the midst of my agony, I felt Jessica squeeze my hand. Then, after one last torturous moment, the pain was gone. But though the discomfort had subsided, my torment was not over. I collapsed back on the couch as the nausea that had been plaguing me since I woke up rocketed to a new level.

"Hey, look!" Jason suddenly said, temporarily pulling me from my misery. Looking up, I saw him pointing anxiously at the screen. Gingerly sitting up I saw that Avril and I were no longer alone in the den. Corpus was now kneeling beside us. I quickly turned to look at the floor in front of me. His body was still sitting cross-legged on the rug, his eyes shut, his hands still folded neatly in his lap.

"Can you see me?" the version of him on the screen asked, not looking at us. Instead he was peering around as if not sure where he should be facing.

"Uh, yeah," Jason said excitedly. "Can you see us?"

"No," Corpus replied. "It's one-way reception. So, uh, how's Oliver doing?"

"I think I'm going to be sick," I groaned before either of my friends could answer.

"Was it that bad?" Jason asked, casting a nervous glance at me, before returning his gaze to the screen.

I swallowed hard, not saying a word.

"Oliver, what's the matter?" Jessica turned away from the screen to give me a closer look, her face riddled with concern.

"I don't know." Leaning forward in my seat, I cradled my stomach with my right arm while my left gripped the arm of the couch. "I haven't been feeling well since I woke up. It must be something I ate."

"Oh, my god!" Jessica gasped, her eyes going wide as she shot a look at Jason. "Are you allergic to doughnuts?"

"No, but if they have too much sugar in them, I get really sick."

"Oh, no!" Her hands flew to her mouth.

"Why? What is it?"

Jason went over to the low wooden table beside the couch and picking up a white cardboard box. "You kinda ate all the glazed doughnuts in here."

"What?!" I gasped in shocked disbelief. "When?!"

"Corpus made you do it," Jason said, looking at the version of the alien on the transparent screen. "When you passed out in school, he took over your body and made you eat the glazed doughnuts."

"Hey, don't put all the blame on me!" Corpus said angrily. "You guys could have told me your friend doesn't eat sugar. How was I supposed to know?"

"But he never told us!" Jessica exclaimed, turning to look at me. "You never told us you can't eat sugar."

I groaned, wrapping both arms around my middle. "Surely you guys must have noticed. The sandwiches, the salads? You think I do that for fun?"

"I did think it was a little weird," Jason said thoughtfully. "But we're all a little weird, right?"

"I'll be right back." Jumping up, I hurried from the living room. Dashing down the hall to the bathroom, I shut the door and stopped in front of the sink. After a second or two my stomach heaved violently and all the half-digested doughnuts I'd been forced to eat came rushing back up. Once my stomach was void of all unwanted substances, I washed my mouth out several times before returning to the living room to rejoin the others. When I got back, Jessica was still on the couch, waiting for me, but Jason had moved to the armchair opposite the couch, a glum expression on his face.

"How are you feeling?" Jessica asked when I sat down beside her.

"Not so good. It will take a while for my stomach to settle down."

"I'm sorry about having to strong-arm you earlier," Jason suddenly said, casting me an uneasy look. "I know how much school means to you. You forgive me, right?"

I shrugged it off. "Of course. You were just looking out for me and that's what matters. I'm lucky to have friends like you."

For a moment the room was silence then Jessica, looking mildly unsure asked, "Oliver, why didn't you ever tell us you couldn't eat sugar?"

"I don't know. People already think I'm weird as it is. I didn't want to add this."

"I don't think you're weird," she said softly.

"Yeah, well you're my friend. Besides, you have your own unique qualities. But I know people think I'm peculiar because I like school. If normal kids don't like school, what kind of kid can't eat sugar?"

"I'm sure there are lots of people out there who can't eat sugar," Jessica said bracingly.

"Take diabetics, for example," Jason said matter-of-factly. "I'm sure you'd fit right in."

"So what's this about Corpus taking control of my body?" I asked, trying to change the subject. "Why don't I remember this?"

"You were unconscious," Jason explained, glancing at the alien's body which was still positioned cross-legged in the middle of the room. "You fainted in Mrs. Waterberry's class."

"I can't believe that," I sighed absentmindedly. "How did she take it?"

"She was going to call 911 until Corpus saw what was going on and got you out of there."

"By the way how are you feeling now?" the alien asked from the transparent screen, now sitting beside Avril as she slept.

"Better."

"Good," he said, getting up and gently sliding the female centaur's head off my chest. "Because you could be in for a bumpy ride."

"How do you mean?"

Corpus was now kneeling beside my unconscious form. "I want to remind you all once again that nothing like this has ever happened before. Anything I tell you is my best logical guess. I don't know what the effect of trying to bring this version of you out with me will have, but I think it's best to warn you of any possible complications."

"Treat it like a Band-Aid," Jason said, sitting up in his seat. "Just get it over with."

"Whatever," the alien muttered, taking my hands in his and closing his eyes.

I felt slightly dizzy for a moment, but otherwise nothing happened. On the screen I remained just as unresponsive as ever. Then I felt something warm start trickling down my upper lip. I pressed my finger to the spot and, on taking it away realized it was blood.

"Oh, my god, you're bleeding!" Jessica cried, staring at the steady flow that was now emanating from my right nostril.

"Corpus, what's going on?" I asked, stemming the flow only to have it replaced with more.

"What's happening?" he asked, releasing my arms.

"My nose is bleeding!" I cried, now panic-stricken as the blood continued to come. "And it's getting worse!"

"Just a moment," the alien said, then with a slight twinge of pain, he disappeared from the screen and the version of him that had been cross-legged on the floor opened its eyes. He quickly got to his feet and came over to the couch. By now my hands were covered in blood as I continued to desperately try to stop the bleeding. Jessica and Jason were using tissues to prevent the blood from dripping onto the front of my shirt and the couch.

"Do something!" Jessica cried when the alien stopped beside Jason, his face stricken upon seeing what was happening. "Make it stop!"

Chapter 10

I wasn't kidding when I said I didn't know the full effect of trying to remove Oliver's body from the world he and Magnum Opus had created, but I wasn't at all prepared for what actually did happen. When I heard Oliver and Jessica's cries of shock and panic I knew something wasn't right. I quickly extracted myself from Oliver's mind and what I saw made my skin crawl. There was a river of blood traveling down Oliver's upper lip, over his mouth and down his chin. Jason and Jessica were doing their best to mop up the bleeding, but they were falling behind. And as the blood continued to run, Oliver's once rich complexion was starting to fade. I stood frozen beside Jason, unable to think straight. In fact, if Jessica hadn't screamed at me to do something, their friend might have bled to death.

Dropping to my knees, I quickly started rummaging around in my bag, looking for the IRD. The moment it flashed into view, I grabbed it, hurried back to the couch and pressed the orange icon on the side. A green band of light came out the end and gradually ran up and down the surface of Oliver's face. After a few seconds, the bleeding stopped.

Ten minutes later we were all, once again sitting in the living room staring at each other in silence. Oliver had spent another five minutes in the bathroom cleaning up after another one of my mistakes. Now he sat on the couch in silence, his face still unnaturally white, and dark circles around his eyes. Jessica was sitting beside him, her feet pulled up under her and her hands anxiously grasping Oliver's arm as if she was afraid if she didn't hang onto him he might fall apart. Jason was back in the armchair, a grim look on his face as he stared at the floor. I, however, was sitting cross-legged in the middle of the room, fidgeting nervously with one of my shoelaces. I wasn't sure how much more of the silence I could take. I wanted to apologize, but I wasn't sure where to start. It seemed to me that after everything that had happened to Oliver over the last twenty hours, a simple "I'm sorry" wasn't going to cut it. Though, I did feel like at least some of what had happened wasn't entirely my fault. But right when I decided to take full responsibility, Jason grunted, "Nice going, Mandayus," in a voice just loud enough to hear. Even though I knew there was no way he could possibly know what he'd just done, I couldn't stop myself from exploding.

"Well," I hissed, whipping around to face him. "It's interesting you should say that, because when I think about it 99.9 percent of anything that goes wrong is your fault!"

"Oh, yeah?" Jason demanded, sitting up in his chair. "How so?"

"Oh, I don't know. You played keep-away with the machine when we first met in the parking lot, you were the one who gave me the doughnuts to feed Oliver, and you told me to just get on with it when I told you about the possible risks. I think it's sick the way you blame everyone else for whatever goes wrong when more times than not you are the one to blame!"

"Hey, I'm not the one who brought that godforsaken thing onto this planet," Jason shot back, his face turning red. "I didn't possess Oliver and force him to eat an entire box of glazed doughnuts, and I definitely didn't try and remove him from his own mind! That was all you, buddy!"

"Guys, stop it!" Jessica yelled from the couch. "Fighting about this won't solve anything! Jason why do you always have to be such a—"

"—Wait!" I gasped, getting to my feet and staring at Jason wide-eyed. "What did you say?"

"You want to fight?" he challenged, also getting up. "I'll pound your head into the ground, little man."

"If he can take control of bodies, I'm sure he doesn't have to worry about you pounding him into the ground," Oliver sighed wearily from the couch. "Jason, if I were you I'd be careful."

"*Oh, yeah?*" he hissed, slamming his left fist into his right palm. "I'd like to see him try. I'll knock his block off!"

"Look, I'm not trying to fight," I said, folding my arms impatiently. "I just realized something."

"What?" Jason demanded menacingly.

I went over to the arm of the couch where the cerebral scrutinizer was still displaying the image of Oliver and the female centaur fast asleep.

"We already know that this place now resides in Oliver's brain," I said, staring at the screen. "So, it's only reasonable to assume that this version of Oliver," I pointed to the Oliver lying beside the centaur, "Is just a representation of him in his own mind. If this is true, then of course it would be irrational to try and remove it. But there is only one way to test if this theory is correct."

"How?" Oliver asked, looking wary.

"I would have to re-enter your mind and try and remove something else. If it is possible to take out a stick or a leaf, then it will be clear that we're facing much bigger problems that I had anticipated."

"Why?" Jessica asked anxiously.

"Because then there's no way I can separate Oliver from this world without risking further damage." I replied. "It's like Jason said. Trying to remove his mind from his body is logically impossible. Had I used my full power... it probably would have killed him."

Chapter 11

JASON

I don't like Mandayus-Corpus. He is snooty, pompous and self-important. Despite his current stature, I knew he looked down on us. I could see it in his eyes. Perhaps humans weren't smart enough, or we weren't powerful enough. It didn't matter. Since his arrival, Corpus had caused nothing but trouble. Not to mention I didn't trust the guy. He was annoyingly evasive and extremely hostile. What did we really know about him? So far everything he's told us is circumstantial. I didn't understand why Jessica couldn't see it. No doubt her love of aliens had her blinded to his potential threat. Still, after seeing the way he reacted to Oliver's situation, it was clear the alien cared. Sitting cross-legged on the floor he looked just as miserable as the rest of us. All I could do was hope that his intentions were good.

"So what are we supposed to do?" I asked as we all stared gloomily at the transparent screen. "We can't take Oliver out of that place without killing him, but he also can't live with it in his mind. That seems a little like catch-22, doesn't it?"

"Before you get all crestfallen, I think you should remember that this is all just speculation," Corpus said, going to the center of the living room floor and sitting cross-legged once again. "I think it best we make sure my theories are correct before we give up. Oliver are you ready?"

"Just do it," he sighed, looking as if he'd given up a long time ago.

The alien closed his eyes and once again the look of intense pain crossed Oliver's face. Then, after a few seconds, he relaxed as the alien appeared on the screen.

"Here goes nothing," I muttered as Corpus picked up one of the large leaves that made up the floor of the shelter. A moment later he disappeared from the screen. All eyes shifted to the center of the room where the alien opened his eyes just in time to see the leaf he'd picked up appear in his hands.

"Oh, no," he whispered, turning the leaf over, a look of total despair in his eyes.

Jessica wrapped her arms around Oliver's neck and began to cry. Corpus continued to stare hopelessly at the leaf. Quite frankly I couldn't believe they were all giving up so easily. There had to be another way out. This couldn't be the end.

"Come on!" I said, looking around the room at all the dismal faces. "There's gotta be something we can do. This can't be it."

"What would you suggest?" Oliver asked, looking at me as if my optimism was causing him further pain.

"I don't know," I said, grabbing the pages of Oliver's story, which Corpus had left on the floor, and flipping through them. "You know this world better than I do. There must be some loophole. Some way out!"

"The cave!" Jessica cried, pulling away from Oliver and wiping the tears from her eyes. "Of course! If Artayus the Great used it to come here, why can't you?!"

"Yeah, but the cave doesn't always work," Oliver said. "Many centaurs have tried to get it to reveal its secrets, but only a few in the history of the Ancient Kingdom have ever been able to enter. Why should I be any different?"

"Because you wrote this story!" I exclaimed, starting to get irritated. "You made the whole thing up! You should know better than anyone how the cave works!"

"I thought I did," Oliver muttered, looking confused. "But being in that jungle must have affected me somehow because now I can't remember."

"It's time to wake up," a soft dreamy voice suddenly said, making everyone jump. "The sun is shining."

"Who said that?" I asked, looking around the room in surprise.

"I think it was her," Jessica said, pointing at the cerebral scrutinizer and all eyes turned to the transparent screen where the female centaur was no longer asleep. She was still lying beside Oliver's motionless body, only now she was gazing down at him with an affectionate look in her beautiful green eyes.

"Come on," Avril cooed, brushing his hair out of his face. "The day is waiting and there is lots to be done."

Oliver still didn't move and a worried look slowly began to creep into the centaur's eyes as she started to shake him. "Come on, Oliver, wake up!"

We all stared in shocked silence as the centaur became frantic. She shook him a few more times then put her ear to his chest. Satisfied that he was still alive, she leaned back and stared at him for a moment as if trying to decide what to do. Finally she propped him up in a sitting position. Running her slender fingers along his jaw, she whispered something in his ear. She then pulled a small bottle from a pouch on her belt, opened his mouth, and poured the contents in. Almost immediately, the Oliver sitting on the couch made a weird sound in the back of his throat, a look of dread streaking across his face. After trying to resist the urge, he swallowed hard. As he did so, the version of him on the screen followed suit, gulping down the mysterious substance.

"What was that?" Jessica asked nervously as Avril gently laid our friend back down on the ground beside her.

"I… I don't know," he replied, staring unblinkingly at the screen.

"Some sort of medicine most likely," Corpus said, also looking uneasy. "But if it's designed to revive you, I think we're in trouble."

"Why?" I asked.

"I think it's become clear that these two parts of Oliver's mind cannot co exist simultaneously. In other words, while that part of him remains unconscious in that world this part can become conscious and vice versa. I can only assume forcing that part of him to wake up while he is still conscious in this world could be very hazardous."

"So what do we do?" Oliver asked.

"I'll have to put you to sleep before that part of you wakes up," Corpus said, getting up and walking over so the two were face to face.

"And how are you gonna do that?" I asked.

"I'm going to hypnotize him," the alien replied. "Oliver, just stare into my eyes. Don't worry, this will not hurt."

Oliver and Corpus stared hard into each other's eyes and after a moment his eyelids began to flutter and within seconds he slumped forward, unconscious once again.

"That's scary," I muttered as Jessica laid our friend out on the couch. "You guys have way too much power over the mind. What is it like on your home world; people just possessing and knocking each other out right and left? There must be anarchy."

"Actually, no," Corpus said as Jessica gently placed Oliver's hands on his chest. "Don't get me wrong, every civilization has its criminals, but a lot of those mind tricks are only possible if both parties are willing. For example, if Oliver hadn't wanted me to hypnotize him, all he would have to do is look away. Eye contact is essential."

"Yeah, but still," I said, folding my arms. "What about the whole mind-control thing? You don't need eye contact for that. Can't just anyone do it?"

"Yes, but it's against the law," Corpus explained, starting to sound impatient. "Only trained personnel are allowed to commandeer someone's body. If you do it illegally, you get reprimanded."

I arched an eyebrow. "So if your people found out that you possessed Oliver, you would get sent to jail?"

"I could," the alien admitted uneasily. "But I've broken so many laws since my arrival, it really wouldn't make any difference. If all of this isn't fixed by the time the ship comes back for me, I will be kicked out of the Spacing Program for sure."

"What other laws have you broken?" Jessica asked curiously from beside the couch.

"Well, verbal contact with life forms with IQs above forty is ill-advised," Corpus said. "And only creators are allowed direct contact with Magnum Opus. Just those two things are enough reason for them to take away my navigation license."

"But it wasn't your fault the machine got in your bag," Jessica said. "You said it was kept in the security room under lock and key. Someone must have put it in your bag."

"Yeah," Corpus said, his shoulders sagging. "But I can't prove it."

Just then, the Oliver on the screen groaned and shifted in his sleep. Seeing that he was waking up, Avril leaned toward him, apprehension dominating her face.

"Oliver, are you okay?" she whispered, and he slowly opened his eyes, looking at her. For a moment he appeared confused then he seemed to relax and sat up.

"What was that?" he asked, running his tongue over his lower lip.

"It's juice from the roots of the honey tree. It acts as a stimulant."

"How'd you make me swallow it?"

"Just a little spell," the centaur said proudly. "I learned it from my mother."

"I have to go!" Oliver suddenly said, making a move toward the entrance of the shelter, but Avril placed a firm hand on his chest.

"Not so fast," she said. "Clearly you're not well. I think you should take it easy."

"You don't understand. I can't stay here."

"What do you mean? Where do you have to be in such a hurry?"

"I have to leave this place." Once again Oliver tried to leave, but the centaur still wouldn't let him pass.

"But you said you were going to help us," she reminded him. "You told me you could help Quaymius."

"Well, I was wrong," our friend said, his eyes darting around. "Guys, can you hear me?"

"Yes, Oliver," Jessica answered, leaning closer to the screen. "We're still here."

"Who are you talking to?" Avril asked, looking around the den.

"Nobody," Oliver replied, looking back at the centaur. "Look, after everything that's happened, I'm not ashamed to admit I'm scared. Corpus, is there any way you guys can come here? I don't want to be alone."

"Uh, I think so," the alien said, looking momentarily surprised. "Uh, Jason what are the odds of someone walking in on us in the next unforeseeable amount of time?"

"If we go up to my room, zero," I replied. "My dad never comes in there."

"Okay, good." Corpus grabbed his bag and the cerebral scrutinizer. "Let's go."

Chapter 12

Jessica

Carrying Oliver's body up the stairs to Jason's room wasn't easy, but in five awkward minutes we made it to the second floor. With me at our friend's feet and Jason gripping him under the arms, it was up to Corpus to open the bedroom door. The alien fumbled with the brass knob for a second or two before finally turning it. Once inside, Jason and I half dragged half carried Oliver to the bed. For someone so skinny he was extremely heavy. After placing our friend on the mattress, Jason locked his bedroom door just in case. As the two of us caught our breath, Corpus told us to get comfortable so he could transfer us to the Brambee Forest.

"The process will be pretty much the same for you as it is for Oliver," he said as I laid down on the bed beside Oliver and Jason sat down on the floor with his back against the wall. "Your bodies will remain here while your minds will be moved to a new location."

"Will it hurt?" Jason asked, looking nervous as Corpus sat cross-legged on the floor.

"It shouldn't." he frowned, folding his hands in his lap. "All I'm doing is connecting your two minds with Oliver's. That way we will all be able to enter this world together."

"Quick question," Jason said as the alien was about to close his eyes. "Will we be able to get killed while we're in his mind? For example, if someone attacks us in there, will we die or will we return back here?"

"I'm not sure," Corpus replied thoughtfully. "Because of the unique way in which this place was formed, its laws are a mystery. We will have to wait and find out."

"I don't like the sound of that," Jason said, tilting his head slightly. "Maybe this isn't such a good idea."

"Come on," I said impatiently. "Where's your sense of adventure? Just the other day you were complaining because life was too boring. Now that you have the chance to experience the prospect of danger and the heart-pounding, mind-numbing feeling of anticipation you want out? Stop being such a baby."

"Hey, I don't want to die, okay!" Jason stated, his voice elevating. "I wanted excitement, yes, but not death."

"Death is not guaranteed," Corpus pointed out. "It's just a possibility."

"I don't like the sound of that."

"What about Oliver?" I asked, glaring at him. "What about all the times he's almost died? He hasn't complained once! After everything that's happened to him, I think the least we can do is be there for him. But if that's too much for you then fine, stay here. Just know that if things were reversed Oliver wouldn't think twice!"

"Fine." Jason gave in and I could tell he was a little ashamed. "I'll come."

"All right then," Corpus said, closing his eyes. "Let's do this." No sooner were the words out of his mouth, everything went dark and a strange sensation swept over me. It wasn't a bad feeling. In fact it was quite the opposite. I felt warm, like I was being wrapped in a gentle summer breeze and carried away. I seemed to drift on the air like a feather; weightless and free. I was so intrigued by the experience, I was mildly disappointed when my feet hit solid ground and the warm feeling inside me disappear. Somewhere nearby I heard a thud and a groan as Jason, too, landed on solid ground, but apparently not as gently. My vision slid into focus just in time to see him picking himself up off the ground.

"That was unbelievable!" I exclaimed as Corpus appeared beside me. "I've never felt anything so wonderful in my entire life!"

"Are you kidding?" Jason grunted, brushing himself off. "That was by far the worst thing I have ever been forced to endure!"

I glanced at the alien who was staring fixedly at the ground. "That's interesting. I thought it was lovely."

"So what do we do now?" Jason asked, looking around at the surrounding vegetation. "How do we find Oliver in all this?"

"That shouldn't be too hard," Corpus said, also looking around. "I tried to bring us within a few feet of that centaur's refuge. He should be around here somewhere."

"Oliver?" I called, cupping my hands to my mouth. "Oliver, can you hear me?"

"I'm right here." He appeared from under what had at first glance looked like an ordinary bush.

"Where's Avril?" I asked as he got to his feet and started pulling small twigs and leaves from his hair.

"She went to get her mother. Apparently she's familiar with maladies. We should get going. She said her mother's isn't far from here."

"So exactly where is this cave?" Jason asked as we started off through the thick jungle.

"It's at the center of the Brambee Forest," Oliver said matter-of-factly. "On the other side of the river."

"And how far is that?"

"Several miles. The forest is very big."

"Several miles of this?" Jason demanded, looking bewildered as he fought his way through a particularly stubborn group of vines. "You can't be serious!"

"Yep." Oliver ducked under a low-hanging leaf the size of a refrigerator door. "But isn't it beautiful?"

"Oh, that changes everything!" Jason looked like he was ready to kill someone as a branch Corpus had pushed out of his way came back and slapped him in the face.

"Shh." I put my finger to my lips. "Do you guys hear that?"

Everyone stopped moving and the sound of distant hooves became clear.

"Who is that?" Jason whispered, fear saturating his voice.

"I don't know," Oliver said, looking wary. "It could be anyone."

"How come you know so little about your own story?" Jason demanded irritably. "Don't you remember who was where?"

"It's a bit more complicated than that," Corpus said, staring in the direction of the hoof beats. "Now that this place has been made real, things no longer have to go exactly the way Oliver wrote them. Our presence here alone could bring on a major change."

"Yeah," Oliver agreed. "When I first arrived here, everything seemed to be exactly the way it was in my story, but then I met Avril at the edge of the forest. No doubt that will have some effect."

"So what do we do?" I asked.

"Try and stay low," he replied. "Make sure no one sees us."

"Why?" Jason asked apprehensively. "What do centaurs do to humans?"

"I'm not sure," Oliver mused. "But if the king gets his hands on us, he'd probably have us executed."

"What? Why!" Jason gasped.

"Because he's spent the last fifty years acting under the pretense that Artayus was a liar and a traitor. How would it look to the people if it turned out Artayus had been telling the truth? There would be anarchy."

"I think we should have some sort of disguise," Jason said nervously. "I don't want to be executed."

By now the pounding of hooves had faded away into the distance and we continued through the jungle.

"What would you suggest?" I asked.

Jason shrugged. "I don't know. Something that makes us not *look* human."

"That's going to be a bit…" Oliver abruptly cut off when Jason stopped dead in his tracks and let out a bloodcurdling scream.

"What is it?" Oliver gasped, wheeling around.

Jason didn't move a muscle. He just stood there, glued to the spot, his eyes popping from their sockets as he stared at something overhead. Slowly the rest of us turned our heads to follow his gaze. Coiled in the branches of a tall thick tree, about twenty feet up, was a massively huge snake. I read somewhere that pythons were known to get as long as thirty feet and weigh up to 300 pounds. This snake was about three times that size. I gripped Oliver's wrist fearfully as it looked down at us with menacing yellow eyes.

"I don't think you have to worry," Oliver whispered, staring up at the snake as sweat collected on his brow. "I know it looks frightening, but it won't hurt us."

"Are you sure?" I couldn't take my eyes off the horrific creature.

"Yeah." As if the snake could understand him, it rested its head on the branch and closed its eyes. "See," Oliver said, letting out a sight of relief. "Perfectly harmless."

Jason stared at the snake for a moment longer then quickly hurried on, his face as red as a ripe tomato.

After we'd been walking a while, the trees began to thin and the sound of rushing water reached our ears. Oliver opened his mouth to say something when we heard voices coming from the other side of a nearby hedge. Crouching low, we peeked through the branches to see who was on the other side.

Standing near the edge of the river was a tall lanky centaur. He was accompanied by a faun, who was sitting on a large black rock and a mermaid, who was sitting on the riverbank, her long bright orange tail halfway submerged in the rushing water. At first glance I thought there was something oddly familiar about the three of them. Looking closer at the mermaid, I realized that she looked almost exactly like me, only her hair was a dazzling golden blond and her skin was much paler. The centaur mirrored Oliver except for his sandy blond hair which was a lot longer. That and his equine ears. Finally my gaze shifted to the faun, who of course, resembled Jason with his shiny black hair and hazel eyes. The only difference was the slightly better build, long goat-like ears, and a shiny black goatee.

"What the..." Jason squinted through the branches at the faun version of himself. "What the hell is going on?"

"Oliver based his three main characters on us," I said, trying to fight back a giggle as Jason's hand went absentmindedly to his chin. "I think it's impressive."

"You would." he continued to stare at the faun. "He made you look good. I, on the other hand, look..."

"We all look good," Oliver said, a pink hue surfacing under his rich complexion. "I worked hard on those descriptions."

"I can see that," Jason said as the mermaid started twirling a lock of her beautiful golden hair around her finger.

"I think I just found the solution to the disguise problem," Corpus remarked, also staring at the greatly enhanced replicas of us.

"What's the solution?" Jason asked, eagerly tearing his eyes from the riverbank to look at the alien.

"Trying to remove Oliver from this place was a fiasco," Corpus said matter-of-factly. "It didn't work out at all the way I'd hoped."

"Thanks for reminding us," Jason said with a false smile. "What's your point?"

"I think that so long as his mind stays within the boundaries of this world, I should be able to move it to any location so long as I know the exact point in which I wish for him to end up. And because we're all just mental projections of ourselves made solid, I should be able to manipulate your structure."

"I still don't get it," Jason said.

"I think I can make the three of you take the place of your fictional counterparts."

"Really?" I turned my attention away from the riverbank. "I'd love to see what it's like to be a mermaid! How does it work?"

"It will kind of be like switching bodies except that this version of you will no longer exist."

"Great!" I said, starting to get up. "Let's do it!"

"Not so fast," Jason interrupted, holding up a hand. "Corpus, how do you know this is even going to work?"

"I don't," the alien said bluntly. "But rest assured, I highly doubt any mishaps will be painful."

"And how do you know that?"

"Come on, Jason," Oliver said impatiently. "You wanted a disguise, here you have it. Why does there always have to be a problem?"

"All right fine." Jason gave in, folding his arms across his chest. "But when this guy turns us all into worms or something, I will gladly say I told you so."

"Here goes," Corpus said, closing his eyes.

After a moment of silence and a slight dizzying sensation, everything came back into focus, but when I opened my eyes I knew something was wrong. Jason was still kneeling in front of the bush, Oliver seemed to have vanished and there was a girl with long blond hair who looked just like me where I used to be.

"Oh, no!" Jason gasped, looking down at himself before giving me a weird look. "This can't be happening!"

"What's going on?" I asked, noticing that my voice was surprisingly deep. "What's happening?"

"Oh, my god!" my clone exclaimed, looking at Jason while frantically pulling at her hair. "I can't believe this!"

"Corpus, I think you need to try again," Jason said, his voice uncharacteristically calm as he massaged his stomach.

"Don't you dare say I told you so," I warned, glaring menacingly at him, but to my surprise he stared at me in alarm. Quite frankly his lack of anger and aggression was starting to puzzle me.

"I wasn't going to," he replied, studying me pensively. "By the way, take a look at yourself."

I looked down at my hands. They were larger than before and my skin was a few shades darker. My eyes shifted to my clothes, but they weren't mine. Now my much larger frame was draped in Oliver's garments. Finally my hands went to my hair. It no longer reached passed my shoulders. Instead it stopped around my ears. Could it be? Did I now inhabit Oliver's body? My fingers drifted to my jeans…

"Oh, my god! I'm a guy!" I squealed, forcing my new voice to an unnatural pitch. There was no doubt about it. This body was definitely not female.

"You don't say," my clone grunted, her face twisted in irritation. "And I'm a girl."

"Oliver?" I inquired even though I already knew the answer.

"Guess again," she said, folding her arms.

"Not Jason."

"Right you are," he replied. "And not too happy to be here."

"Corpus, it didn't work!" Oliver in Jason's body said, looking unhappy. "We've just swapped places with each other."

"Shoot." the alien looked at each of us in turn. "I was afraid that might happen."

"But now that I'm here…" Jason loosened my scarf from around my neck. "I really don't get you, Jess. How can you stand wearing this thing in this climate?"

"*Stop that!*" I hissed, grabbing his arm. "What I choose to wear is my business."

"Cool it, Olive— I mean, Jessica," he said, pushing my hand away. "I'm burning up."

If ever there was someone I didn't want in my body it was Jason. I could just imagine his negativity tainting my soul. The thought made me shutter… until I remembered whose body I was in. My curiosity instantly took hold. In my quest to understand humanity, I have often envision the world through other people's eyes. Kneeling in the grass, my attention immediately turned to my current form; Oliver. Placing my hand on my chest, I could feel his heart beating just beneath the surface. I always knew he was different. Now I could feel it. He had a definite presence; an energy that radiated from his being.

"You're not surfing the crimson wave, are you?" Jason suddenly demanded, pulling me from my thoughts, my scarf now fully removed.

"What? No!"

"Are you sure?"

I chose to ignore him. "Corpus, can you fix this? I don't want that *thing* in my body."

"Yeah," Oliver in Jason chimed in, pulling the material of his shirt away from his chest.

"His body is no picnic either."

"Okay, give me a moment. This is a lot harder than it looks." the alien took a deep breath and closed his eyes.

Chapter 13

OLIVER

There are no words to describe what it's like inhabiting your best friend's body. Opening my eyes, I quickly knew the three of us had swapped places. For starters, my clothes were more restricting than I remembered. Already with the notion of a possible mishap, I quickly put two and two together. I was Jason, he was Jessica and she was me. Being a dreamer, I have imagined many things, but I've never imagined this. I would be lying if I said I've never contemplated a world where I was devilishly handsome, however, those fantasies didn't include body swap. When it comes to physique, Jason and I couldn't have been more different. Kneeling behind the bush, I couldn't stem my curiosity. Hesitantly running my hand over my abdomen, I could feel the muscle underneath. I've never had abs before. Jason isn't absurdly buff, but he is definitely brawnier than me. Even so, in this humid atmosphere, his clothes were downright suffocating. And to make matters worse, right when Corpus was about to give the transference another shot, Quaymius became aware of our presence.

"I think I heard something." A twig snapped as the centaur took a step toward the bushes. "Who is that?"

Quite suddenly he emerged from around the hedge, his bow drawn, and an arrow pointing straight at my chest. A second later, Duke appeared at his side, a thick branch clutched in his hands and a fierce look in his eyes.

"If it's Followers again I want a piece of…" his voice trailed off when he saw the four of us.

"What is it?" Naomi called from the riverbank.

"I'm not sure," the Rebel replied, eyeing Jessica in my body suspiciously. "They're not like anything I've ever seen before."

"They must be spies," Duke said, glaring at me. "Probably sent by the king to capture us. I say we dispose of them."

"Corpus, you might want to hurry up with that disguise thing," Jason in Jessica's body said nervously. "These guys are all over us!"

"It takes extreme concentration." The alien's voice shook as sweat built up on his forehead. "Correct me if I'm wrong, but things are a little hectic right now."

"We don't kill unless we absolutely have to," Quaymius said, his keen grey eyes shifting from one of us to the next. "Besides, if they're spies they could be useful."

"Bring them out into the open," Naomi called. "I want to have a look."

"Move it!" Duke grunted, shoving me hard in the back. "Let's go."

One by one we were all led out onto the riverbank and into the light. When Naomi saw us, her beautiful blue eyes became wide with surprise.

"By the great pearls of the sea, what are those?" she breathed, her hand going to her mouth.

"What are you?" the faun demanded, stepping forward so our faces were only inches apart. "Did the king send you here to spy on us?"

"No!" Jessica in my body insisted, her eyes wide. "Please, don't hurt us. We're not the enemy!"

I still couldn't get used to seeing her in my body. Regardless of my current state, it felt like having a twin. Except that Jessica was clearly ill-at-ease. Standing hunched over, her right hand would make the occasional journey up to the side of her face. When she remembered my hair wasn't long enough to twirl, it would promptly return to her side.

Quaymius stared at Jessica for a moment before turning his attention to Duke. "What do you think?"

"We should tie them up. They could be dangerous." With that, the faun left the clearing to fetch some rope. Returning a few minutes later, he proceeded to tie our hands behind our backs. When he got to me, he made sure the ropes were extra tight. Now that my friends and I were bound, Quaymius lowered his bow and returned the arrow to the quiver on his back.

"What about that one?" he nodded at Corpus who Duke had neglected to bind and who was now fidgeting nervously with the hem of his shirt, looking more vulnerable than ever. "He doesn't look like an impostor."

"He's only a child," Naomi said softly, looking the alien up and down. "So young and innocent."

"It's too risky to let him go," the faun said firmly. "He might be young, but he knows where to find us. That information could be very dangerous in the wrong hands."

Now that Jason's, Jessica's and my hands were firmly secured behind our backs, the centaur and the faun started examining us. Duke started with me, sinking his fingers in my now black hair. As his nails scraped my scalp, it took me a second to realize he was searching for horns. Clearly puzzled, he migrated to my face where he began tracing Jason's hairless chin. Treading a path around me, the faun moved to my clothes, his rough hands going from my collar to my sleeves, his curious fingers sampling the material as he went. Then, crouching down, he turned his attention to Jason's shoes. Noticing the laces, he pulled on the end of one, causing it to come untied. As the faun did the same with my other shoe,

Quaymius was giving Jessica in my body the same treatment. Circling her several times, the centaur looked in her eyes and ears, examining her hair and forced her to open her mouth. Of the three of us, the only one who wasn't getting body searched was Jason. Perhaps the Rebel and his companion didn't feel comfortable examining a girl. Corpus was all but forgotten. Satisfying his shoe curiosity, Duke straightened up and started checking my pockets. It wasn't long before he stumbled across Jason's wallet. Looking intrigued, his opened it and started removing its contents; a driver's license, a school ID, a social security card, a twenty dollar bill, etc.

"Garrett, Jason Matthew," he read, squinting at the driver's license. "Male, black hair, hazel eyes. Your name is Garrett?"

"My… his name is Jason," Jason in Jessica muttered under his breath.

Duke eyed him for a moment before returning his attention to me. "Why do you have three names? Are they aliases?"

"No," I replied and, unable to think of an answer he would understand, fell silent.

"What are you exactly?" the Rebel asked, his gaze shifting to Jason in Jessica's body. "You look like us, but different."

When none of us answered, Duke grabbed a handful of my hair, forcing me down on my knees. "I believe my friend asked you a question. What are you?"

"We're humans!" I gasped as several hairs were inadvertently yanked free.

The faun let out a sharp laugh. "Yeah, right. What are you really? What did the king ask you to do?"

"We're not spies," I groaned as he tilted my head back, compelling me to look at him.

"Oh, yeah, then what are you?"

"I told you. We're humans."

"*Don't lie!*" the faun hissed and his resemblance to Jason was uncanny. "Humans have never set foot in this world."

"As far as you know."

A muscle worked furiously in Duke's jaw as he continued to eye me menacingly. "If you're so smart answer me this. If you truly are human, why do you so happen to look like us?

"But we don't look like you," Jessica said desperately. "Not exactly. We're not fauns, centaurs or mermaids. We're just ordinary people."

"Be that as it may," Duke replied, poking me in the chest with his free hand. "We still look uncomfortably alike. How do we know the king didn't cast some sort of spell to trick us? For all we know he's waiting right now in the bushes to ambush us."

"Oh, my god," Jason in Jessica's body suddenly said. "Oliver, tell me I'm not really like that. I'm not that skeptical, am I?"

"You'd be surprised," Jessica grunted. "I've been trying for years to get you to broaden your mind. Now you know how Oliver and I feel."

"What's going on?" Duke demanded, looking suspicious as he relinquished his grip on my hair, his focus switching to my friends. "What are you talking about? Is this some sort of code speak?"

"That's enough!" Quaymius declared, swiping an arrow from his quiver, re-notching his bow and aiming it menacingly at Jessica. "I don't know what you guys have planned, but you will not succeed."

"This is madness!" I cried, hardly able to believe my eyes. "We are not planning anything! We are not the enemy. We're here to help you!"

"That's it!" Lunging forward the faun grabbed Quaymius's sword from its holder and placed the blade against my neck. "I don't want to hear another word out of you!"

"Corpus, can you get us out of this mess?" Jason pleaded as the Rebel's arrow shifted to him.

"All right!" the alien yelled, gritting his teeth and a second later I felt Duke's grip loosen on my collar as everything went black. After a few seconds, my vision gradually came back into focus. Jason and Jessica were gone. All that remained were their fictional counterparts, both looking down at themselves in amazement. Lowering my own eyes, I saw that I too had changed. I was now wearing Quaymius's small dark-green vest and the leather belt that held his sword. His bow and quiver of arrows now hung over my shoulder. Slowly reaching up, I felt the grey bandana he wore around his head. It had worked, I was now the Rebel. Corpus had successfully transferred us to the proper places.

After getting over the initial shock of being Quaymius, I was quick to remember that the centaur and I hadn't been that different to begin with. Granted, his hair was a lot longer than mine and I was now a few feet taller than before. The major change was from the waist down.

"Wow!" Jessica exclaimed, moving her tail gracefully back and forth through the water and running her fingers through her long golden hair. "This is unbelievable!"

"It is different," Jason mused, sitting down on the rock and examining his cloven hooves, his fingers combing the short cinnamon brown fur on his legs. "Better." he added with a smile as his eyes shifted to his more muscular abdomen and torso.

"What about you, Oliver?" Jessica inquired, turning to look at me. "What's it like being a centaur?"

"Strange," I replied, taking a few steps forward. "Walking on four legs will take some getting used to." For practice I started making a circle around the small clearing.

"Mandayus-Corpus comes to the rescue again," the alien said triumphantly, his hands behind his back.

"And not a moment too soon," Jason said, his fingers now stroking his slick black goatee. "Another second and we would've been history."

"What about Quaymius's accent?" I asked, stopping in the middle of the clearing. "If people hear me they'll know something's not right."

"Don't worry about it," Corpus said, studying each of us with curiosity. "Everyone who inhabits this world will be able to hear it even if we cannot."

"Accent or not, I'm just glad we got out of that before we were all killed," Jason sighed, unfolding his arms and resting his elbows on his furry knees.

"They wouldn't have killed us," Jessica said calmly, her palms gliding over her shiny, smooth scales.

"How do you know? That Duke character looked like he was itching to shed some blood."

"True, but they don't believe in capital punishment."

"Since when did you get so structured?" Jason asked, looking suspicious. "A moment ago you were begging for your life."

"I wasn't begging," Jessica said flatly. "I was simply trying to appear innocent."

Jason snorted. "Yeah, right. And I'm not a faun."

"So, Corpus," Jessica said, choosing to ignore him. "How exactly does—" but before she could finish, the alien's eyes rolled back in his head and he collapsed on the ground, motionless.

"Oh, my god!" I hurried over to where the alien lay and crouching down beside him.

"Is he okay?" Jessica asked, crawling across the grass on her belly to join me.

"I don't know." I lifted the alien's head up off the ground. "He just fainted."

"This is it!" Jason declared, his lower lip trembling. "First Corpus bites the dust, then the rest of us get picked off one by one."

"Corpus, wake up!" Jessica urged, patting him lightly on the cheek. "Come on."

"What...?" he slowly opened his eyes. "What happened?"

"You passed out," she informed him. "But don't worry. You're going to be okay."

"I'm not so sure," the alien whispered, gingerly sitting up and I noticed that he was a lot paler than usual.

"What do you mean?" Jessica asked, surveying him more closely. "You were fine a minute ago."

"It seems that with enough mind power, I am able to do a great deal here," Corpus said calmly. "Many of the rules no longer apply. But it is starting to take a heavy toll. I am running out of energy. If I don't rejuvenate soon, I fear something terrible will happen."

"How do you rejuvenate?" Jason asked.

"Sleep usually. I just need to rest for a while and I should be okay."

"So," Jessica ventured after a moment of silence, studying Corpus with a mild look of curiosity. "If the rules here don't apply, would it be possible for us to see your true form?"

"It might have been," he said wearily. "But I don't think I can muster up the energy now."

"Of course not," Jason grunted, a sarcastic air to his tone.

"Hey!" Jessica said indignantly. "Obviously he's not well," then turning her attention back to the alien added, "That's too bad, I can't help wondering what you really look like."

"I think you would be disappointed if you found out," Corpus said, his gaze lingering on Jason for a moment. "My race does not look all that interesting."

Uncertainty flashed across Jessica's face. "How do you mean?"

"I…" the alien started to say, but he cut off as a look of searing pain crossed his face and he pressed the heel of his palm against his forehead.

"Corpus!" Jessica cried, looking like she was going to have a heart attack.

Tears welled up in his eyes. "I'm sorry. I think my problem might be a little more serious than I had originally hoped."

"What do you mean?" I asked.

"The mind is a complicated thing and when pushed too far there can be major side effects." Corpus sobbed, burying his face in his hands. "There's a reason most people don't use mind tricks right and left back home. Mind-control is a difficult practice and when not done correctly it can have major repercussions. One of the reasons it became illegal was for public safety."

"You never mentioned that before," Jason said, his eyebrows shooting up.

"I didn't want to complicate things."

"But if the things you've been doing are dangerous to your health, then why did you do them?"

"I was trying to fix the mess I made. If I don't get everything under control here before the fleet returns, my days in the Spacing Program will be over."

"You're not going to die, are you?" I asked as Corpus wiped the tears from his eyes. "You're going to be okay, right?"

"I hope so," he whispered. "I can't be sure of anything until I get some sleep. But if that does not work, I may have to leave this place for a while. Energy is essential to my survival and if I do not find a way to rejuvenate, I will perish."

"In that case, I think you should stay here," I said, surveying our surroundings. "I don't know what lies ahead. If anything happens you'll be safe here, plus we'll know where to find you."

"Are you sure that's a good idea?" Jason asked, concern creasing his brow. "I think we should stick together. There's strength in numbers."

"Technically that's true, but there's no way to know what's going to happen. Should we get out of here alive, Corpus is the only one who can help me. I can't afford to let anything happen to him. But don't worry," I added. "The king's men hardly ever come this far into the jungle. We'll be fine."

"Guys," Jason said, a hint of desperation in his voice. "I've seen hundreds of movies and if there's one thing I've learned, it's that splitting up is never a good idea."

"Relax," I said, attempting to put his mind at ease. "This is not a movie, we are not pre-destined to a worst-case scenario."

Jason didn't say anything, but it was clear he was less than happy with leaving Corpus behind.

"Don't worry," Jessica said bracingly. "I'm sure we'll be all right. Oliver knows this place like the back of his hand. We should be fine."

"So what do we do now?" Jason asked, standing up. "Do we keep looking for the cave?"

"That's pointless until we figure out how it works," I said, adjusting the leather strap across my chest. "In my story, the answer to the cave is supposed to be in the Old Library. There should be some kind of pattern in those books. I just can't remember what it is. If we look, I might be able to find something. But first I think we should find some place to rest. I for one have been up for pretty much the last twenty-four hours straight."

After saying goodbye to Corpus, we started east along the riverbank toward the ocean. I knew it wasn't safe to move around too much in the forest and that we'd probably be much better off if we found a secluded place to stay.

"So where are we going?" Jason asked after a few minutes silence.

"To the faun refuge," I replied. "It's a lot bigger than a centaur's den and much better hidden."

"The faun refuge," Jason mused. "Why didn't I think of that?"

*   *   *

While Jason and I wove our way through and around the shrubs and bushes along the bank, Jessica swam gracefully in and out of sight amid the river's frothy depths. Every now and then she would jump out of the water like a dolphin or do cartwheels and somersaults under the surface. It was like I was seeing her for the first time. In the past, I have always admired Jessica for her fascinating personality, but now I found myself taking her physical appearance into account. Suddenly she wasn't just smart, caring, and understanding, she was also beautiful. The odd thing was she hadn't changed a bit. True, her hair was more radiant and her skin was fairer, but her features remained the same.

"Would you mind not making that look so easy?" Jason suddenly said, cutting into my thoughts as he fought his way through a thick web of vines that wouldn't let him pass. "Some of us weren't so lucky."

"I'm sorry," Jessica replied, stopping a few yards up the river and smiling happily, her arms folded on the mossy bank. "I can't help it if the water and I move as one. It's like we were made for each other."

"Go figure," Jason grunted sarcastically as I stopped to see if he needed help. "Water and mermaids? Nah!"

"You're just jealous," Jessica said, tossing her beautiful golden hair and giving Jason a smug look. "I can tell. You always use sarcasm to hide the way you feel."

"Whatever," he muttered as I helped untangle him from the vines. "I just don't see why I couldn't have been something cool."

"What do you mean?" I asked, untangling one of his horns.

Jason looked exasperated. "Isn't it obvious? You can just walk right through these weeds because you're a horse. Jessica can swim effortlessly through the water because she's a fish. But what can I do? I'm just a puny little faun. I mean look," he added gesturing to the small cuts and scratches on his chest and arms. "I'm getting all torn up!"

"First of all I'm a mermaid, not a fish," Jessica said heatedly, unfolding her arms. "And second, those scratches are nothing compared to what some of us have had to endure."

"What are you talking about?" Jason demanded indignantly. "I have gone through a lot. Maybe even more than you!"

"I wasn't talking about me!" Jessica said, reaching absentmindedly for her scarf only to find it wasn't there. "That is so typical of you, Jason; the whole world revolves around you. Why are you so self-centered? You're not the only one with problems, you know!" With that she disappeared into the water.

"That's unbelievable!" Jason exclaimed his eyes as round as saucers, finally freeing himself from the vines. "I can't say one word without her flying off the handle."

"I'm sure she has her reasons," I sighed, continuing along the river.

"I don't know." Jason glanced at the mermaid-free water for any sign of Jessica before hurrying along beside me. "I know we've had our differences, but this seems worse."

"Whatever you say." I wasn't really listening.

"So where exactly is this faun refuge?" Jason asked, examining a small cut on the back of his hand.

I took a look around. "Well, assuming that everything I put in my notes is now a part of this world, there should be a waterfall somewhere along this river."

Chapter 14

JASON

I had a bad feeling about this. The body swap thing was bad enough. Who knew scarves could be so smoldering? I felt like I was getting strangled by Satan himself. And let's not forget the run-in with that faun and his friends. Talk about looking in a fun house mirror. In stereo! Finally, after knowingly entering a hostile environment, we left a member of the group behind. Who does that? Corpus could be irritating at times, but he was still the strongest among us. After what Oliver said about the centaur king, we needed strength. Why test our luck? So that Anaconda look-a-like was harmless? Small comfort. Leaving the alien behind was the first step in an already badly laid out plan. Just because we knew where we were, didn't mean this couldn't turn into *Lost*. As far as I was concerned it was just a matter of time before an irate polar bear or a menacing pillar of smoke attacked us. Or something equally terrifying. This may not have been a movie, but it was sure playing out like one.

I don't know how long we walked along the riverbank, but right when I was about to tell Oliver I couldn't go any farther, he suddenly stopped, his grey eyes surveying the surrounding vegetation.

"Did you hear that?"

"What?" I stopped dead in my tracks, my heart leaping into my throat.

"I thought I heard footsteps," Oliver whispered, squinting into the jungle. "I think we're being followed."

"Oh, my god!" I whimpered, moving closer to him. "Is it good guys or bad guys? I thought you said the king's men don't come here."

"Usually they don't, but every now and then they make an exception."

"Great. We're done for."

"Not this time," Oliver concluded after a moment's silence. "Whoever they were, they're gone now."

We continued along the riverbank for a few more minutes before he stopped again only this time he looked excited. "Can you hear that?"

"Not again!" I pleaded, feeling defeated. "I don't hear anything!"

"It's the waterfall! We're not far now!"

We followed the river until it reached a twenty-five to thirty foot drop off a rocky ledge. The rushing water cascaded into a small pool where it settled before continuing on through the trees. From our spot at the top, we could see Jessica in the water below, swimming lazily in circles, waiting for us.

"How'd you get down there?" I called, scanning both sides for a safe route.

"How do you think?" she replied, stopping in the middle of the waterhole and looking up at us.

"Oh, my god!" I exclaimed, taking a step back. "You can't be serious!"

"Don't be such a baby," Jessica said, tracing circles on the surface of the water in front of her. "It's not that bad."

"I'm not being a baby," I muttered stubbornly. "I just don't think—"

"Then jump!" Jessica declared, watching me as if she expected me to chicken out.

"Fine!" I took a deep breath, closed my eyes and leapt off the edge of the waterfall. It seemed to take forever to hit the surface below, but I didn't open my eyes until I was completely submerged. Despite the humidity of the surrounding jungle, the water was pleasantly cool. All around me bubbles spiraled upward. The pool must have been at least 15 feet deep, but after the small air pockets dispersed, I could see the bottom clearly. If not for the smooth pebbles below, I might have mistaken it for a swimming pool. Ignoring the aquatic life, I quickly swam to the top, taking in a lungful of air.

"Now it's your turn…" I started to say looking up to where Oliver was still standing, only to find he had already removed Kay whatever's quiver and belt, tossed them to the bank below and was now galloping toward the edge of the waterfall. He lunged off, his front feet stretched out in front of him in a graceful arc, his arms up in the air. Hitting the water with an award-winning splash, our friend doused me and Jessica in a huge tidal wave.

Once the aftermath of Oliver's plunge died down, I had a chance to look around. Sweeping the wet hair from my face, I found myself floating in the middle of what looked like one of those nice lagoon-like getaways you see in snapshots. As if protecting this peaceful oasis from prying eyes, the jungle tightly surrounded it from all sides. The only thing allowed in was the sun, reflecting off the spray from the tumbling water, casting a rainbow across the waterfall. The surface of the pool rippled and shone and tiny white butterflies danced along the shore.

"Isn't this place just amazing?" Jessica murmured and I realized she'd been watching me.

"Uh." It occurred to me that for the first time in my life I had nothing to say.

Jessica smiled knowingly. "I know."

"It's behind there," Oliver suddenly said. Looking up I saw that he was no longer in the water. He had climbed out and now stood on a low overhang north of the water hole that circled around the pond and disappeared behind the waterfall. As he gestured to the cascade, a shower of droplets fell from his underbelly and tail onto the glistening rock.

"What is?" I asked, feeling somewhat annoyed with myself. I couldn't believe I'd let Jessica catch me off guard like that. I had a reputation to uphold.

"The faun refuge. It's behind the waterfall."

"Great!" I eagerly swam to the edge of the pool and climbed up onto the ledge. "I feel like a sitting duck out here."

"What are you talking about?" Jessica asked, twirling a lock of hair around her pinky as she floated idly in the water, studying me with mild curiosity.

"Oliver heard someone moving through the jungle earlier," I replied, avoiding eye contact. "It could be the enemy."

While the two of us walked along the ledge, our hooves clicking softly, Jessica swam under the waterfall to meet us on the other side.

"I thought you said this was the faun refuge," I said, disappointed as I ran my hand over the smooth damp rock that met us.

"It is," Oliver insisted, looking around. "But it has some kind of spell protecting it. Only fauns can enter."

"You mean like a magic password?" Jessica asked, folding her arms on the ledge. "That's so cool!"

I made a face. "A magic password? What is this, *Ali Baba and the Forty Thieves?*"

"No," Oliver muttered irritably. "The catch isn't the password, it's the fact that only you can get us in."

"Whatever," I smirked, trying to keep a straight face. "So what's the password?"

"I don't know," Oliver said, studying the wall pensively. "I haven't gotten that far."

"What do you mean gotten that far?"

"In my story."

I couldn't suppress my bewilderment. "How is that possible?!"

"Calm down, Jason," Jessica said soothingly as she floated on her back in the small space below us. "I'm sure there's a logical explanation."

"There is actually," Oliver affirmed. "Like I said, I haven't gotten that far. Everything in this place either appears in the beginning of the story or is included in my notes. Anything that I didn't think was worth writing down I just memorized, and now I can't recall any of it."

"Great," I groaned, collapsing against the moist wall. "So we're stuck here until either someone decides to come out and find us or…" Just then, from the other side of the waterfall, we heard the sound of someone making his or her way through the forest. The rustling of leaves was coming from the north bank and whoever was lurking beyond the bushes was getting closer. "Or we're caught and murdered for the cause," I finished heatedly.

Oliver pointed to the other side of the waterfall, mild trepidation flickering across his face. "Do you think we should take a look?"

"*Are you crazy?*" I hissed. "*I'm not going out there!*"

"Come on," Jessica whispered, her eyes sparkling. "Where's your sense of adventure? This is way better than any of those movies you watch."

"Yeah, except that no one ever died watching a movie."

"You don't know that." She was obviously enjoying this. "What if they had a heart attack or something?"

"You know what I mean. I'm not going out there."

"It might be a faun," Oliver reasoned. "Someone who knows the password."

"Or it could be a horde of centaurs sent to kill us."

"I already told you the king's men don't come this far in."

"You said they *hardly* ever come in this far," I corrected. "It's not worth the risk."

"Fine." Oliver pulled his sword from its sheath. "Jessica and I will be the heroes." With that, he went back along the rocky ledge to the other side of the waterfall while she went under it.

"Yeah, a couple of dead heroes!" I called, but I don't think they heard me. A moment later I heard Jessica's voice.

"Uh, Jason, I think you might want to see this."

Great, I thought, *what kind of trouble have they gotten themselves into now?*

I cautiously made my way back along the overhang to the other side of the waterfall.

After resurfacing, it looked as if Jessica hadn't made it very far from the waterfall. She was still so close the spray was pelting her in the back of the head, only she didn't seem to notice. She was too busy staring at something in front of her. Looking up I saw a figure standing on the bank a few yards from where Oliver stood, his sword frozen in he left hand as he, too, stared dumbfounded. Taking a few steps forward it only took me a moment to see why the others were so transfixed.

"Mom…?"

Chapter 15

JESSICA

Jason's statement wasn't 100 percent off. The figure that had just emerged from the bushes and now faced us on the shore did appear to be his mother, only now, like him, she was a faun. It had been a long time since any of us had seen Mrs. Garrett, but she looked just the way I remembered; long black hair falling gracefully around her pretty young face, big beautiful brown eyes, and smooth dark skin. The only difference now was that from the waist down she had furry goat legs, long goat-like ears, and small horns sticking out the top of her head.

"Oh, Duke, honey there you are!" Jason's mom said, bringing me back to reality as she hurried over to hug him. "I was starting to get worried. Thank goodness you're all right."

Jason just stood there like a statue while the faun version of his mother continued to embrace him. The look on his face was a mixture of shock and disbelief.

"Oh, hi, Quaymius," Jason's mother said, just noticing Oliver, who was slowly returning his sword to his belt. "How are you?"

"Uh, fine," he muttered, glancing nervously at me.

"And, of course, Naomi," Mrs. Garrett continued, following Oliver's gaze. "You're also doing well, I trust."

"Yes," I replied, brushing my hair out of my face and swimming forward a few feet out of the waterfall's reach. "I'm fine…" I was about to call her Lorenza but stopped. Given the fact that Jason's mother was now a faun, no doubt her name had changed as well. "I'm fine," I repeated.

"Well, come on inside," Mrs. Garrett said, hurrying passed Oliver and gesturing for us to follow. "It's not safe to linger out in the open too long."

Before following her, Oliver quickly gathered Quaymius's equipment from the grassy area where it had landed when he discard it. Still eyeing the female faun uncertainly, he fastened the belt around his waist before sliding the quiver of arrows over his head. Once we were all safely concealed behind the waterfall, Jason's mother placed her palm flat against the damp rock, closed her eyes and murmured "open." I expected Jason to make some comment about how he expected the password to be more complicated than that, but he didn't say a word. He just stood there, surveying the female faun with overt disbelief. I assumed it was because he was still getting over the shock of seeing his mother again. He stared at her as if he feared she'd disappear should he blink.

The moment Jason's mother removed her hand from the wall, the rock seemed to melt away, revealing a long, dimly lit passageway. The only light came from a few torches randomly placed along the walls. I hoisted myself up onto the rocky ledge, Oliver lifted me up onto his back, and the four of us entered into the depth of the faun refuge.

We walked in silence down the long passageway. The only sound was the soft echo of hooves on the cold stone floor and the rhythmic dripping of water off the flickering walls. After we'd been walking for some time, a light appeared at the end of the tunnel. I expected the passageway to open up into a cavern or some kind of room, but instead we found ourselves stepping out into a grassy clearing. There were small shops and booths everywhere with vendors selling fruit and vegetables. In the distance, trees swayed gently in the afternoon breeze, only partly concealing small huts and burrows as the sun hung low in the clear blue sky. It looked as if the passageway we'd just exited led to a secret village, hidden away from the rest of the world.

"Well, I'll see you youngsters later," Jason's mother said, giving him a quick peck on the cheek. "Try to stay out of trouble." With that she disappeared into the sea of commotion, her long black hair swinging behind her.

"Wow, we have to check this place out!" I gasped, clutching Oliver's waist tightly and, in my excitement, slapping him hard on the side with my tail.

"Okay, okay," he groaned, trying to loosen my grip around his middle. "No need to get violent."

"Sorry. It's just that this is really fascinating. I mean how is this possible?" I looked around at all the fauns as they went about their business, paying us no mind. "I thought we were in a cave. Aren't we under the river?"

"It's an enchantment," Oliver explained, also looking around. "It provides the fauns with a very life-like place to live, a place the king can't find them."

"Jason, even you can't deny this place is cool," I said, watching as a young faun tried out a new flute from a rack of neatly carved musical instruments. "Jason?" It wasn't until then that I realized he was no longer with us. Looking around I spotted him standing a few feet away by a booth piled high with interesting looking fruit, a far-off look in his eyes.

"Are you okay?" I asked as Oliver hesitantly approached.

Jason didn't respond. Instead he picked up a piece of fruit and started turning it over in his hands, staring at it as if they were alone in the universe.

"Jason?" I reached down, putting a hand on his shoulder. He looked up and to my surprise there were tears in his eyes. "Oh, my…" I pulled back in shock. In all the years I've known him I never thought I'd see Jason cry.

"What is this?!" he demanded, glaring up at Oliver, a look of both hurt and anger in his eyes. "What is she doing here?"

"Hey, man, calm down," Oliver said, clearly surprised. "I didn't know Duke's mother would look like that."

"Yeah, right!" Jason spat, tossing the fruit back onto the pile before turning his back on us. "How could you not know? You made this place up. You deliberately and meticulously molded every aspect of its characteristics to fit your perfect little story. Now you're telling me you didn't know?"

"Well, I didn't," Oliver insisted in a small voice. "I guess if Corpus were here he'd probably say something about the aspects of this world being generated by the less conscious part of my mind. I hadn't intended for Duke's mother to look like yours, but I guess somewhere in the back of my mind, that's what happened. I honestly had no idea what to expect. I don't even remember half the fleeting ideas I've had for this story, but somehow they played a part."

"Stop it!" Jason cried, wheeling around, his eyes wide and desperate, his hands clenched into fists. "Just stop it! I am sick and tired of hearing about all the things you didn't know would happen, or didn't expect to be here. I don't want to hear about all the things you can't remember. I'm tired of being scared all the time, and I am sick of trying to find a way to get you out of this place! I just want to go home. I've had enough!" Jason then turned and ran off into the crowd, disappearing among the fauns.

"Wow!" Oliver's voice was full of disbelief. "I assumed he'd cave eventually, I just never dreamed it would be under these circumstances."

"We have to find him."

An hour later, we found Jason sitting on a rock outside the village. His elbows rested on his furry knees as he turned a smooth, tiny pebble over and over in his hand, his mournful gaze fixed on the ground. When Oliver stopped in front of him, he didn't look up. Instead he just shook his head and laughed, as if silently mocking himself. I noticed that in his moment of pain, Jason's newly acquired ears were laid back. Sort of the way a puppy's are when it's being scolded. I would have found this endearing if he hadn't looked so heartbroken.

"There's no way out of here," he muttered, speaking only half to himself. "I tried, but no matter which way I go, I always end up back where I started. This forest is like a loop, folding back on itself over and over again."

"If you want to leave the faun refuge you have to go back through the tunnel," Oliver said apologetically.

"Yeah, I kinda guessed that," Jason grunted, glancing up at him resentfully. "But who knows what's lurking out there? So much for knowing this place like the back of your hand."

"I'm sorry about all this." Oliver was clearly struggling to think of something comforting to say. "I know this must be real hard for you."

"Just leave me alone," Jason said, throwing the pebble on the ground.

"Here, let me," I whispered in Oliver's ear and, taking his hand, I lowered myself onto the ground next to Jason.

"Okay." Oliver looked relieved. "I'll just be over there." He gestured at a small water hole a few yards away.

"This is all a bit surreal, isn't it?" I murmured as soon as Oliver was out of earshot, indicating the trees and the flowers with a small wave of my hand. "I'm sure having trouble believing it."

Jason glanced at me, but didn't say anything.

"I know I can seem a bit optimistic sometimes, but that's just to cover up how scared I really am."

"What are you talking about?" Jason asked darkly. "You never get scared."

"Of course I do," I said in disbelief. "We all get scared, even me. As exciting as this place is, I'm still constantly dreading what will happen if the plan doesn't work and we can't get Oliver out of here. I've read what he has so far in his story and I know we'll be in big trouble if we get captured. But I try to stay positive. That's how I master my fears. Things don't always have to go wrong, they can also go right."

"You never cease to amaze me," Jason sighed, shaking his head. "I wish I could see the world through your eyes."

"Technically you already have," I said, trying to humor him.

"Yeah." Jason nodded and I noticed the corner of his mouth twitch ever so slightly. "That's something I'm definitely not going to forget any time soon."

For a moment I thought I'd succeeded but then his face fell yet again.

"What is it?" I asked when he didn't say anything.

Jason looked away, seeming slightly embarrassed to be seen in this state, but when I remained silent his eyes gradually made their way back to mine, and in that moment he seemed to completely let go.

"I never thought I'd see her again," he whispered, tears steadily trickling down his face, and I knew he was talking about his mother. "I think about her all the time, of course, but I had learned to accept the fact that she was never coming back, and now…" his voice trailed off and he looked at the ground, no longer able to maintain eye contact.

"I can only imagine what seeing her again must have been like for you," I said, placing a hand on his leg and realizing his fur was much softer than I had expected. "When I resurfaced in front of the waterfall, it was like I'd gone back in time. I couldn't believe my eyes."

"And Oliver?" Jason asked. "How'd he react?"

"I think he was just as surprised as I was, if not more. I think he's beginning to realize just how little control he has over this world. Image-wise, a lot of it seems to be fueled by his subconscious."

"Kinda like a psy-moon," Jason muttered, wiping the tears from his face.

"A what?"

"A psy-moon," he repeated. "It changes its terrain to match your subconscious." When I continued to look confused Jason shook his head in frustration. "Never mind, it's just something I saw on *Red Dwarf.*"

"So are you going to be…" I started to say when a bolt of pain shot down my tail. "Ow!"

"Are you okay?" Jason asked, looking worried as I gingerly shifted my weight.

"My tail is getting dry!" I exclaimed, running my fingers lightly over my now dimming scales. "Obviously mermaids aren't meant to stay out of the water for long periods of time."

"Well, there's water over there," Jason said, hastily getting to his feet, and scooping me up in his arms. "I'll take you." And he carried me over to the waterhole where Oliver was idly skipping rocks across the smooth surface, causing it to ripple.

"What's going on?" he asked as Jason gently lowered me into the water.

"Don't worry," I said as I felt the cool liquid move up my tail, making the pain fade away. "I've just been out of the water too long. I'll be fine."

"Good." Oliver glanced uncertainly at Jason. "Well… so long as you'll be okay." And I knew he wasn't talking to me.

"I'll be fine," Jason replied after a moment's silence. "Sorry about earlier."

"No problem," Oliver said, looking relieved.

Chapter 16

OLIVER

That evening we sat around the campfire only half listening as one of the elder fauns told an ancient faun fable to the youngsters, the firelight reflecting off his face as he spoke. The moon hung low in the night sky while dozens of fireflies danced over the forest floor. I could just make out the random points of light flashing in and out of view from where I lay, my upper half propped up on my elbow.

"This is all so magical," Jessica whispered softly. She was currently lying next to me, our bodies touching as sparks from the fire flew up into the air. "Sometimes I forget there's a real world out there, beyond this place."

"Yeah," Jason agreed from where he sat, his back up against a nearby tree. "We're here, but our bodies are still in my bedroom."

Without warning Jessica's face fell. "I wonder what my parents are doing right now. All this happened so fast I didn't get a chance to tell them I'd be spending the night at your house. They're probably worried."

"My mom probably doesn't even notice I'm gone," I said absentmindedly, staring into the flames. "She spends so much time working, she hardly has any time for me… not that she ever did."

"Sounds a lot like my dad," Jason said flatly. "He's never home. Ever since Mom left it's like he's not the same person anymore. We might as well be living in two different countries."

The three of us fell silent for a moment, listening to the others as they continued their evening routine. All around us fauns sat in small clusters randomly scattered across the grassy clearing. Some were families while others appeared to be friends or lovers. Peering through the flickering light, I noticed that a few of them were casting Jason curious looks. Of all the fauns at the campfire, he was the only one sitting alone. At one point a couple of what I assumed were Duke's friends had waved him over, offering him a place among them, but Jason quickly declined. It amazed me that after all the time I spent writing about this world, how little I now knew about it.

"So what is the story behind all this?" Jason asked after a few minutes, gesturing at the forest around us. "Why do the fauns have to live here?"

"Now that's an interesting story," I replied, thinking back to my notes, relieved to have a question I could answer. "Since the dawn of time, the relationship between the fauns and centaurs has been stormy at best. But for the most part, the two races have been able to live in a relative state of peace. Before the arrival of Artayus the Great, the centaurs lived in the valley and the forest, while the fauns preferred the more rough terrain of the mountains. But every now and then disputes would break out over the location of the border between the two regions. Over time, the centaurs pushed the fauns farther and farther back into the mountains 'til they were completely cut off from their source of food and water. About fifty years ago, fed up with the centaur's poor treatment of their race, a group of fauns decided to leave their home in the Burly Mountains and take residence in the Brambee Forest. Unfortunately, they decided to make this bold move during the reign of the young King Mytus, who was highly conceited and determined to rule with an iron hoof. Already having banished the unicorns and Pegasi from the forest, King Mytus had a very short fuse. The moment he received word that the fauns had broken the Agreement of 1756, he went into a rage and declared war on the fauns. An order was immediately issued to the surrounding villages to every male seventeen and older, fit to join the army and fight for his king."

"What did that have to do with Artayus the Great?" Jessica interjected.

"Before he came along, the Kingdom of the Centaurs was divided into two groups; the Preservatives and the Revolutionaries. The Preservatives mainly consisted of the rich, who believed that wealth and power should remain within the family, whereas the Revolutionaries were comprised mainly of the poor people, who thought that letting the wealth circulate throughout the population was necessary to balance out the division between the two factions. There were many disputes between the two parties, but for thousands of years they were the only two groups within the centaur community. However, as different as these two parties were, there was one thing that always united them; their devotion to the king. In the Ancient Kingdom, loyalty to the king was a very large part of one's status in the community. Those who carried out the lord's will blindly and without question were considered guardians of the his rule and were rewarded for their service. Often, medals were bestowed upon such individuals as an example to the public. But in a place where there is no change, a story can't possibly exist, thus the arrival of a young centaur named Artayus.

"Artayus didn't have the faintest clue what he was getting into the day he joined the army. Eager to serve his king and uphold his family's honor, the young man set off for the castle. Of course, it only took a few days of battle for him to see the insanities of war. For one, it was costing too many lives. The death toll alone was quickly reaching the thousands. Both fauns and centaurs alike. Furthermore, the Brambee Forest is a hundred square miles. There was plenty of room for both races to co-exist. Like they did in the days of Lord Arcron. So Artayus did something no centaur had ever dreamed of. In full violation of his oath to the kingdom, he committed the first act of treason in recorded history. For the better part of a year, the young man helped the fauns escape the brutal blows of the centaur army. With the help of the mermaids, he built the faun refuge where they took shelter. Over time, the king began to suspect that his enemy was receiving aid. He immediately called back his troops, determined to find the guilty party. With Lord Mytus on his tail and with no hope of ever returning home, Artayus was on the run. Fortunately, he was not alone. Along with the fauns he'd managed to rescue, he had also gained the aid of other centaurs who believed that the king was being barbaric and unjust. By the end of the year, a third group had emerged. The Rebels."

"So what happened to Artayus?" Jessica asked, looking completely engrossed.

"In the months that followed the battle, King Mytus put all his time and energy into finding the one who betrayed him. There were whispers in the surrounding villages of a brave young warrior known as Artayus the Great. Enraged by his increasing popularity, King Mytus was determined to have him executed. One day, more or less a year after what would later be called the Faun-Centaur War, Artayus was yet again running through the forest, pursued by the king's men. The faithful servants usually stopped after he crossed the river. Not today. This time they continued to chase Artayus deeper and deeper into the jungle. Before long the Rebel began to feel desperate.

"Artayus was well aware of the mysterious cave at the heart of the forest. Like every youth in the kingdom, he had heard of its strange and mysterious powers. Now nearly in the middle of the jungle, the young man had no choice but to put his faith into finding this cave. Like most people, Artayus didn't really believe in its powers, but he hoped that it would at least provide shelter from the king's men. The Followers arrived at the cave a moment after Artayus disappeared inside. They searched everywhere, but he was nowhere to be found. The news of Artayus the Great's mysterious disappearance quickly spread throughout the kingdom. For five long years his name was murmured with curiosity and fascination. Thus, his legend grew.

"One day, Artayus re-emerged from the forest telling tales of a world quite different from the Kingdom of the Centaurs. He spoke of beings called humans who drove metal carts and flew in medal birds. To the village folk, the Rebel sounded delusional, his rants recalling the ancient myths. Still, it was well-known how much King Mytus loved power. He also loved the idea of having more land to rule. Intrigued by Artayus's stories and the exciting possibilities they offered, the king told the young Rebel that if he could prove this world did indeed exist, he would spare his life. So Artayus took the king and an army of his men to the cave. But, like so many times before, it showed no signs of life. And so Artayus the Great was executed in the village square and the hope he gave the fauns and Rebels who dwelled within the forest might have been lost forever if not for his son…"

"Who is his son?" Jason asked.

"Perseus," I replied. "He died several years ago in the king's dungeon."

"So Quaymius's entire family is either locked up or dead?" Jessica concluded.

"Well, no. Perseus had two sons. Mortis is one of them."

"Who's the other?" Jason inquired.

"Jupiter," I said half-heartedly. "He didn't really agree with the way his father and brother lived their lives. He preferred living in town. In fact, Quaymius has never met him. He doesn't even know he has an uncle. Jupiter wasn't really a part of my stories. He is more of a background character."

"Wow," Jason breathed as the fauns around the campfire got up and dispersed to their various huts. "I can hardly believe you put all of this together. It's like a movie that came to life. Other than the death hazard, this place is actually kinda cool."

"Leave it to Oliver to do something amazing," Jessica said fondly and she took my hand in hers, her beautiful eyes gleaming in the firelight as she gazed up at me.

"Uh, yeah." I pulled away, embarrassment tinting my cheeks. "That's what I'm here for."

"Duke?" The three of us looked up. A female faun about our age was standing a few feet away. We'd been so wrapped up in our conversation we hadn't noticed her approach. I recognized her as one of the ones who had waved Jason over. After casting me and Jessica a brief look, she went over to where he was seated and knelt down. Placing a hand on his chest, she leaned over and whispered something in his ear. Jason abruptly jerked back, a look of mild disgust on his face.

"Uh, thanks, but I think I'll stay out here tonight."

What I'm assuming was Duke's girlfriend looked incredulous at our friend's strong reaction. "You've been gone all day! I was hoping we could spend some time together."

Jason shook his head, looking more uncomfortable by the second. "Thanks, but no thanks. I'm good right here."

Duke's girlfriend looked at me. I had the feeling she wanted to say something, but after an unreasonably long pause she got up and hurried away. I didn't know what to think of her. She wasn't in any of my stories. She wasn't even in my notes. I didn't even know her name. The longer we were here, the less this world felt like a product of my creation. I may still possess some general knowledge about certain topics, but for the most part we were strangers. That bothered me.

Jason couldn't have looked more relieved. "That was awkward. I think she wanted to have sex."

"What's wrong with you?!" Jessica snapped. In the dying firelight I noticed that she looked unusually upset. "Why does your mind always have to go to the gutter? Maybe she just wants to talk."

"At this time of night? Yeah, right."

"Not everyone is like you."

"Hey, you didn't hear what she whispered in my ear!"

The conversation didn't sound over, but I was desperately tired. After the longest day of my life, I really needed to get some sleep. Folding my arms on the grass, I lay my head down and closed my eyes. If my friends continued their dispute, I didn't hear it. I was out within seconds.

The next morning, I woke to the sound of splashing. Peeling my face from the dew-sprinkled grass, I found Jessica in the small pool a few yards away doing cartwheels, her fins glistening in the sunlight. For a moment I lay silently watching her. I couldn't help being mesmerized as she moved effortlessly through the water. Since we were young, Jessica has always been spirited. Seeing her now reminded me of that. This place was bringing something out in me I'd never felt before. Jessica and I have been best friends since kindergarten. Why was I just noticing her now? Embarrassed by the feelings that were stirring within me I felt the need to say something.

"Why are you up so early?"

Ringing her golden curls over her right shoulder, Jessica turned to look at me. Her cheeks were flushed and she was out of breath. "Do you know what time it is?"

"No, what time is it?"

"I don't know," she said, making a face. "I haven't known since we got here. I just assumed you did. How else would you know it was early?" Was it just me or was there a hint of hostility in her voice? "I mean, how can you accuse me of getting up early if you don't know what time it is? For all we know it's three o'clock in the afternoon."

"The sun isn't very far from the horizon," I pointed out, a little intimidated. "That would be the first clue."

"Oh, sorry," Jessica grunted, a lock of hair whizzing rapidly around her index finger. "I didn't realize I was speaking to the expert."

"Jessica, is there something wrong?" I asked, propping myself up on my elbows. "You seem a little off."

"I'm fine," she stated flatly, folding her arms and turning away. "Never better."

"What's all the commotion?" A few feet away Jason groaned from where he now lay, his back up against the tree. His voice was heavy with irritation and judging by the dark shadows beneath his eyes, he hadn't slept well last night.

"Jessica's upset about something."

"I wasn't causing a commotion and I'm not upset," she said, not looking at either of us.

"Good, then maybe I can go back to sleep," Jason grunted, shifting position and shutting his eyes once again. "I didn't get much sleep last night."

"Why? What's wrong?" I asked.

"Nothing," Jason muttered, not opening his eyes. "I had a weird dream is all."

"What kind of dream?"

"Donno know. Just weird."

I turned my attention back to Jessica. She was still sulking, her blue eyes fixed on the rippling water. "Are you going to tell me what's bothering you?"

She turned to face me, no longer looking irritated. Now she looked sad. "It's nothing. I just wish you could be more sensitive, that's all."

What did that mean? Was she upset because I didn't intervene when she and Jason were arguing? That couldn't be it. I seldom interject when they fight. Maybe it was because I pulled away when she took my hand. That wasn't fair. The moment was so… bizarre. How'd she expect me to react? Not sure what Jessica meant, but not wanting to upset her further, I didn't press the matter. Maybe Jason was right, maybe she was acting strange.

All morning Jason seemed bothered by something, but every time I asked him what was wrong he would just shake his head. Did it have something to do with Duke's girlfriend? He had been pretty weirded out by that. Perhaps it was something Jessica said after I went to sleep. Their disagreements could get pretty heated. When Jason continued to deflect I stopped asking. After breakfast, we packed some food for our journey and filled a canteen with water for Jessica's tail. Saying goodbye to Duke's mother, we dodged another encounter with his girlfriend before leaving the faun refuge. On our way through the forest, we stopped by Quaymius's shelter. There I retrieved his cloak before the three of us continued on our journey to the library.

*   *   *

"It was about my dad," Jason said out of the blue about half an hour later as the three of us we made our way through the jungle. He was walking a few feet ahead of me while Jessica rode on my back. "The weird dream I had, it was about my father."

"What happened in the dream?" Jessica asked and I could almost hear the gears in her head switch on.

"It probably didn't mean anything," Jason mumbled, shaking his head. "I've been under a lot of stress lately."

"What happened?" Jessica prompted, gripping my shoulders so I would stop.

Jason scratched his head, his expression pensive as he turned to face us. "It started out just like any other dream, then all of a sudden it changed. I was sitting at a table with my father and a woman I've never met. We were eating Chinese and she asked me what my plans were for the summer. I said something that made her cry and my father jumped to her defense…" Jason's voice trailed off as he started to look self-conscious.

"It's okay," Jessica said, her voice barely above a whisper. "Keep going."

"He demanded that I apologize," he continued, his gaze fixed on the ground. "I remember him reaching over and putting his hand on hers. That's when I realized what was going on." Jason cleared his throat. "My father was dating and this was his girlfriend. I felt angry and betrayed. I couldn't believe he was replacing my mother with this woman. The next thing I knew I was on my feet, yelling. All the hurt and frustration I felt over the years just poured out of me."

"Then what happened?" Seated on my back, Jessica was outside my line of sight, but her voice was full of fascination.

Jason frowned, uncertainty in his eyes. "I donno know. I woke up after that and couldn't get back to sleep."

"Do you think your feelings toward your father provoked this dream?"

"I do not know," he stated flatly. "I do not know how I feel about him."

"How would you feel if he started dating?"

Jason made a face. "He wouldn't. He loves my mother too much."

"That wasn't my question."

"I don't know how I'd feel!" Jason said, sounding irritated. "I haven't given it much thought."

"Sure you have."

"No, I haven't!"

"Come on, Jason," Jessica urged, raising her voice. "How would you feel if your father started sleeping with other women?"

"I wouldn't let him!" Jason yelled, tears filling his eyes. "I wouldn't let him!"

"Your father's a grown man," Jessica pointed out, her voice calm once again. "He can do whatever he wants. How would you stop him?"

"I don't know," Jason whispered, closing his eyes, and leaning against a nearby tree. "I don't know, but I can't just sit back and let some woman take Mom's place. I just can't."

"And there it is," Jessica said.

"What are you talking about?" Jason peered up at her through defeated eyes. "There what is?"

"The truth. The answer to the question you've been unwilling to ask yourself. Whether you were willing to admit it or not, a part of you always knew there was a chance your father would date again. You knew you didn't have the power to stop it and so you were forced to hide inside yourself."

"You tricked me," Jason muttered, looking self-conscious.

"No, I got you to tell the truth," Jessica said. "I gave you the power to admit how you truly feel."

"Do you think that dream has any bearing on reality?" Jason asked uneasily.

Jessica shrugged. "In a place like this, who knows. Corpus said the usual rules don't apply. It's not inevitable that your father will find someone, but it is possible. And now that you know how you feel, I suggest you take this time to prepare."

A few minutes later, we continued through the jungle, nobody saying a word. I was just beginning to think the silence would follow us all the way to the village when Jason suddenly spoke, mild amusement in his voice.

"You know, Jess, I've gotta hand it to you. You'll make a great therapist someday."

"Thanks," she said courteously. "That means a lot coming from you."

"Don't think this means I'm gonna change or anything," he continued nervously. "I'm still the same guy."

"Believe me, Jason, I know."

He clearing his throat loudly. "Okay, good. So long as you understand that."

"Oh, I understand."

A couple of hours later, the jungle began to thin as we reached the edge of the forest. Stepping out of the woods, the three of us found ourselves standing at the edge of the beautiful valley that stretched out before the royal palace. Each blade of grass swayed lazily in the evening breeze. The sun's evening light cast a golden glow over the tall grass, giving the valley its name.

"Guys, we're here," I said, taking in the sight.

"Wow!" Jessica gasped from her seat on my back. "This is *so* amazing!"

I couldn't suppress a smile as long blades of grass gently tickled my ankles. "It's one thing to imagine something. It's completely different to actually see it."

Jason peered out across the terrain. "What's the big deal? It looks like an ordinary sunset."

"Have you ever seen a sunset highlighting the impressive structure of a centaur-built castle before?" Jessica asked, her grip around my waist tightening.

"No, but it's still a sunset."

"Whatever you say." Obviously she didn't think it was worth arguing over. "Personally, I've always found something incredibly fascinating about the construction of castles. Unlike modern buildings, they feel more down to earth. More natural."

I nodded in agreement

"Whatever," Jason sighed, weaving back and forth through the sea of golden grass.

* * *

By the time we made it up the hill to the village, the sun had almost completely disappeared behind the mountains. Other than the random passerby, the streets were empty. The only presence was the king's guards, who could be seen standing at street corners, on

113

the lookout for people like us.

"Okay," I whispered, stopping behind a small hut on the edge of town and pulling Quaymius's cloak over Jessica and myself. "This is where we need to start being careful. If the king's Followers catch us, we're finished."

"Do all centaurs live in these tiny little huts?" Jason asked, gesturing at the surrounding houses.

"No," I replied, waiting for one of the closest guards to turn his back. "The nicer houses are closer to the middle of town." Then with a slight smile, I added. "I always pictured them being rustic and Tudor. They look so earthy."

"Where's the Old Library?" Jessica asked urgently from under the cloak.

"On the other side of town." I looked cautiously around the side of the hut. "I think it's safer if we go around the outside of the village. The guards are stationed everywhere in town. It will take longer, but I don't think they will look for us there."

"How do you know?" Jason asked, standing back a few feet, looking apprehensive.

"Because I always had Quaymius go through town. He's more daring than I'd care to be."

Quietly, we made our way around the outer perimeter of the village, careful to stay in the shadows. After silently creeping behind buildings for the better part of an hour, we finally made it to the Old Library.

"Here we are," I whispered, looking up at the ancient structure. "We made it."

"Why have you come here?" a voice suddenly demanded and the three of us froze.

Chapter 17

I knew that using mind tricks was a bad idea. How was I supposed to know it would leave me feeling this bad? I was completely drained. Sitting on the riverbank I waited, hoping that the exhaustion would abate. Unlike humans, my people don't have to sleep for a minimum of eight hours every day. We are able to obtain our energy for longer periods of time. In fact, Earth time, we only sleep once every six months. But because we don't sleep as frequently, we remain unconscious for much longer; twenty-four hours, more or less. I knew I didn't have time to take a twenty-four hour nap, but when the drained feeling didn't pass after an hour, I knew I had to get some shuteye. Carefully extracted myself from the centaur world, hoping I wasn't causing Oliver any pain, I re-entered the human world. When I was back in Jason's bedroom, I got up and looked around. It wouldn't be easy sleeping in human form, but I would have to try. Going over to the wall, I leaned up against it, tilted my head back, and closed my eyes. After I'd been sleeping for several hours and could already feel my energy returning, there was a knock on the door, pulling me from my slumber.

"Jason!" the doorknob rattled. "Come on out. There's someone I want you to meet."

I pulled away from the wall. *Oh no! What do I do? Didn't Jason say his father never bothers him here?* While I tried to figure out what to do, his father continued to knock on the door.

"Okay, now I'm starting to get worried." The doorknob rattling again. "Jason, if you don't open this door in ten seconds I'm coming in, okay? I'll knock it down if I have to." And he began to count, "1… 2…"

This can't be happening! My eyes swept the room. Oliver and Jessica lay side by side on Jason's bed while he sat on the floor, propped up against the wall. If Mr. Garrett came in he'd know something was wrong. I couldn't let that happen. Hurrying over to the closet, I slid inside and shut the door behind me. *Here goes.* I sat down and crossed my legs. In the past, commandeering bodies hadn't gone well, but it seemed that I was getting the hang of it. Hopefully, if I was careful and didn't overdo it, I would be able to keep any negative side effects to a minimum. So, placing my hands on my knees, I closed my eyes and carefully took control of Jason's body. With any luck he would be unaware of what was going on. As soon as he was under my control, I made him stand up and go to the door.

"No, don't come in," I said through Jason, putting his hand against the door just in case. "I'm fine. I was just—" I glanced around the room, "—listening to music with my headphones on."

"Okay, good," Mr. Garrett said from the other side, sounding relieved. "Uh, can I talk to you for a second?"

I wasn't sure what to say. First of all, whatever Jason's father had in mind sounded like something the real Jason would want to hear. Second, I wasn't sure how much longer I would be able to keep the emotion in his voice, making him sound like a ordinary human being and not a 'zombie.'

"What is it?" I asked, knowing I couldn't delay any longer. Maybe this wouldn't take long.

"Uh, could we talk face to face?" Mr. Garrett inquired, sounding more uncomfortable by the second. "You know, father and son?"

I swallowed nervously. Putting an ordinary amount of emotion in Jason's voice was hard, making him appear normal was far more difficult. It had been hard enough making Oliver presentable on the short trip out of the school. If Jason's father planned on talking for more than a few minutes, I didn't know if I could do it.

"Please," Mr. Garrett begged from the other side of the door when I still hadn't responded.

From inside the closet I took a deep breath and let it out. I didn't know what the relationship was between Jason and his dad, but I sure didn't want to be the one to make it worse.

"Okay," I replied as Jason and I opened the door and slid out. "What do you want to talk about?"

"I know the two of us haven't really spoken in a long time," Mr. Garrett said, looking at me with troubled eyes. "Ever since your mother left I've sort of distanced myself from you, but I want to change that. I want to be the father I haven't been for a long time. I want to be there for you."

"Really?" I decided to keep it simple.

"Yes." Hope flickered in his eyes. "Jason, I loved your mother and I will always love her, but I think we can both agree that she is never coming back. I've spent five years watching that front door, hoping she would return, but she hasn't. I think it's time we both moved on with our lives."

In the two minutes I stood there listening to Jason's father, I learned more about him than in the last twenty-four hours combined. I was finally able to understand Jason in a way I never thought possible. I finally understood the mystery behind those curious hazel eyes.

"That makes sense," I murmured, more to myself than to Mr. Garrett, but he smiled all the same.

"I'm glad you agree. There's someone downstairs I want you to meet."

I felt the calm steady gaze I'd been giving Mr. Garrett gradually slide off Jason's face, but it wasn't because of what he'd just said. I simply didn't have the expertise to maintain the appearance of emotion. I tried to get Jason to smile over and over again, but nothing happened. When Mr. Garrett saw his son's face suddenly go blank, he started to look worried.

"You're okay with that, right?"

"Yes, of course," I replied, but to my dismay Jason's voice was completely void of expression.

"Are you sure?" his father asked, now looking scared.

Shoot! How do criminal masterminds do it? Inside the closet, I gritted my teeth and focused all my energy into getting Jason to show an emotion, any emotion.

"I said okay!" I yelled at Mr. Garrett through his son and I felt his eyebrows narrow in anger.

"All right," his dad said, looking relieved and I could only assume to him any emotion was better than none.

Anger wasn't what I was looking for, but it would have to do. Interestingly it was relatively easy to convey.

I followed Mr. Garrett down the stairs to the living room, Jason's eyes still narrowed and a slight frown on his face. It seemed that maintaining a look of mild irritation was far easier than trying to spontaneously juggle several different emotions at once. I had no idea what Jason's reaction would be if he found out his father was dating. Knowing him, he probably wouldn't take it very well, but I still didn't like the idea of deciding for him. However, fearful that his face would go blank again, I made no attempt to smile as Mr. Garrett introduced me to Emily, the new secretary at his office.

"Hi!" She greeted me with overzealous enthusiasm, shaking my hand as she stood up from the couch. "Your father has told me so much about you!"

I would like to have at least used positive words, some sort of reassurance that I was okay with the situation, but I feared anything I said would be misinterpreted in the stiff, unfriendly voice I was forced to use. I didn't want Jason to appear threatening or aggressive. However disappointed Emily and Mr. Garrett might be at his son's disapproval, no doubt they would take far more comfort in that than downright hostility.

"Really?" I made it sound more like a statement than a question. "What did he say?"

"Uh, just that he's proud of you and he's lucky to have you as a son," Emily replied, casting her partner an uneasily glance.

"Right." I turned to Jason's father. "Is that it? Can I go now?"

"Well, I was kinda hoping we could all go out to eat together," Mr. Garrett said, fidgeting nervously. "Get to know each other a little better."

"That's a great idea!" Emily agreed. "What did you have in mind?"

"I was thinking Chinese," Jason's father said, glancing at me. "Is that okay with you, son?"

"I'm not hungry," I said stiffly. At precisely that moment, Jason's stomach growled loudly, making a liar out of me. It was only then that I realized how famished he actually was.

"That settles it," Mr. Garrett said, grabbing his coat. "I want everyone in the car in five minutes."

I didn't know what the effects of operating in the centaur world without real world food had on the body, but it couldn't be anything good. Since it was clear that Jason's system longed for nourishment, it was probably best to feed him.

"Fine. Whatever." I grabbed his coat and headed out the front door.

On the way to the restaurant, I started trying to think of ways to extract the centaur world that Magnum Opus had put in Oliver's head should he and his friends ever escape. I had no idea how I would go about this, but I knew that getting him out of there would be pointless unless I could somehow free him of that place. The longer that world resided in his mind the more damage it would cause, eventually leading to his death. Unfortunately, the best solution I could come up with was to somehow design and build some sort of device that was capable of removing that world. But even if I could locate an energy source strong enough to power such a machine, I had no idea where I would even start. I was not an engineer, I had no idea what kind of parts I would need to make something like that. Even if I did, the odds of successfully constructing a gadget capable of eliminating the centaur world from Oliver's mind (without killing him in the process) were minute.

When we arrived downtown, Mr. Garrett parked the car and the three of us climbed out. During my preliminary sweep of this area, I only got momentary peeks through the occasional store window. Now I would get a close up look at public dining. Back home, I have eaten in public settings before. Given my father's position, on many occasions I have accompanied him to fancy dinners and banquets, but I have never experienced anything quite like this. On the inside the restaurant was small. Very small. At various tables and booths people sat hunched over eating from ceramic plates. When we entered, a seemingly young girl greeted us. She could have been anywhere from 14 to 24 years old. I wasn't sure. According to a small plaque on her shirt, her name was Wen. After asking how many were in our party, she led us to a small table in the back. Before leaving, she passed around three thin fold-out booklets. At the top it read 'menu' in fancy letters.

"Would you like anything to drink?" our server asked as Mr. Garrett and Emily calmly scanned their brochures.

"I'll take water," the secretary said, smiling politely.

Jason's father flipped to the back of his menu. "I'll have a beer." He seemed confident in his request, but when Emily cleared her throat, he quickly changed his mind. "Uh, make that tea instead."

Surveying the beverages, I ordered the first soda product listed. As she wrote down my order, I noticed Wen give me a shy smile. Informing us that she would be right back with our drinks, she turned and left.

"So who was that kid I met this morning?" Mr. Garrett asked, dragging my attention away from our surroundings.

"What kid?"

"The little blond one. I don't recall seeing him before."

"Oh, uh, just a friend," I replied, not sure what to say.

"He looked a lot younger than your other friends."

"He's one of those… What do you call them?" I grappled for the right words. "Child geniuses. He was just helping out with a science experiment."

"What kind of experiment?" Emily asked.

"Uh, sleep cycles."

When both adults continued to look confused I added. "How uncomfortable locations affect our sleeping patterns."

Satisfied with this response the two smiled and nodded. Just as she'd promised, our server was back with our drinks. Once she had placed all the cups on the table, she pulled out her notepad and asked if we were ready to order. Emily requested the coconut shrimp while Mr. Garrett settled on the General Chicken.

"And for you?" Wen asked, turning to me.

"Uh, I think I'll try the steamed vegetables."

"Seriously?" Jason's father stared at me like I had lost my mind. Remembering what happened with Oliver and the glazed doughnuts, I became nervous. "I'm not allergic, am I?"

"No, I've just never known you to choose veggies over meat."

"Oh. I can order something else if you would prefer."

"No, it's fine." It was clear Mr. Garrett wished he hadn't said anything. "Order the vegetables. It's good you're eating healthy."

The wait for our food was in silence. I couldn't sense their emotional state, but I still had the feeling both adults wanted to speak. Emily kept opening her mouth then shutting it. I also caught her shoot Mr. Garrett these intense looks before jerking her head in my direction. Personally, I invited the silence. It was better than awkward conversation. With any luck, no one would utter a word for the rest of the evening. No such luck. Not long after our dinner arrived, the secretary started to speak.

"So, Jason, what kind of books do you like to read?"

I couldn't pretend to know the answer to that. The only literature I recalled seeing in his room were small, nondescript paperbacks. Most of them looked like they hadn't been touched in ages. If anything, Jason preferred magazines. They littered his floor. But, not wanting to risk displaying any inconsistencies his father might notice, I just shrugged and continued eating.

"What about movies?" Emily asked, obviously determined to find something to talk about. "Your father says you love watching films. What genre do you like?"

I still didn't respond.

"I like comedy," she chirped. "My favorite comedian is Will Ferrell. What about you? Do you have a favorite actor?"

The term 'actor' was lost on me, but I was starting to get an idea of what Emily was talking about. On my first night here, I got a general overview of human entertainment. I wasn't entirely sure what they entailed, but movies were one of them. Based on the posters that plastered Jason's walls and his occasional film reference, I concluded that a movie was a very primitive version of VRSS. For me, the Virtual Reality Software System is a means of escape. It would seem that movies served a similar purpose. I didn't want to speculate on Jason's motives, but I had to say something.

"I don't know about a favorite actor, but my walls are covered with an assortment of posters from a number of different movies."

"That's impressive," Emily said, looking relieved. "Why do you enjoy films so much?"

"Because unlike life, movies don't let you down." I looked up at her, allowing the emotion to drain from Jason's voice. "No matter what happens, you know there's going to be a happy ending… at least most movies have the decency to do that. All I want is to escape from my problems and believe in something different, something better, if only for a moment. Is that too much to ask?"

"I guess not." the secretary looked unnerved. No one spoke for several minutes after that. In the meantime, I stared out the window, watching as the sky grew steadily darker, wondering how the others were doing, and if I would be able to get this mess fixed before the fleet returned. This would be my third night on Earth and Marcus had said they would be returning in three days. Tomorrow was my last day. Time was running out.

"So what are you learning in school?" Emily suddenly asked, cutting into my thoughts. "Anything interesting?"

"Not really." I let my gaze shift back to my plate. Despite Mr. Garrett's misgivings, the steamed vegetables were really good. "We're reading stuff like 'Good Country People' and 'Story in an Hour.'" I was also amazed at the portions that I was given. There was no way I could eat all this. "I don't know how Mrs. Waterberry expects us to interpret what authors who lived back in the 1800s had in mind when they wrote stuff like that." I was only half finished and Jason's once starving belly was already feeling overburdened.

"I felt the same way when I was in high school," Emily said bracingly as I set down my eating utensil, not wanting to risk regurgitation. "I also don't understand how the school system doesn't expect these younger generations to start developing back problems with the amount of books their teachers are assigning. Over time, those history books just get bigger and bigger. They must weigh a ton by now."

"They don't weigh that..." I started to say, but stopped. I just had an idea. Time was running out. Even if I still had no idea how I was going to help Oliver, the least I could do was start trying to find a solution. It was time to stop feeling sorry for myself and start doing something. Just because Jason's body was stuck having dinner with his father and his new girlfriend didn't mean that I, Mandayus-Corpus, couldn't be working on a way to fix Oliver's problem. After all, controlling two bodies was like walking and talking.

I crawled out of Jason's closet on my hands and knees, went over to my duffle bag, and pulled out my *Space Navigation* book, feeling rather foolish for not thinking of this before. There was loads of information in there that might help me. After all, the book covered anything and everything remotely related to navigation.

I flipped the book open and started thumbing through the pages, only stopping when I got to a section entitled "All You Need to Know About the Navigation System and How It Works." Up to this point it never crossed my mind to wonder what systems looked like or how they operated. They just had to function. Now I was eagerly hunched over the page, taking in everything the book had to offer. It was incredible! The book had labeled diagrams of the computers I used to calculate the distance of every star or galaxy in the local vicinity. It explained how those computers transferred the information I gave them into digital, three-dimensional maps. There was even an emergency section on how the computers were able to extract data from neighboring ships in the unlikely event that all the systems aboard the mother ship were down. The device in the computer responsible for extracting this data was something called the prong.

This is it! I thought, my hands sweating with excitement, *this is the answer!* Eliminating the world Magnum Opus had created in Oliver's mind wasn't the solution. That was too complicated and far too dangerous. It would be much easier and far safer to find a way of relocating it.

I was in the process of reading exactly how the prong worked when Emily started talking to Jason once again, and, still being in control of him, I could hear her as if she was standing right beside me in his bedroom. I might have been able to control two bodies simultaneously, but I couldn't concentrate on two different things at once. I reluctantly stopped reading to focus my attention on her.

"I'm sorry, what did you say?"

"I was just wondering if you were planning on getting a job during the summer," Emily said. "I remember when I was your age. I spent my summers life-guarding at the local swimming pool."

"Sorry," I grunted, eager to get back to my book. "I don't know what I want to do this summer."

"Don't be silly," the secretary said, brushing her hair out of her face. "Every teenager knows how they plan to spend their summer. It's the time of year you look forward to the most."

"Well, I don't," I said shortly. "I've had other stuff on my mind."

"Come on, Jason." Emily sounded desperate for the first time that evening. "You have to lighten up sooner or later."

"No, I don't," I said coldly, wishing that she'd leave me alone. "I don't have to do anything. I don't have to like this, I don't have to answer your questions, I don't even have to like you. I did you the courtesy of speaking to you, but I don't have to do that either. I just want to be left along! Please, just leave me alone!"

Emily opened her mouth in a silent cry of shock, her eyes wide. Then she dropped her fork, placing her hand over her mouth, trying to hold back the sobs that threatened to burst forth.

"Jason Matthew Garrett, you apologize right now!" his father said angrily.

"Or what?" Jason demanded, clenching his hands into fists and I realized to my horror that I was no longer in control. Something else was driving him to say the words that now burst angrily from his mouth and I couldn't stop it! Had Jason woken up? Was this actually him yelling at his father? That was impossible. Neither Jason nor Jessica could exit the centaur world without my help. And yet he kept yelling at his father, only now he was on his feet. "What will you do, Dad? Will you shut me out again? What can you do that's any worse than what you've been doing for the last five years? What punishment can you press upon me that would make me feel any worse than I've felt since the day she walked out? Do you really think that I can forget about her that easily? Do you really think that I can just sit back and let some other woman take her place? Well, I won't, Dad. I won't." With that, Jason stormed out of the restaurant. I wasn't able to regain control of his body until he was in the back seat of the car, still breathing heavily.

"Jason?" I whispered through him, not sure if I expected a response. "Jason, are you there?"

Nothing.

"Jason!" I said more urgently, "Jason, can you hear me?"

Still no answer.

What the heck just happened? I wondered, looking around in alarm. If that wasn't Jason, who was it? I sat in the car for several minutes pondering the strange events that had just unfolded before remembering I had important work to do.

Chapter 18

JESSICA

Okay, I admit it! I had a crush on one of my best friends. I have for some time. Did that make me crazy? Maybe. I was definitely crazy for acting on it. The way Oliver reacted when I took his hand you'd think I'd stung him. I might as well have for all the good it did. I tried to hide my disappointment, but I failed miserably. To make matters worse, I lashed out at Jason in the midst of my frustration. On a lighter note, I did achieve the unthinkable. After dozens of failed attempts, I finally got Jason to open up. To be honest, I was beginning to think that would never happen. Perhaps there was hope for him yet. As we ascended the hill to Sunset Village, I was still dwelling on the events of the previous night, but at least I had something to feel good about. And seeing the Old Library filled my chest with hope. We were just getting ready to enter when a voice spoke to us from out of the darkness. Standing in the shadows cast by the ancient, crumbling statues that guarded the entrance, stood the silhouette of a centaur. It was impossible to determine who stood there, concealed in the shadows, only that her voice was full of hate and anger.

"Who are you?" Oliver demanded, his hand casually inching toward Quaymius's sword.

"Who do you think?" the shadow responded coldly. Slowly stepping out of the darkness, she allowed the moonlight to fall like a pale curtain across her face.

"Avril?" I couldn't see Oliver's face from my seat on his back, but I could definitely hear the surprise in his voice. "What are you doing here?"

"I could ask you the same thing." Quaymius's friend surveyed him with hurt frustration. "I thought you already came here or was there a new breakthrough that I was not made aware of?"

"Were you the one following us down by the river?"

"I wanted to know why you didn't return the night before last."

Oliver shifted his stance uneasily. "It was late. I didn't want to bother you. I had no luck the last time I was here. I thought I'd bring my friends."

"Do you not consider me a friend?" Avril gazed at him, the cold look in her eyes melting away only to be replaced with tears. "Why are you always shutting me out? I only want to help."

"I'm sorry, but this is very dangerous. I don't want you to get hurt."

"I'm not a child!" the red-haired Rebel declared, her eyes ablaze. "I can take care of myself. I can help you," then, casting me a scornful look, she added, "Much better than she can."

"I don't deny that what you're saying is true," Oliver said, clearly trying to find a way out of this. "But we're less likely to get caught if there are fewer of us."

Avril stared at him for a moment, then, lowering her voice she spoke in what I'm assuming was Polytaurus. Despite my growing fear, I couldn't deny that it was a beautiful language. Obviously she didn't want Jason or I to eavesdrop.

"Well?" Avril prompted when Oliver didn't respond. He clearly had no idea what she'd said. To avoid suspicion, I quickly cut in.

"I don't think this is the best time to be discussing this. We should get inside."

"I agree," Jason said, looking around nervously. "It would be a shame to get this far only to be caught."

We entered the Old Library together with Oliver in the lead, Jason in the middle, and Avril bringing up the rear. When we arrived in the main lobby, which was a large circular room with a smooth marble floor, I slid Quaymius's cloak away from my face to have a better look. My mouth fell open in awe as I took in our surroundings. Every aspect of the library mirrored Oliver's description perfectly. The books that lined the walls seemed to go on forever; thousands of torn and tattered documents that looked as old as the library itself. Halls branched out in every direction, their ancient shelves sagging under countless pages of literature. Cobwebs hung everywhere like white wispy curtains, clinging to the books as if trying to shield them from unfriendly eyes. The only light in the room came from an old chandelier that hung from the ceiling. Most of its candles had gone out, but a few still flickered, casting a pale orange glow on the surrounding walls.

Oliver stopped in the middle of the room, looking down each hallway in turn, as if trying to figure out which way to go.

"Wow," Jason murmured, coming to a halt to his right. "Is this where they keep all their books?"

"The Old Library does not just contain books," Avril said, casting him a disapproving look. "It also guards the records of our history. All the great achievements and battles of our past are kept safe here."

"Because that's what every crook is looking for," Jason remarked sarcastically. "History books."

"For your information, there are plenty of people who want to steal or even destroy the documents that are kept in this place."

"Why?" I inquired.

"Because, with the information that is kept within these walls, one could become very powerful," the Rebel said as if she were talking to a child. "The king himself would have this place destroyed if he thought anyone was mad enough to try and read every book here."

"Why doesn't anyone?" Jason asked.

"Are you kidding?" the centaur snorted, glancing at Oliver as if wondering how his friends could be so ill-informed. "Nobody could read all these books, not even in ten lifetimes. The chances of anyone stumbling across anything that would do them any real good are infinitesimal."

"Are what?"

"Very small, minute."

"Where's the guardian?" I asked, realizing that something was missing.

"Who knows," Oliver replied, still looking around. "He comes and goes like the wind. By the way," he added, gesturing to the hall directly in front of us. "The place we're looking for is this way."

After traveling down the long, dark hallway for what seemed like an hour, but couldn't have been more than a couple minutes, we arrived at the room that contained all the myths, fairy tales, and legends of this world.

"Finally," Jason gasped as we hurried inside, his arms wrapped around himself. "I was starting to feel like I was being buried alive."

We quickly made our way over to the side of the room containing the English version of the stories.

"Curious," Jason remarked, looking over some of the titles on the bookshelf. These in particular mirrored several human tales, including *Alice in Wonderland*, *Beauty and the Beast*, and *Peter and the Wolf*. The only difference was that all the human characters had been replaced with centaurs.

"I thought it would make this world easier to understand if its stories were similar to ours," Oliver said under his breath as Jason ran his fingers over *Little Red Riding Hood*, *Cinderella*, and *Sleeping Beauty*.

We then started pulling books off the shelves and looking through them.

"Remember," Oliver announced as he gingerly flipped through the pages of a desperately torn and tattered paperback. "We're looking for clues that might lead to discovering the cave's secret."

We had only been looking a few minutes when Jason called our attention to the book he had in his hands.

"Hey, look at this," he said, sounding mildly amused as he flipped it open.

"What is it?" Avril asked eagerly, looking up from her book.

"*The Adventures of Quaymius the Almighty*," Jason read, looking the book over with increasing interest. "It's a collection of stories told by various people about Quaymius."

"So?" Avril looked disappointed.

"Since when was Quaymius almighty?"

"Since always," Avril replied, giving him a dark look before smiling lovingly at Oliver. "There are lots of stories about the wonderful things that he has done over the years."

Jason paid her no mind. "Whatever. This first story is entitled, 'The Ranger:' Once upon a time there was a young man who lived in the forest. He had a free spirit, he did whatever he wanted; he was bound to no one. He was neither a part of the system nor society; he made his own laws, he followed his own rules. He came to be called the Ranger, for no one knew his real name. Few believed in him. They thought he was a myth, a legend that someone had created. I believe in the Ranger, one might even say it was I who started those stories…"

"Are you sure this is about Quaymius?" I asked skeptically. "It sounds awfully old."

"It is a legend, it is meant to sound old," Avril said, giving me a distasteful look. "And it wouldn't be a good story unless some of the facts were embellished."

"There's more," Jason said eagerly, and continued to read. "The first time I saw the Ranger was during the Last Crusade against the unicorns…"

"This story isn't about Quaymius," I interrupted for a second time, remembering something Oliver had said. "King Mytus had already banished the unicorns before Artayus came along fifty years ago. This tale either got mixed in with ones about Quaymius or someone is giving him credit for something he didn't do."

"What is wrong with you?" Avril hissed, glaring daggers at me. "Do you not think that Quaymius is capable of great things?"

"Well, no I mean yes," I said, taken aback. "I'm just saying, of all the great things he has done, this was not one of them. I don't even know why we're wasting our time with this! We're supposed to be trying to find answers about the cave!"

I expected Avril to have some retort, but she just stood there staring at me. It was impossible to know what she was thinking and after a moment, without saying a word, she turned back to the bookshelf and continued looking. Breathing a silent sigh of relief I, too, continued my search.

Half an hour later, I was thumbing through the same book Quaymius had read, making silent notes to myself when it hit me. In a moment of overpowering realization I knew how the cave worked. After carefully re-reading a few lines from a couple of the stories, I was sure I had the answer.

"I've got it!" I cried excitedly, slamming the book shut. "I know how the cave works!"

"How?" Jason asked, already looking defeated.

"It's so simple." I was surprised I hadn't noticed it before. "What do all of these stories

127

have in common?"

Before anyone could answer the door burst open, revealing six centaurs in emerald green cloaks. The one in front was slightly shorter than the others, but what he lacked in height he made up for in looks. His eyes were cold and fierce, he had dreadfully pale skin, and his jet-black hair was pulled back in a pony-tail. The only thing that made him seem less threatening was his beautiful chocolate-colored fur. Beside him stood a tall, lanky centaur with white fur and blue eyes, the evil look on his face struggling to hide his beautiful features. Behind them were a grey, a light-brown, and a black centaur. I couldn't tell what color fur the last one had, but of the six, he appeared to be the youngest.

"By order of the king, you are under arrest," the fierce-looking guard yelled as the six of them rushed forward into the room. The white centaur pulled me off Oliver's back while the other five surrounded Avril and my friends. The chocolate guard and the grey one circled Oliver while the light-brown one and the black one closed in on Avril. The remaining Follower grabbed Jason from behind, forcing his arms behind his back.

"Let me go!" I screamed, twisting and squirming in the white centaur's powerful grip as the others also tried to escape. The only one who wasn't making any attempt to fight off her captors was Avril. She just stood there, as still as a statue while the black and light-brown Followers held her from either side.

After the fierce-looking centaur had chained Oliver's wrists together with iron cuffs and bound his ankles in leather shackles, he proceeded to do the same to Avril. But before he even got the restraints out, she suddenly collapsed on the floor... Well, she didn't exactly collapse. The following sequence occurred so rapidly I hardly had time to realize what transpired before it was over. First Avril relaxed her hindquarters, allowing herself to go into a sort of sitting position, but instead of stopping there, the rest of her body followed. This happened so suddenly the two Followers holding her were taken off guard, thus allowing her to slip through their fingers. I half expected Avril to fall in a heap on the floor, but instead she sort of gracefully twisted her body in the air as she went down, permitting her to roll onto her back. Reaching out with her hands, the young Rebel grabbed the light-brown centaur around the ankles, pulling his feet out from under him, while at the same time kicking out with her hind legs, knocking the black guard into one of the bookshelves, sending books flying in every direction.

Keeping the roll going, Avril turned completely over, using the momentum of the fall to bring herself back up on her feet. A second later she was galloping toward the exit, grabbing books off the shelves and flinging them over her shoulder as she went. This last act appeared to be last minute because none of the books she threw actually hit anyone. The next thing I knew, she was gone.

"Catch her!" the fierce-looking Follower yelled as the black and light-brown one attempted to regain themselves. "She must not escape!"

As the two guards disappeared from the room, the fierce-looking one turned to look at the rest of us, his eyes alight with a fire that made the hairs on the back of my neck stand on end.

"At last I have you," he hissed, his hungry eyes falling on Oliver. "I guess Quaymius the Almighty is not so mighty after all. Too bad your little red-headed friend decided not to bail you out this time. When the king learns of this I will be rewarded above all others!"

"This is not over," Oliver said, his teeth clenched, his eyes narrowed.

"Why do you still fight?" the fierce-looking centaur demanded, approaching our friend so their faces were only inches apart. "No one can defeat the king!"

"I must do what I know in my heart is right." It was no surprise that Oliver could play a convincing Quaymius, but though I doubted the Followers could see it from where they stood, I noticed his hands were shaking.

"Perhaps you should have killed us when you had the chance," the fierce-looking centaur said, and only then did it dawn on me that he, the grey one to Oliver's left, and the white one holding me, were the three Followers Quaymius threatened in the forest. I could only assume the same thought passed through Oliver's mind because, for a split second, a look of fear crept into his eyes. But a moment later it was gone.

"I am not a monster," he whispered, his gaze dropping to the floor. "Regardless of what the king throws at me, I will never take the life of another."

"Well, it doesn't matter now," Arsenic said, surveying Oliver with thoughtful eyes. "Tonight was your last rebellion against the king. Did you really think you could come back here unnoticed? The king sees all. You shall hang just like your great-grandfather!"

"Stop it!" I cried, no longer able to stand seeing my friend tormented like this. He might have been able to fool these guys, but he couldn't fool me. "Leave him alone!"

"Kobalt," Arsenic snapped to the white centaur, who was still holding me firmly around the waist. "Take her down to the ocean. Merpeople take no part in our affairs. Then, send word to the king that Quaymius has been captured at last."

"No!" I screamed, struggling with all my might as Kobalt carried me from the room. Unfortunately, I wasn't strong enough to free myself from the Follower's iron grip, and even if I was, there wasn't a whole lot I could have done. My physical form made doing anything on dry land difficult, if not impossible.

The white centaur carried me through the village, across the Golden Valley, and all the way to the Blue Ocean.

"Sorry, my lady," Kobalt said in a hard toneless voice before tossing me into the water and taking off. As I resurfaced I could hear the distant sound of his hooves pounding the earth as he returned to the castle.

I knew I didn't have a moment to lose. I had to find a way up to the royal palace. No doubt Jason and Oliver were on their way there now to be held prisoner until the king decided what to do with them. I immediately started swimming along the shore, looking for the river that emptied out into the ocean. The one that would lead me to the place where we left Corpus.

Swimming up the river proved to be a lot harder than I had originally hoped. Fighting against the current took everything out of me, and within half an hour I was exhausted and yearned for a break. However, I decided I wouldn't stop until I reached the faun refuge.

After what seemed to take forever and my tail felt as if it would fall off, I finally reached the small pool before the waterfall. Relieved, I slowly crawled up the bank, planning to take a half-hour break before continuing up the river. I lay down on the grassy shore, my tail still in the water, and rested my head on my arms. I wondered what had become of the others. They had probably reached the castle by now. Would the king have them put to death straightaway or would he wait? I tried to push away the horrific thoughts that raced through my mind. Oliver said that the king had Artayus executed in the town square as an example to the people. Surely after ten years he'd want to do the same to Quaymius. Chances are King Mytus would wait until dawn before carrying out Quaymius's fate. As for Jason, to the king he was just another prisoner to add to his collection. Odds were my friends had at least eight more hours. Hopefully by then I would come up with a plan. So, with this comforting thought, I relaxed and closed my eyes.

Chapter 19

JASON

After using some sort of stop, drop and roll technique to escape, the red-haired beauty was gone. A moment later so was Jessica. Now it was just me and Oliver standing in that creepy old library. My arms were cuffed behind my back and the centaur standing beside me had a firm grip on my arm. Oliver had two centaurs watching him; one mean-looking one who seemed to know Quaymius pretty well and another with grey fur and a long scar running down his right forearm. Unlike mine, Oliver's wrists were chained in front of him. However, that didn't give him much of an advantage because, unlike mine, all four of his ankles were shackled.

After the centaurs pursuing Avril and the one carrying Jessica had left the room, the three guards holding Oliver and me led us out the library entrance.

I can't believe this is happening! I thought desperately as my friend and I were led from the Old Library to a cobblestone path that snaked up the hill to the castle. *One minute we were inches from finally escaping this place and the next we were taken prisoner!*

I walked in silence, wondering what was going to become of us. I've seen a lot of movies depicting prisoners during the middle ages. I'd become quite familiar with the techniques used to torture people, so I couldn't stop the flood of horrific possibilities that rushed into my head. Everything from the rack to the pillory went through my mind. Not to mention the things kings of more distant times did to their prisoners for entertainment. Would they put us in a giant arena and make us fight other prisoners as gladiators, or worse, huge hideous monsters? I could only imagine what horrors awaited our arrival.

As we continued along the path, the castle grew larger and larger over the hill until it loomed above us like some sort of monstrous fortress. Once we reached the top of the hill, the ground leveled out, revealing the base of the palace walls. I saw that the drawbridge had already been lowered to allow us entrance. It crossed over a deep trench that surrounded the castle. As we made our way across the drawbridge, I nervously looked over the edge at the still, black water below. At one point I was sure I saw something move just beneath the surface.

As we neared the end of the drawbridge, the iron grate blocking our path slowly rose and we passed through into the gatehouse. Once inside, the iron grate slid down behind us, eliminating any possibility of escaping, and the drawbridge rose back up. Now we could only move forward, through the heavy wooden doors that blocked our path, leading into the grounds. The moment those doors opened, the guards led us through the outer wall into the courtyard. While the king's men steered us toward the main entrance of the royal palace, I looked up at the walls that surrounded us. Stationed along the top, about twenty feet apart, were heavily armored centaurs carrying bows and arrows. Some of them surveyed the activity within the castle walls but most faced outward, keeping a lookout for intruders.

"Take him to the dungeon," the mean-looking centaur said to the young one, stopping us in the main hall. "The king will be awaiting our arrival."

"Yes, sir," the guard holding me said, and led me down a dark corridor that branched off the main hallway. Looking over my shoulder, I was able to get one last fleeting look at Oliver before he disappeared from sight.

We descended a long, winding staircase that went on for so long, I was sure we must have been deep underground by the time we reached an ancient iron door. The guard pulled out a ring of old skeleton keys and unlocked the door, causing it to creak mournfully as he pushed it open. Looking around, it appeared as if the guard had taken me to what only could only be described as the darkest, dankest part of the castle; there were fauns and centaurs by the dozens chained along the walls, their heads hanging, looking as if they'd given up on life a long time ago. Only a few of them even bothered to raise their heads as we passed by. When we reached the far wall, the guard chained me up with a pair of rusty iron shackles that were connected to the wall. Only then, did he un-cuff my hands from behind my back.

After he left, I slid down to the cold stone floor, my back against the wall. All around me sat sad miserable creatures. Hadn't Oliver said some of these guys had been imprisoned here for as many as ten years? Some more? How long would I be trapped in this cold dark dungeon? Would the days turn into weeks and the weeks into months? Would I be all but forgotten? What would happen to my body in the real world if I was trapped here forever? What about my friends? If they managed to escape, would they come back for me or would they just leave me here?

Tears of despair filled my eyes as I started thinking about my father and the dream I'd had. I thought about Jessica and what she'd said in the forest. To be honest, I'd planned to reject any new girlfriend my father might acquire, real or imaginary, but now it seemed pointless. All the bitter thoughts I'd harbored against him no longer had any meaning. I found myself regretting that I'd never gotten the chance to straighten things out between us. Now, by the looks of things, I never would.

It wasn't long before what little warmth that was left in my body faded away and I began to shiver. Wrapping my arms around myself, I tried to maintain body temperature. But, between the icy floor beneath me and the even colder stone wall behind me, it was a losing battle. I attempted to pull my knees up to my chest, hoping that the soft fur on my legs would help keep me warm, but every time I tried to bring my legs up close to my body, my hooves would slide on the smooth surface of the floor. Deciding that I would probably be less cold if less of my back was touching the wall, I turned so only my left shoulder was touching the wall. This worked for a little while until my left arm started to go numb.

I spent the next several minutes shifting and turning. But no matter how I sat, I could not get comfortable. And to make matters worse, hunger started gripping my insides as the hours since my last meal began to multiply.

"I can't believe this," I groaned in frustration as my stomach began to rumble softly.

"Duke?" someone whispered from somewhere nearby, but forgetting whose body I was in, I ignored them.

"Duke, is that you?" the voice repeated and, looking up, I saw a faun about my age staring at me through the dimly lit room. It was hard to make out her features, but she was clearly looking at me. In fact, most of the prisoners on this side of the room were watching me. I guess my discomfort had captured their attention.

"Do I know you?" Evidently I was supposed to recognize her.

"It's me, Luna," she said, crawling as close as her shackles would allow. "You were really young when the three of us were imprisoned."

"The three of you?"

"Yeah." Luna gestured to the two fauns beside her. "Your brother, Cantus, and our father."

"Oh."

"How's Phoebe?" Duke's father asked anxiously. "Have you been taking good care of her?"

"Who's Phoebe?"

"Wow, you must really be hungry," Luna said as my stomach gave another desperate cry. "You're delusional. It's been ten years and I still remember mother."

"She's fine," I muttered. "Do they feed you guys down here?"

"I'm afraid you'll have to wait, little brother," Cantus said from where he sat, his back against the wall. "Feeding time is in the morning."

"They only feed you once a day?"

"We're prisoners. What do you expect?" grunted a nearby centaur, whose hair was so dirty I couldn't tell what color it was originally. "Maybe you should have thought about that before you went and got yourself captured."

"It's not like I did it on purpose," I mumbled irritably. "Things didn't go the way we planned."

"What do you mean? What were you doing?" Luna asked.

"We were in the Old Library and we got ambushed." I wished that she would stop asking questions. I just wanted to try and go to sleep, hopefully speeding up time until morning.

"Who was with you?" someone asked.

"Quaymius and Naomi," I said, my head drooping, my eyes half shut, hoping they would get the message.

No such luck.

"Quaymius?" a female centaur a few feet away from me gasped. "They captured Quaymius?"

A murmur went through the room and any faun or centaur who hadn't been paying attention before was all ears now. Before I knew it, I was being bombarded with questions. Some of them in a language I didn't even understand.

"Where did they take him?"

"What's been happening out there?"

"Why weren't you more careful?"

"What were you guys doing in the Old Library?"

"Hey, guys," I whispered weakly, curling up against the wall, my arms wrapped around my middle. "I have no idea where Quaymius is or what's going on out there. In case you haven't noticed, I'm down here with you, probably for the rest of my life. However long that is. Please just leave me alone."

Since it was clear I wasn't going to say anything more tonight, everyone fell silent. They could tell I'd been through enough for one day. Obviously these guys knew when to leave well enough alone. Relieved, I closed my eyes and tried to ignore my cold, hard surroundings and the hunger that clawed at my stomach. I really didn't feel like going over everything that had happened in the last few hours. If I was going to die down here, I would rather do it in peace. Maybe if I was lucky, death would find me quickly.

Chapter 20

As I watched the youngest of the Followers drag Jason off to the dungeon, I felt a bolt of fear run down my spine. Everything was spinning out of control. First I lost Corpus, then Jessica, and now Jason. It was unbelievable how quickly a figment of my imagination had turned into this real and hostile place. After Jason was taken away, I was escorted down the main hall, a Follower on either side, to a magnificent marble staircase. Even in the midst of the ever-increasing dread, I couldn't help noticing how impressive this castle was. The carpets (which stretched down the length of every hallway) were made of pure silk, shimmering with greens, reds, and purples. Glimmering marble statues stood guard at every entrance and exit. There were dozens of portraits along the walls depicting all the great kings and queens of the past. Looking around, I truly felt like I was in a fairy tale.

As Arsenic and Almaeon led me along the second floor hallway, everyone in our path stopped and stared. One of the servants even dropped the silver tray of dishes she was carrying. The sound of delicate ceramic dishes shattering echoed up and down the halls. I also couldn't help overhearing some of the whispered comments made in my wake: "It's him, they've caught him at last!" "I can't believe it. After all these years." It was clear that after a decade, the capture of the great-grandson of Artayus the Great was a big deal. It probably wouldn't take long for the news to spread throughout the entire castle. And, assuming that Avril had managed to escape, word would undoubtedly spread through the Brambee Forest like wildfire.

When we'd finally reached the end of the hall, the two Followers stopped outside two large double oak doors. They were dark brown with fancy engravings and shiny gold handles shaped like winding ferns. This had to be the king's chambers.

Almaeon and I stood in the hall while Arsenic went in to announce us to the king. On his return, he cast me a gleeful look before leading me forward. I must admit I didn't know what to expect. Of all the time I spent describing Lord Mytus's evil deeds, I never stopped once to consider what he looked like. When I set eyes upon him for the first time, I must say I was surprised. Although King Mytus had all the looks of a wealthy man, he did not possess the physical traits of a villain; he wore numerous robes and shawls. His fingers were laden with gems, emeralds, and diamonds. And though he possessed long black hair that tumbled down his shoulders and his eyes were as black as night, he looked pretty ordinary. There was nothing mean or evil about him. He didn't even look old. I knew he must have been in his sixties since he was young fifty years ago, but he didn't look it. I would have pegged him somewhere in his early to mid-forties. If it was any consolation, from the waist down he was build like a draft horse, the muscles under his smooth black fur flexing as he moved. I half expected the floor to creak under his immense weight as he approached me.

As terrified as I was, I still couldn't believe that I was standing in the presence of King Mytus himself, lord of the centaurs. True, he was one of the bad guys, but that didn't make seeing him in the flesh any less exciting.

"Quaymius, son of Mortis, great-grandson of Artayus the Great," King Mytus said, slowly circling me, his black eyes studying me with great intensity. "When my men told me you had been captured, I hardly dared to believe it. I wondered, 'Could it be true, could they really have caught you at last?' I was sure there must have been a mistake, but here you stand before me as plain as day. Do you have any idea how long I have been waiting for this moment?"

"Since the day you captured my parents," I replied hesitantly, still not sure whether to show fear or awe. "You haven't thought of anything else."

"That is correct." Lord Mytus looked mildly impressed. "For ten long years I have awaited this day and now it has arrived. Now I can crush the Rebels once and for all. Without you as a source of hope and inspiration, they will not stand a chance. At last I can silence all those who oppose me!" King Mytus watched me intently, his eyes boring into mine. "Not many have evaded me. You managed it for ten long years, but you have not been the longest. For roughly eighteen years now your uncle has escaped my clutches."

"My uncle?"

"Jupiter." Of course, Mortis's brother. "Today I have caught you and someday I will capture him too."

"What are you going to do with me?" Even as I as asked this I already knew the answer. Perhaps now was a better time than any to show fear.

"Everyone must know that I have defeated you." King Mytus turned to look out the window. "Everyone must know that you are no longer a threat. From the foot of the Burly Mountains to the sandy shores of the Blue Ocean, everyone must know that I have won. In a kingdom such as this, it is important to maintain order. The moment the people sense that their king is no longer in control, pandemonium reigns. Therefore, it is crucial to show the people that the guilty shall be punished. I must show them what happens to those who defy their king. Apparently the message was not received when I had Artayus hanged in the village square. Perhaps this time they will pay closer attention!" As he said these last words

Arsenic stepped forward, unrolled a scroll of parchment and began to read:

"Quaymius, son of Mortis, you are hereby sentenced to death at high noon tomorrow in the village square, by order of the king. Your method of death will be to hang in the gallows until you are dead. If there is anything you wish to say before the time of your execution, you will be given one minute to do so. Long live the king!"

King Mytus turned to face me once again. "Because tonight shall be your last night in this world, you will be treated as a guest in this castle. We will have to remove your weapons, but rest assured, you will be able to wear them during your final moments." As he spoke, Kobalt stepped forward and removed Quaymius's bow and quiver of arrows from my shoulder. He also took my belt, freeing me of anything I might use to defend myself. Only after I was weapon-free did Arsenic unfasten the cuffs around my wrists and the shackles around my ankles.

I've never taken archery or learned how to use a sword, but I felt better knowing that I still had the means to defend myself. Now I felt completely defenseless surrounded by all those armed guards.

"You will stay in the guest's chambers on the third floor," King Mytus continued, watching me with cold emotionless eyes. "If there is anything you need, a servant will be there to provide it for you."

Arsenic and Almaeon took me to the guest room upstairs. They told me that it would be foolish to try and escape because guards would be posted outside my chamber doors all through the night. Once they left, I found myself in a room that wasn't quite as luxurious as the king's chambers, but it was still very nice. The floor was covered with soft carpet. There was a handsome lamp on a wooden desk next to a beautiful stained-glass window. In one corner there was a wardrobe the size of my bedroom, and in the other stood a magnificent four-poster bed. It had dozens of beautifully embroidered quilts and blankets, all shielded behind a transparent veil that hung lazily around the bed.

I was so mesmerized by the room, it took me a moment to notice the young female centaur standing in the corner. Her hands were clasped in front of her while she stood as still as a statue, observing me. She had brown hair that came down a little passed her shoulders, her big brown eyes caught the light from the chandelier overhead, making them sparkle. She looked like she couldn't have been more than a year or two younger than me, but she was so petite her frame couldn't conceal the magnificent grandfather clock that stood behind her. When our eyes met she gave me a shy smile, but otherwise didn't say a word.

"The king sent you here?" I asked, feeling a little self-conscious.

"Yes, sir," the young servant said, bowing her head. "I am to get you whatever you wish, so long as it doesn't conflict with the circumstances of your imprisonment."

"What's your name?"

"Iris," she said, her cheeks turning red.

"Do you know who I am, Iris?"

"Everybody knows who you are, sir," she replied, watching me shyly. "Your legend has spread to all four corners of the land."

"Then you know why I am here?"

Her face fell. "Yes, sir. I do."

"You don't have to call me sir. Olive—Quaymius is fine."

"Olive Quaymius?" Iris looked confused.

"Just Quaymius."

"Is there anything I can get for you, Quaymius?" the servant asked eagerly.

"Not at the moment." I went over to one of the large stained-glass windows, not comfortable with the idea of giving someone orders. "Maybe later."

"Yes, sir. I mean Quaymius," Iris murmured while I unlatched the window and pushed on it to see if it would open. Sure enough, I'd barely touched the wooden frame when the window swung open, revealing the outside world. Looking down, I could see the courtyard three floors below. The guards patrolling the grounds looked tiny from where I stood. Seeing that it would be impossible to escape this way, I shut the window and latched it. When I turned around, Iris was still standing in the corner, watching me.

"You know, you don't have to stay there," I said, glancing at her awkwardly. "You can move around if you want."

"Thank you, Quaymius." she relaxed her muscles, took a few steps forward then stopped. From the look on her face it was clear she wasn't sure what to do.

"How long have you worked here?" I asked, trying to fill the silence.

"Since I was five," the female servant replied, weaving her fingers together. "I have been here ten long years. My family has served the great kings of old for many generations."

"Do you like it here?"

She shrugged. "I don't know, I guess. I mean, this is all I know. There are times I have wonder what it would be like living outside the castle walls, but those are just silly dreams. Besides, my mother says that I should be proud of what we do. She says that it is a great honor to serve the king."

"King Mytus?"

"She also says that someday things will be like they once were, when Lord Arcron ruled these lands. She says that he was a king worth being proud of. He was one of the greatest rulers who ever lived."

"He was a great leader," I mused thoughtfully. "A great king. Many were compelled to follow in his footsteps. At times like these we could use someone like that."

"Yes," Iris agreed, looking up at me. "Someone like you. You give hope to so many people. I think you would make a great king."

Now it was my turn to blush.

"I don't know about that," I muttered, looking away. "I'm not really the leader type."

We both stood in silence for several minutes. I could tell Iris wanted to say something, but it appeared as if she wasn't sure what. I, too, was pulling blanks. Finally, when all I could think of commenting on was the weather, the servant said, halfheartedly, "Are you sure there's nothing I can get for you, Quaymius? The chefs have cooked up a real banquet down in the kitchen."

"No, really I'm fine. I wouldn't want to trouble you."

"It's no trouble. That's what I'm here for."

"Are you sure?"

"How about this," Iris offered, seeing how uncomfortable I was. "You're not asking for anything. I was already on my way down to the kitchen and while I'm there I'll bring back something to eat. How does that sound?"

"Well, since you were already going…" I said with a smile.

"It's settled, then." Iris cast me a triumphant smile before exiting the room.

Twenty minutes later she returned, wheeling a cart stacked high with food; an entire roast pig, mountains of mashed potatoes with rivers of gravy. Glazed ham, sun-dried sausage, poultry and sea food. Loaves of freshly baked bread, a dozen different cheeses, exotic fruits and vegetables as well as beverages including orange juice, cider and beer. There was everything I possibly could have imagined and more.

"There you go, Quaymius," Iris said, taking a step back. "Enjoy."

"Aren't you going to eat?" I asked, looking at the mountains of food. "There's enough here for an entire village."

"Oh, no." She shook her head vigorously. "I couldn't possibly. This is for you. It's your last meal."

I slid the cart across the floor toward her. "There's no way I'm going to be able to eat all this myself. I need help and if this is to be my last meal, there is no one I'd rather share it with than you."

"But the king never permits us to…" Iris started to say, looking overwhelmed, but I cut her off.

"I am not the king."

"Oh, Quaymius," she gasped, looking down at the feast as if seeing it for the first time. "I have heard of your greatness, but never in my wildest dreams did I ever imagine… I don't know what to say."

"You don't have to say anything." I picked up a silver fork and handing it to her. "Just eat."

Iris and I stood on either side of the cart, eating and talking and laughing, for the better part of an hour. I got so wrapped up being with her, I momentarily forgot about my friends. It wasn't until she asked how I'd managed to get caught after all this time that I remembered why I was here. Because of me, Jason was now locked away in the dungeon. It was undoubtedly cold down there and he was probably very scared. I had no idea where Jessica was. Arsenic had told Kobalt to dump her in the ocean. Who knows where she was now. Knowing Jessica, she was probably doing everything she could to find a way back up here. It struck me like a punch in the gut that there was a very good chance we would all die in here.

"I'm so sorry, sir!" Iris gasped, her voice rising several octaves when my face fell. "I didn't mean to upset you."

"It's nothing." I tried to force a smile. "I was just thinking."

The silence that followed seemed to last forever. I watched the servant as she slowly finished what was on her plate. It was clear that she wished she hadn't spoken. I hated the fact that she blamed herself for my unhappiness, but I doubted anything I said would convince her otherwise. Looking around the room, I tried to think of something to lift her spirits when my eyes fell on the wardrobe that was set back against the wall.

"You know," I said, setting down my fork and taking off Quaymius's cloak and bandana and letting them fall to the floor. "I've been wearing the same clothes since I was little. I think it's time I changed my style, don't you?"

"I don't know, sir," Iris replied in a voice just barely above a whisper.

"No, really," I insisted also removing Quaymius's vest. "I think it's time for a change. Around all these well-dressed people, I feel so naked."

"Well, you kind of are now," the servant said, the corner of her mouth twitching slightly.

"Yeah…" I looked thoughtfully around the room. "There has to be a solution to my problem." Then pretending to just notice the wardrobe I said, "Let's see what's in here. Clothes fit for kings, no doubt." Iris giggled as I walked over and pulled open the door. Reaching inside, I extracted a fancy feather hat and set it on my head. "No?" I also pulled out one of the classic green cloaks with the silver trim and the silhouette of a centaur. "Perhaps this will help." I draped it around my shoulders and turned to face her.

"Wow!" she exclaimed, stepping around the cart and approaching me for a better look. "You really make that outfit look good. Better than anyone around here, anyway."

"Here," I said, putting the hat and cloak away. "You try something on."

"I couldn't." Iris shook her head, taking a step back. "I'm not allowed."

I arched an eyebrow. "Even on my last night on Earth?"

"Well, if you put it like that way…" the servant extracted a shimmering white gown from the wardrobe and pulled it over her head.

The material fell over her petite frame, the hem coming to her knees. She turned in a circle, letting me see it from all angles.

"It's not complete without this." I removed an expensive-looking silver headdress from a wooden bust and carefully set it on the centaur's head.

"Wow," she whispered, looking at herself in the full-length mirror next to the wardrobe and running her hands over the soft material. "This is so beautiful. I can't believe I'm wearing it. I feel like royalty."

"You look like royalty," I murmured, staring at her. "More than anyone around here, anyway."

"Really?" Iris examined herself more closely.

"Really." I took her hand and led her over to the window. "I bet you've never done this before." Flipping up the latch, I pushed it open. Iris gasped at the beautiful landscape before her, her face lit up by the moonlight that filtered in. Her hair fluttered gentle in the evening breeze. I watched as her eyes traveled from the starry sky to the mountains in the distance.

Iris stepped forward, placing her hands on the windowsill, closing her eyes and tilting her head back as the wind gently caressed her cheek. "I've dreamed of doing this for so long," she whispered, her lips barely moving. "It was unbearable to be so close yet so far away."

"I've heard the view from this point is breathtaking," I said, looking down at the village beyond the castle walls. It was distinguishable by the many lights in the window of the houses, looking like a sea of fireflies.

"My sister will never believe this!" Iris opened her eyes, looking down at the small huts behind the castle, just inside the wall. "It's her birthday today."

"How old is she?"

"She's five now," the servant said sadly. "She will start working in the castle tomorrow. Tonight is her last night of freedom."

"Would you like to spend it with her?" I could see the longing in her eyes.

"I'm supposed to be here, serving you," the servant said, still staring out the window. "I can't just leave."

"Your job is to make me happy on my last night in this world," I said softly. "I couldn't be happy knowing that you won't get to see your sister on her birthday. You've done more than enough for me. If you really wish to serve me, do whatever makes you happy."

"Oh, Quaymius." Iris turned to look up at me, tears in her eyes. "I don't know how I could ever thank you enough. Nobody has ever treated me with such kindness."

Chapter 21

MANDAYUS-CORPUS

When we pulled into the driveway, Mr. Garrett told me in Jason's body to go to my room. He said he didn't want to see me again until I was ready to apologize for what happened in the restaurant. Having no choice but to assume that the phenomenon that occurred earlier really was Jason, I decided to honor his wishes. I would wait for him to return to set things straight with his father. It sounded as if they had a lot to talk about. So, after returning Jason to his room, I got to work. First I copied the diagram of the prong and made a list of the materials needed to duplicate it, then I scrolled through the first aid manual to get information on the cerebral scrutinizer. I hoped that if I was able to combine the technology within the two gadgets, I could somehow create a machine that was safe to use on Oliver. I spent several hours designing a blueprint for the device. It was particularly hard because I had to keep in mind that the materials I would be using were human-made and therefore not as practical or advanced. My only option was to find equipment that performed basically the same task as what I needed. In this respect, several of Jason's magazines came in handy. More specifically the ones concerning electronics. By three in the morning, I had a relatively long list of things I would need to purchase. Since I didn't have access to currency at this late hour, I decided to take a break until morning. Rolling up the finished blueprint, I slid it under Jason's bed. After sitting on the floor for a few minutes wondering how long it would take to get a hold of all the things on my list, I remembered how hungry I had felt as Jason, and decided that Oliver and Jessica could probably use something to eat.

The next morning, I checked on the humans. Still thinking about what had happened the other night at the restaurant, I elected to start with Jason. However, hooking him up to the cerebral scrutinizer and looking at the transparent screen, I didn't see anything to satisfy my curiosity. What I witnessed only increased it. From what I could tell, the faun version of Jason was in a dark room. The only light came from a few primitive light fixtures that flickered feebly along the walls. He was sitting on the floor, surrounded by dozens of fauns and centaurs, his ankles shackled, his arms wrapped around himself, and his head bowed. I called his name several times, knowing that the other people in the room would not be able to hear me, but he did not move. If it hadn't been for the fact that I could see him breathing, I would have thought that he was dead. Moving on to Oliver and Jessica, I knew that whatever happened in the restaurant would have to wait.

Chapter 22

Jessica

When I woke up it was morning. The sun's first light filtered gently through the trees, reflecting off the surface of the pond, and somewhere in the forest I could hear birds singing. As I rolled onto my side, the events of the previous night flashed back in an instant. *Oh, no!* I sat up straight. I had only planned to take a half hour break! How could I have overslept? I had to find a way to get up to the castle! Slipping into the water, I swam to the other side of the waterhole. My best hope was to continue up the river to where we left Corpus. Maybe he could help me. It took me about half an hour to crawl up the side of the hill to the top of the waterfall, but once I was back in the water it didn't take me long to reach the black rock.

"Corpus?" I called, looking around frantically. "Are you still here?" But he was nowhere in sight. I floated in the water for several minutes calling his name, but he didn't answer. For all I knew Jason and Oliver were dead, and the alien was nowhere to be found. Losing all hope, I folded my arms on the riverbank and started to cry.

"Jessica?" a voice suddenly said out of the blue. "Jessica, what happened?"

"Corpus!" I yelled, raising my head and looking around. "Where are you?"

"I'm in Jason's bedroom." He sounded as if he was standing right in front of me. "I'm using the cerebral scrutinizer. What happened?"

"We got separated last night," I said, wiping the tears from my face. "We were in the Old Library and we were ambushed. They took me down to the ocean and I don't know what happened to the others."

"I checked on them," Corpus said. "Jason is in what appears to be a dungeon, no doubt somewhere in the castle. I'm not sure where Oliver is. The scrutinizer showed him sleeping in a well-furnished room on an elegant, four-poster bed. Does that make any sense to you?"

I pondered this for a moment. There was no way Oliver could have escaped, was there? The Followers hadn't wasted any time shackling him. Even if he had somehow managed to free himself, he'd want to keep a low profile. I doubted any rich family would want him shacking up with them. There had to be another explanation. Of course there was the chance that he was in a room in the castle. But how? I thought for a moment, trying to remember anything I might have read concerning executions in the past.

"In some cultures it was customary to provide those condemned to death with certain comforts before they were scheduled to" I said hesitantly. "In the United States people on death row are given their favorite foods before they are executed. No doubt King Mytus is honoring this custom and allowing Quaymius to have a good night's sleep before he dies."

"Oh." the alien sounded perplexed.

"Corpus!" An overpowering sense of dread invading my mind. "I have to get up to the castle before it's too late!"

"I wish I could help you," he said, his voice shaking slightly. "But I can't. Entering that world drains too much of my energy."

"Isn't there anything you can do?"

"Sorry. If I keep using up my energy, I won't have the power to get you and Jason out of there when the time comes. There must be something you can do."

"Like what? I'm a mermaid. I can't walk on solid ground!"

"But I can," a voice suddenly said from somewhere beyond the bushes and a moment later, Avril stepped out into the clearing. Her spicy red hair billowed in the morning breeze, her almond-shaped green eyes fixing me with a steady, determined gaze.

I looked up at her with uncertainty. "I thought you hated me."

"I do not hate you, Naomi," the Rebel replied, flicking her hair back with a long slender finger as she continued to study me. "That would be unfair seeing as I don't know you. But even if that were the case, I would never allow my feelings to get in the way of saving Quaymius's life. At first I did possess some feelings of resentment toward you, but the determination you demonstrated in the Old Library the other night proved to me that you care about him just as much as I do. You were able to solve a mystery that my people have dwelled on for centuries. If that isn't devotion, I don't know what is."

I wasn't sure what to say. "Oh, I just… I mean, I thought…"

"You did figure it out, didn't you?" Avril asked, arching an eyebrow. "You do know how the cave works, don't you?"

"Yes," I replied. "Yes, I know."

"Good." Bending at the waist, she held out her hand. "Then let's go save our friends."

*　　　*　　　*

"So do you know what's going on up at the castle?" I asked from Avril's back five minutes later as we made our way through the jungle to Sunset Village.

"Rumor has it that King Mytus is planning to have Quaymius executed at high noon. I spent most of last night traveling all over the area, informing all the Rebels and our allies of the terrible news."

"Will the whole village be there? You know, for the execution?"

145

"Everybody from all the surrounding villages will be there," Avril replied. "Except Rock's Peak," she hastily added. "I didn't go there. The inhabitants there are a little shady. But I did send word to all the other villages. A lot of people didn't believe me when I told them. They wanted to see it for themselves."

"I can hardly believe this is happening," I said, staring sadly at the ground. "It's like a nightmare I can't escape. I've known Olive—Quaymius my whole life. I don't know what I'd do if anything ever happened to him."

"Do not worry," Avril said bracingly. "If King Mytus thinks that he can get away with this, he has another thing coming. Fifty years ago, we weren't equipped for this kind of thing. Now we are. Now we have the power to stop him."

The Rebel's words of comfort made me feel a lot better. I didn't know what the forest dwellers were capable of, or how much influence they had, but Avril made them sound pretty powerful. I only hoped that she was right.

"So who were you talking to earlier?" she asked, stepping over a log.

"What?" I didn't know what she was talking about.

"Back at the river," she clarified, pushing a branch out of the way. "Before I came out into the clearing, I heard you talking to someone."

I wasn't sure what to say. "I was… uh, talking to myself."

"You were asking someone for help. I heard you. You said 'isn't there anything you can do?' then after a pause you said, 'like what, I'm a mermaid, I can't walk on solid ground.' It didn't sound like you were talking to yourself."

"I don't know what you're talking about," I insisted, shifting uncomfortably on her back. "I wasn't talking to anybody."

"It's okay," Avril assured me. "I think I understand. This is going to sound crazy, but the other day I ran into a human. He told me he came here from his world. He said his name was Oliver and that he could help Quaymius. I took him back to my shelter and the next morning he started speaking to someone I could not see. I assumed it was someone from his world, but I never found out. Not long after that he disappeared. You don't have to lie to me, Naomi."

"Okay," I admitted after a moment. "I was speaking to the human world. Oliver is doing everything he can to help your people."

"This is good news," the Rebel said, a hint of excitement in her voice. "Two days ago I had my doubts that the human world even existed. Don't get me wrong," she quickly added. "I believe in Artayus and what he did for the fauns, but I was not sure what I thought about the cave. There have been so many stories told about it for so many centuries. It just seemed unreal. But now I know that Artayus was telling the truth and that has given me renewed hope."

We traveled in silence for about ten minutes before Avril asked, somewhat timidly. "If you don't mind me asking... how does the cave work?"

This time I didn't hesitate, knowing that I could trust her "That place truly is mysterious. After looking at all those stories, I was able to come up with only one logical explanation. True, it was difficult reaching my decision with all the tales that were either inaccurate, nondescript, or inconclusive, but I'm pretty sure I figured it out. Once I weeded out the questionable fairy tales, it became evident that the only thing that remained constant was the manner in which each centaur entered the cave. For example, Artayus was able to enter while being pursued by the king's men. In *The Tale of the Centaur and the Cave*, the Great One entered when being attacked by some angry griffins. It all adds up!"

"I'm sorry. I don't get it," Avril said, confusion in her voice.

"Don't you see the pattern? All those people were only able to enter the cave when their lives were in danger. The cave is a refuge. It protects you in a time of need. That's why no one else has ever been able to enter; curious and inquiring minds are not enough. A person's life has to be in imminent danger."

"By the great gods!" Avril stopped dead in her tracks "That makes so much sense! I can't believe I never saw that before!"

"Actually, it's easy to see how one might be led astray," I said matter-of-factly. "A lot of those stories are either about centaurs who were never heard from again or they were meant to give some kind of moral or sage advice; we either never hear the circumstances in which some individuals entered the cave or the story is fudged to get a point across."

"Wow!" the centaur breathed, still sounding mystified as she continued through the forest. "This is unbelievable!. After all these years the cave's secret is finally uncovered. This will really help set Quaymius free."

"You're not going to tell the king, are you?"

"What? No, of course not," the Rebel said indignantly. "He probably wouldn't believe me anyway. Whatever we tell him, he must hear it from someone he trusts."

"So what's the plan?"

"I'm not sure yet." Avril sounded pensive. "But whatever it is, it must take place at exactly the right moment. Timing is everything. If King Mytus gets the news too soon, he will leave Quaymius in the castle, making it impossible to get to him. But if we tell him too late, well... you know what happens."

"When we get to the village, we'll need to find you a disguise," she continued as the trees began to thin. "The king might have let you go once, but I'm not sure he'll be so welling next time."

"What kind of disguise?"

"I do not know." The Rebel glanced at the shore as it came into view through the trees.

"But we had better think of something fast. When we get into town, there cannot be any mistakes."

"Can't you just pull a robe or cloak over me? That's what Quaymius did."

Avril shook her head. "No, that would be too obvious. There will be a lot of people there and we cannot take any chances." Then she added as sort of an afterthought. "If only we had some mermaid magic."

"Some what?"

"Mermaid magic," she repeated. "Quaymius told me about it. Don't worry, I haven't told anyone," she quickly added, then said in a wistful voice. "That would solve all our problems."

"How does it work?" I asked, thinking fast. "I only heard about it in passing."

"You mermaids really are something," Avril mused, her voice full of admiration. "Possessors of some of the most powerful magic around. It's a shame there is so little communication between our two worlds. You can thank King Mytus for that. The particular brand of magic I am referring to allows the drinker to take on any form he or she desires. If we had some, we wouldn't have to worry about sneaking you around."

"Well, why don't we?" I asked, my heart starting to race.

"You think you can convince your uncle to give you some?" the Rebel asked, stopping and turning her head to look at me.

"Sure, why not?"

"Okay." Avril turned and headed for the shore. "Just be quick. We only have about two and a half hours to get to the town square."

When we arrived at the Blue Ocean, she lowered me down into the cool crystal water, her hooves sinking in the moist sand. "Be careful," she called, taking a few steps back as the waves came in, threatening to moisten her feet.

"Don't worry," I said, turning to gaze out at the endless horizon beneath the rising sun. "I'll be back in a flash." Without wasting another second, I dove under the surface. I didn't know what to expect as I swam deeper and deeper out into the ocean. Oliver hasn't written any stories about the merworld, but knowing him there were probably at least a couple pages of notes about the place somewhere in his notebook. Despite the circumstances, a part of me was eager to see what mysterious world was concealed in the deep.

After I'd been swimming for about ten minutes and the ocean surface loomed high above me, the murky water started to clear, and I came across what looked like an underwater city. At first it was just a few houses with door frames that were door-less and window frames that were glass-less, then a sea of tall building-like structures drifted into view. They looked as if they were made of coral, but coral like I had never seen it before.

Everywhere there were mermaids and mermen going about their daily lives. I realized it was going to be difficult finding what I was looking for. Scanning the tops of all the building, I couldn't tell which one was the mermaid fortress. They all looked alike.

"Excuse me," I called, flagging down a mermaid that was fifteen feet away, who happened to be passing by. "Maybe you could help me. I'm looking for the palace. Can you tell me where it is?"

She had long black hair that drifted lazily around her face. In the rippling water her features were unclear, but her sadness was not. When she turned to look at me the pain in her eyes was haunting. Looking surprised, she pointed toward the tallest, fanciest coral structures in the distance.

"Of course." Now that it was being pointed out, it was obvious.

"Don't I know you?" she asked, studying me more closely.

"I'm the king's niece," I said before quickly taking off.

It was clear that the merworld was very different from the centaur one. There didn't seem to be as big a gap between the social classes and there was nowhere near as many guards patrolling the streets. The only security I encountered was the two guards stationed at the entrance of the under water fortress. When I approached, they hastily swam aside.

"Uncle?" I called as soon as I was inside, swimming quickly down the main hall. I didn't really expect anyone to respond, but I didn't have a moment to waste.

"May I help you, Lady Naomi?" a young mer-girl asked me as I turned down another hall. She wasn't wearing anything to indicate that she was a servant, but judging by the way she presented herself to me, I assumed that was her role here.

"Yes, do you know where my uncle is? I need to see him right away. It's urgent."

"Why, yes," she replied, seeing my haste. "He's in his study."

I realized I had no idea where that was. "Could you take me to him, please?"

"No problem. It's right this way," the young mermaid replied, not looking the slightest bit surprised by my request.

When we arrived at the low archway leading to a room, the young servant stopped and motioned me forward. "Here you are, my lady."

"Thank you," I said graciously before swimming forward into the room. The sea king was positioned behind a low stone table. He was a powerful-looking man with broad shoulders and long grey hair that drifted around his face. When I entered he was looking at an array of small black pebbles, all with different symbols engraved on the top. As far as I could tell the pebbles were scattered randomly across the surface of the table, however, the sea lord observed them with great intensity.

"Uncle?" I said, moving forward a few feet.

"What can I do for you, Naomi?" he asked, looking up and smiling at me. It was only then I saw that his eyes were a deep, perceptive blue.

149

"I need some mermaid magic. It's important."

"What do you need it for?" he asked calmly.

"King Mytus has captured Quaymius and they're going to hang him at noon if someone doesn't stop him." I decided it would be easier to tell the truth. Hopefully he was familiar with the stories of Quaymius the Almighty.

The sea king straightened up, drifting away from the table as he surveyed me thoughtfully. "You wish to help save him?"

"Of course. He's my friend."

"I understand. I just want you to know the danger you will be in if you follow through with this. If you are caught, King Mytus is unlikely to be lenient with you. Even if you are my niece. He'll put you in his dungeon, along with all his other prisoners."

"I understand," I replied, thinking of Jason.

"Okay," the sea lord said, going over to a shelf and picking up a small glass bottle. "So long as this is what you want, I will not stop you. This magic is very straightforward. Just picture in your mind what you wish to become and it will do the rest." Having said this he swam over to me and placed the bottle in my hand. "This should be enough for one hour."

"Thank you!" I gushed, relief washing over me. I hadn't expected to get a hold of the mermaid magic this easily. "Thank you so much."

"Just promise me you'll be careful," he urged, placing a hand on my shoulder. "I don't know how I would explain it to your father if anything happened to you."

"I promise."

The moment I was outside the fortress, I sped as fast as I could back to the beach. Avril was still waiting for me on the shore when I resurfaced.

"Did you get it?" she asked as she once again hoisted me up onto her back.

"Yes," I replied, holding up the tiny glass bottle. "I got it. He gave me enough to last an hour. I'll use it right before we get into town."

"Incredible," the Rebel said as she took off up the beach toward the valley. "You are amazing."

*   *   *

When we reached the edge of town, it was clear that noon was approaching. All the houses and shops were deserted. There wasn't a soul in sight.

"Okay, we must hurry," Avril said, gently lowering me onto the ground. "After you've changed, meet me in the town square in front of the saloon. Good luck." With that she was gone.

After staring at the bright purple liquid inside the bottle for a split second of concentration, I pulled out the glass cork, and downed the contents. I didn't feel a thing, but it only took a second for the magic to take effect. Everything from the waist down changed.

As a plant grows in fast forward, I watched as my fish tail grew out into the body of a beautiful silver dappled horse. Finally! Now that I was a centaur I could walk on solid ground.

The moment the transformation was complete, I re-corked the bottle and slid it into my now empty canteen. When I got to my feet I was a little unsteady at first, but after a moment or two, I was galloping down the empty streets to the center of town. Seeing the middle of the village for the first time, it was amazing how much it resembled an old western;, everything from the blacksmith shop with smoke curling from the chimney to the saloon.

Continuing toward the town square, I heard the crowd long before I saw it. The loud rumble of voices could be heard from several streets away.

Entering Main Street, I could see the crowd all gathered together. Avril wasn't kidding when she said every village would be there; the sea of centaurs seemed to go on forever. There were so many spectators that not all of them could fit in the open, forcing some to stand in the streets. As I approached, it looked as if the poor population consumed the perimeter of the crowd, while the rich made up the center. There was even a row of guards surrounding them to insure that the lower class didn't get too close. The gallows were at the center of the crowd. It was a wooden structure with a platform positioned about fifteen feet above the ground. There was an additional platform that stood next to it where the king and all his main advisors stood. Among them were Arsenic, the light-brown centaur, and the black one.

When I got to the back of the crowd, I had to fight my way over to the saloon. The moment I got there, the volume of the crowd suddenly went up several notches. Looking up, I saw that Kobalt, the white centaur who had thrown me in the ocean, had just led Oliver out onto the wooden platform of the gallows. Another centaur with copper-colored fur accompanied them, a scroll of paper in his right hand. I noticed that Oliver's wrists were tied, but his ankles were free. He was also fully armed with all of Quaymius's weapons.

Looking up, I saw that the sun was nearing its highest point. It wouldn't be long now. All around me voices were strained as people articulated their concerns. Some silently wiped tears of despair from their eyes, while others bowed their heads, whispering desperate prayers of hope.

As I looked at all the dismal faces surrounding me, waiting for Avril to arrive, I noticed a centaur standing a few yards away, near the edge of the crowd. I couldn't see his face because his head was bowed, his long hair acting as a curtain. There was nothing significant about his appearance. He was just as broken down as the people around him. What caught my eye was the plain silver band he wore around his ring finger. Because of his wretched state, I thought it odd he would own, much less keep, something of that value. I didn't have too much time to think about it though. At that moment Avril appeared beside me.

"It's all set," she said, looking around. "In exactly five minutes our under-cover will announce to the king that she has heard from a reliable source that the secret of the cave has finally been revealed. If all goes well, the king, being eager to solve this mystery once and for all, will leave Quaymius here while he and his men go into the jungle. Before the guards can return Quaymius to the castle, our people will jump them, buying him enough time to escape."

"And if everything doesn't go well?" I asked.

Avril whispered something under her breath, then said, "Pray to the gods for a miracle.

At that point, another guard joined Oliver and the other two centaurs on the platform. He stood behind Kobalt, his arms folded and a dark look on his face. It occurred to me that, when the time came, it was his job to pull the lever that would release the trap door under my friend's feet.

The copper centaur holding the scroll stepped forward and unrolled the paper, preparing to speak. The rumble of the crowd, which had been pretty steady until now, suddenly broke off, leaving behind a heavy silence. He then proceeded to read the long list of crimes Quaymius had committed in his life. When he was done, Kobalt reached over and pulled the noose over Oliver's head.

"Is there anything you wish to say?" the copper centaur asked. My friend's eyes scanned the crowd below him. He didn't look like he was searching for anyone, just desperately trying to come up with something to say. My heart thundered in my chest and tears welled up in my eyes as Oliver stood there silently on that platform. The look on his face made it clear that he had given up. He was accepting his fate.

No! I thought as the silence seemed to stretch on forever. A silence so dense it was a wonder anyone could breathe. *Oliver, don't give up. It's not over yet!*

"Very well then," the centaur said, pulling out a black bandana and tying it around Oliver's head, covering his eyes. Right when the dark-looking guard behind Kobalt was about to pull the lever, a piercing cry came from somewhere to my right.

"Wait!"

All heads turned as a beautiful young maiden tore through the crowd. With long platinum-blond hair and dove-white skin, she was radiant. The fancy garments that draped over her slender Akhal-Teke frame made it clear that she was high-class, however, she didn't show any sign of disgust at the poor state of the people around her. Instead she forced her way through the crowd to the foot of the gallows.

"Wait!, I have news!" she yelled, looking up at King Mytus.

"Persephone, this is hardly the time," Arsenic hissed, glancing nervously at the king. "Perhaps later—"

"No, father!" she declared, her voice trembling. "This is important!"

152

"I am truly sorry, my lord," Arsenic apologized, turning to the king. "I don't know what has gotten into her. She is usually very well behaved."

"It is all right," King Mytus said, studying Persephone with mild curiosity. "I would like to know what is so important at a moment like this. Go on," he continued, addressing Persephone directly. "I am all ears."

Persephone hesitated as hundreds of eyes focused on her. "I just wanted to tell you that I have received word from a reliable source on how the cave at the center of the forest works."

The tidal wave of noise that followed was so loud it was impossible to tell if she said anything after that. Everyone appeared to be talking at once. It was several minutes before the noise had died down enough for any one person to be heard.

"Who might this source be?" the king asked Arsenic's daughter. Unlike some of the people in the crowd, he did not look skeptical. Instead he observed her with a serious air.

"All I can say, my lord, is that he or she is willing to swear on their life that what they say is true," Persephone said, bowing her head. "The proof you seek is at the center of the forest, but you must hurry. Your window closes by the minute."

"Why do you bring this up now?" the black centaur demanded, gazing at the young woman with suspicious eyes. "Why not last week or last month?"

Persephone raised her head to look up at the king. "Fifty years ago, his majesty said that should someone unlock the secret of the cave, he would pardon Artayus for the act of treason he committed against the kingdom. Artayus is gone now, but I see no reason this promise should not extend to his descendants. After all, if not for that act of treason, none of us would be here," and she gestured to Oliver who was still standing on the trap door, the black bandana covering his eyes, and the noose around his neck. "That is what you said, my lord, is it not?"

King Mytus nodded once, not taking his eyes off Persephone. He seemed to be in deep thought. In his moment of absence, his advisors stepped in.

"How do we know the secret of the cave has been discovered?" the black centaur asked, looking dubious. "What if this is a trick?"

"Yeah," the light-brown centaur agreed. "We're supposed to believe the word of a girl? How do we know she is telling the truth?"

"That's my daughter you are talking about!" Arsenic snapped, his voice sharp as a whip. "She has never told a lie in her life!"

"Clydon, Norus, Arsenic, relax." King Mytus said, still watching Persephone with his piercing black eyes. "If she is telling the truth we do not have much time to act. If there is a gateway to another world, I do not wish to pass up the opportunity."

"But, my lord," Norus, the light-brown centaur started, but the king overrode him.

"Kobalt, take Quaymius to the dungeon. If this turns out to be a trick, we can always continue this later."

"Yes, my lord." the white centaur removed the bandana and the noose from around Oliver's head and led him down off the platform. Two other guards accompanied Kobalt as he took my friend back up to the castle.

"On their return, we shall pursue this source of yours," King Mytus said to Persephone. "If you wish to back out, now is the time."

"No, my lord," she said, her face unchanging. "I stand by what I have said."

"Very well then." the king's dark eyes gleamed. "The cave awaits us."

"Oh, no!" Avril hissed. "This is not how things are supposed to happen!"

"What do we do?" I asked, panic gripping my insides.

For a moment she didn't answer, her green eyes darting around as if she was trying to come up with something fast. "I'll be right back," the Rebel finally said and disappeared before I could respond. All I could do was stand there and wait for her to return. If this plan didn't work, we were right back where we started, only worse. It was just getting to the point when I began to wonder if Avril was ever coming back when someone grabbed my arm. Looking up, I expected to see she, but instead I came face to face with a stooped ancient-looking centaur. He was so old and withered it was a wonder he could stand.

"We must go!" he whispered, pulling on my arm with amazing vigor. "Quick! We don't have much time."

"I'm waiting for someone." I tried to pull away, but he wouldn't let go.

"Avril can wait," he said, dragging me away from the crowd. "Right now there are more pressing matters."

"Where are we going?" I asked, looking over my shoulder as the town square and all the people in it disappeared around the corner. "Where are you taking me?"

"There is no time to explain."

"Stop!" I dug my hooves into the ground and pulled back with all my might. "I can't leave! I have to save Quaymius!"

"If you wish to save your friend, you must follow me now!" the ancient centaur said, letting go of my arm and continuing down the street.

"Where are you going?" I called, not sure what to do.

"To the Old Library," he shouted, disappearing around the corner.

"What about Avril and the plan?"

"That was just the first part," the guardian called, his voice becoming more distant. "There is still work to be done."

"Then shouldn't we wait for her?" I asked, reluctantly following him.

"Avril doesn't know about this part," the guardian said as we turned another corner, reaching the edge of town. "She and her group were relying too much on chance and it is imperative that this plan works. Only a select few know about this."

"Who?" I asked, my misgivings starting to fade.

"Those who must remain anonymous for this or future plans to work," the ancient librarian said as we arrived at the Old Library. "Those who know what could happen if the great-grandson of Artayus the Great dies today."

"Why did you include me?" I inquired as the two of us entered the ancient, crumbling structure. "How do you know you can trust me? Do you even know who I am?"

"A fascinating thing, trust. Is it not?" the old guardian mused as he hurried to one of the many bookshelves and started skimming through the titles. "Everyone has his or her own definition for it. For some, the word is symbolic; they use it lightly, more figuratively. Whether or not these people can actually trust a person or situation is irrelevant. They use the word as a means to communicate their own personal feelings or desires." At this moment the old guardian found the book he was looking for. He pulled it out, reached into the empty space and pulled out an old rusty key. After returning the book to its place on the shelf, he motioned for me to follow as he hurried down the hall that led to the room of myths and fairy tales.

"Whereas others," he continued as if there hadn't been a pause. "Use the word more literally. Instead of basing their decisions on feelings or desires alone, they base it on facts; something that can support them." At this point we reached the room with the stories, but instead of going inside, he turned so he was facing the cold stone wall opposite. "I do not know how you decide to place your trust," the old librarian said, placing his palm flat against the stone wall, and looking deep into my eyes. "But I like to base it on facts. So, I guess the answer to your question would be yes, I trust you, Jessica."

I nearly swallowed my tongue. "How do you know…?"

"Your friends need us now," he cut me off and he pushed on the wall. To my surprise it slid back, reveling a long dark passageway.

Chapter 23

OLIVER

I really believed I was going to die. At first I entertained the possibility that, by some miracle or stroke of luck, someone or something would save me. Maybe Avril had managed to escape the king's men and was bringing help. Perhaps Jessica and Corpus had band together and were now on their way to bail me out. But, as time continued to pass and I found myself standing on that platform above the crowd, I finally gave in. What was the point in fighting the inevitable? The likelihood of anything changing in the next few seconds was insurmountable. So I was more than surprised to find myself in the dungeon twenty minutes later, no longer inches from death. After bring me down, Kobalt untied my hands, took me to the far wall, and chained me up. What just happened? Standing on that platform, I recall hearing someone say something about deciphering the secret to the cave. The only person I knew who had successfully done that was Jessica. Was she behind this? I hardly dared to exhale.

Lying down on the cold hard floor, my back up against the wall, I started looking around the room. Most of the prisoners appeared to be asleep. Only a few bothered to raise their head after Kobalt left. Whether or not any of them recognized me, all of them seemed too weak to show it. I squinted at all the despondent faces. Lots of these prisoners have spent the last ten years in here. For most of them this is where they would spend their last days on Earth. Remembering that Jason was brought down here last night, I started peering around for him. With any luck he was okay.

It took me a second to locate him because the light was so minimal. Plus all the prisoners were covered with a thin layer of grime, making it hard to discern their faces. After a second or two I realized that he was sitting right next to me.

"Jason, are you okay?" When he didn't respond, I slid over to have a better look at him. The unconscious form of my friend sat curled up against the dungeon wall beside me. "Jason, are you awake?"

When he still didn't move my heart almost stopped beating as my mind began to weigh the possibility that he never would. Then, very slowly, he raised his head and looked at me. It was amazing how dirty he had become after spending one night in the king's dungeon. I could hardly make out his features under the layer of dirt that covered his face.

"Oh, man," I sighed, relief washing over me. "I'm so glad you're all right. I wasn't sure what happened to you after we got separated. I thought you might have frozen to death down here."

"Just about did," Jason murmured, surveying me through half-shut eyes. "I honestly don't know how I made it through the night."

"How are you holding up?"

"Well, assuming I never need to use my fingers again, I should be just fine." He demonstrated by trying to move one of his digits without success.

"Oh, my god!" Placing his hands between my own I felt how cold they were. If his fingers weren't so dirty they would undoubtedly be blue. "Can you still feel anything?"

"No," Jason replied, looking like he might cry. "If we ever get out of here, my hands will probably have to be amputated."

"Don't say that!" I hissed, rubbing his hands between mine, trying to rekindle some life in his frozen extremities. "I'm sure you'll be fine."

"I don't know," Jason whispered, his eyelids drooping. "I feel so numb. I was so hungry last night, but when they finally brought us food this morning, I couldn't eat. My hands were too paralyzed. It's like that day we accidentally got locked in that walk-in freezer at that meat-packing factory. Remember? On that class field trip back in the fifth grade? It took them forty minutes to find us. Only now it's like I got stuck in there all night."

"If I recall correctly, that was your fault," I muttered, trying to humor him.

"Whatever."

I tried to think of something to make him feel better, however, I wasn't sure if there was anything I could say that would erase the misery he had endured down here. "Don't worry. I'm sure we'll find a way out."

Jason's eyes slid shut. "I don't think I'll make it. Go ahead without me."

"No!" I said, shaking him. "You can't go to sleep. You have to stay awake!"

"It's so hard," he whispered, his eyes still shut. "Please, just for a little while."

"*No!*" I pulled his cold, nearly lifeless body against me. "You can't sleep, not now! Please hold on!"

Jason didn't respond and I was about to call for help that probably would never come, when suddenly the wall to my right seemed to vanish, leaving a dark tunnel in its place. A moment later Jessica was towering over me, only she was no longer a mermaid. Now she was an incredibly beautiful centaur. A few feet behind her, stood an old decrepit-looking centaur, carrying a torch in one hand and a key in the other.

"Jessica?" I breathed, hardly able to believe my eyes. "Is that really you?"

"Yes," she replied, hurrying over to stand beside me, tears of joy in her eyes. "I'm here to save you."

"We must hurry," the old centaur said, coming in and unlocking the chains around my ankles then proceeding to do the same with Jason. "We don't have much time."

"My friend is suffering from hypothermia," I said, getting to my feet, Jason in my arms. "He needs help."

"He'll be fine," the librarian said after studying him for two seconds.

"How can you be sure?"

The centaur gave Jason a firm slap on the cheek and he jerked awake. "Wha... what happened? Where am I?"

"Don't worry," I said, smiling at Jessica. "You're going to be okay."

"You guys go on ahead," the old librarian said. "I have work to do here."

"What are you going to do?" she asked.

The guardian held up the key. "Set these people free, of course. There are many innocent lives in here to save."

"Thank you for all your help," Jessica said. "I don't know what to say."

"Just promise me you three will be careful."

"I promise."

"Now hurry," the librarian said. "No doubt the king's guards have returned to the town square. Oh, and Jason," he added as Jessica and I headed to the dark passageway. "She still loves you."

"What was that about?" I asked as we hurried alone the passageway, Jason still in my arms. "How did he know Jason's name? Did you tell him who we were?"

"No," she said, not looking back. "Somehow he knows who the three of us are. I have no idea how. But that's not important right now. The only way for us to get you through the cave is if we are being pursued by someone or something dangerous. I'm pretty sure that's the cave's deep dark secret; it's some sort of refuge. Now, in order to do this, we have to get the king and hopefully several of his men to follow us to the center of the forest."

"Why several of his men?" Jason asked. As we left the cold confines of the dungeon, he seemed to recover more rapidly.

"Because the more witnesses there are, the harder it will be for King Mytus to deny. We want word to get out that Artayus was telling the truth."

"How can you be sure the king will even follow us into the forest?" Jason was starting to sound more like his old self.

"A couple of reasons," Jessica replied as we exited the tunnel and ran down the hall that led to the main lobby of the library. "First of all, seeing Quaymius's miraculous escape from his dungeon will no doubt send the king into an outrage and he'll be compelled to stop us. Second, King Mytus is legendary for his desire to conquer and control as much territory as he possibly can. If he thinks there is a chance there is land somewhere out there, he will go to any length to get it."

"Wow!" I couldn't help being impressed. "Sounds like you really did your homework, Jessica."

"Well," she said as we galloped across the marble floor of the lobby toward the exit. "I didn't have much of a choice. Of the three of us, I was the only one in any position to do anything."

"I'm going to ask the question that I'm sure is on all our minds," Jason said tentatively.

"And what's that?"

"What if this King Mytus and his men catch us before we reach the cave?"

"That's the tricky part," Jessica replied as we exited the library and headed for the town square. "It is imperative that we are far enough ahead of the king and his man that they don't catch us, but also not so far ahead that they give up and turn back; without their pursuit, the cave will not open."

"So where are we going?" Jason asked.

"To the town square. Hopefully everyone is still there, including the king. With any luck we can bypass the small shops and enter Main Street in full view of the gallows…" It sounded as if Jessica was going to say something else, but she trailed off. Wondering what was going on, I slowed down to look at her, only to realize she had stopped a few feet back.

"What's wrong?" I asked, taking a few steps toward her, but before Jessica could answer her body suddenly began to shrink. Not her whole body, just everything below her waist. Her beautiful equine body rapidly shrunk away, leaving her lying on the ground, a mermaid once again.

"Jason, you and Jessica can ride on my back," I said, not wasting a second. "My arms are getting tired and I'm assuming you're not up to running."

A moment later, both my friends were on my back and we were yards away from entering Main Street. We could hear the loud rumble of the crowd, which probably meant the king and his men were still there.

"Here we go," Jessica murmured, holding onto me tight. "The moment of truth. It will take us a while to get to the center of the forest, do you think you can make it?"

"Yeah," I replied, taking a deep, determined breath. At this point I was willing to run any distance to get out of here.

When we entered Main Street, I stopped and turned to face the crowd. King Mytus was still standing on the high-rise, his advisors at his sides. It looked like he was going over some last minute details of his excursion into the jungle. When I thundered to a halt in the middle of the street he looked up and the heads of everyone in the village square turned.

"How did you…?" the king breathed, staring at me like he'd seen a ghost.

159

"You will never bring me down!" I yelled so that everyone could hear. "You may have silenced my ancestors, but you will never silence me!"

To my surprise the majority of the crowd started cheering, centaurs rearing up on their hind legs, pumping their fists in the air.

"Long live Quaymius!" they began to chant and the look of shock on King Mytus face turned to malice. No fire could have burned brighter than the rage in his eyes.

"No!" he roared, jumping down from the platform, his black eyes burning with pure hatred. "You will not escape!" He then proceeded to barrel through the crowd, barking furiously at his guards to catch me.

"*Okay, go!*" Jessica hissed in my ear and I turned and took off down the street. I could hear the pounding hooves of the king and his men behind us, but I didn't dare look back. I ran through the village all the way to the edge of town, my friends on my back and King Mytus on my tail. I descended the hill, traversed the Golden Valley, and entered the Brambee Forest. I concentrated on nothing but the pounding of my hooves across the ground; each step bringing us closer to resolution. I didn't start getting winded until we were well into the forest. The trees were starting to get closer together, making it harder to run in a straight line. I kept having to weave this way and that around large shrubs and bushes. I didn't slow down, but all the detours plus the additional weight on my back didn't make things easy. Before long I was struggling just to keep pace.

There were several yards of vegetation between the king and us, but we could still hear him and his men in the distance. I felt I had put up a good fight, but I wasn't sure how much farther I could go. Outrunning the king after having escaped the dungeon seemed so much easier when it didn't feel like I'd just run a marathon.

"You're slowing down, man!" Jason exclaimed as we neared the river, digging his hooves into my sides. "I don't know about you, but I don't want to go back."

"You might find this hard to believe," I gasped, each breath a challenge as I continued to charge through the jungle. "But running full speed through a forest with your two best friends on your back is not as easy as it looks. If you care to lighten my load, feel free."

"How do we cross the river?" Jessica interjected. "We can't waste any time."

"Don't worry," I said, veering west. "There's an old fallen tree forest-dwellers use to cross the water. It's been there for decades."

Once we were on the other side of the river I was really struggling.

"You know what," I gasped, finally coming to a stop. "I either need a break or someone needs to get off."

"And by someone you mean me," Jason said.

"Well, you are the one with the legs," Jessica stated. "Besides, judging by how tight you've been hanging onto me, I'd say you've pretty much recovered from your stay in the dungeon."

"Fine." Jason slid down off my back. "Let's go."

"Just a moment," I protested, brushing my hair out of my face while trying to catch my breath. "I still need to take a quick breather. I did just run several miles straight."

"But they'll catch us," Jason said, gesturing frantically behind us.

I looked back the way we came. "Don't worry. We gained a little ground on them. We'll have to wait for them to catch up. Remember it's important they don't fall too far behind." I was going to say something more when I heard Corpus's voice loud and clear as if he were standing right beside me.

"Where are you guys?"

"We're on our way to the cave," I said, eagerly looking around, thinking maybe he had decided to rejoin us. "It shouldn't be much longer now. The king and his men are not far behind."

"Who are you taking to?" Jason asked, looking around, but on seeing no one, studied me like maybe this whole adventure was getting to me.

"I heard Corpus say something."

"How come I can't hear him?"

"I can't either," Jessica said from my back. "But that doesn't mean Oliver isn't telling the truth. It was just like this when I was in the river this morning. I could hear Corpus as if he was right in front of me, but I couldn't see him. It's because he's using the cerebral scrutinizer."

"Yeah." I nodded thoughtfully. "It was just like this when I was in Avril's den. I could hear you guys, but I couldn't see you."

"Then why can't we all hear him?" Jason asked. "We're all here."

"The cerebral scrutinizer can't scan all your heads at once," Corpus explained. "Oliver, you're the only one who can hear me because you're in scanning range."

"Corpus says I'm the only one in scanning range. That's why I'm the only one who can hear him."

"So he's in my room, then," Jason said, suddenly looking annoyed. "What has he been doing while some of us have been locked in dungeons freezing to death?"

"We do not have much time," the alien said, ignoring him. "Remember, Oliver, you are the only one who can theoretically exit this world through the cave. You have to allow enough time for me to get Jason and Jessica out of there before you arrive. But you must also be close enough to the cave that you feel you can get there by yourself. Once I have removed your friends, you will be on your own."

"Let's go," I said, not wanting to bother my friends with the details. "Time is running out."

As Jason and I ran the remaining distance through the jungle, Jessica on my back, I couldn't help but notice what Corpus had said. Until now the cave had been the only way out of here, but the alien had just reminded me that this was all just speculation. There was no guarantee that, even if Jessica was right and the cave did act as a refuge, it would get me out of here. In my present situation, who knows where the cave would take me, assuming it took me anywhere.

Chapter 24

JASON

Trapped in the dungeon, I didn't think I'd ever get to sleep. When I finally did lose consciousness, my dreams were plagued with arctic nightmares. This must be how Chloe Sullivan felt in *Smallville* when she was inadvertently transported to Clark Kent's Fortress of Solitude. I don't know how long my torment continued when warm hands shook me awake. Peering through half-shut eyes I saw Oliver. Was he really here with me or was I still dreaming? I couldn't tell. I wasn't completely convinced of my freedom until we were on Main Street, preparing to outrun King Mytus and his men. Personally, I was more than ready to get out of here. After spending all night in the underworld, sunlight felt foreign to me. But it was an oddity that I could quickly get accustom to.

"All right," Oliver said, coming to a halt as the jungle began to thin, and we could make out the mouth of the cave through the trees. "Here we are, the moment of truth."

"Are you sure this is going to work?" I asked, also stopping. The stiffness in my muscles had left, but I was still very sore and incredibly hungry. "What if the cave doesn't open up? What if something goes wrong?"

"Don't say that," Jessica hissed, her arms wrapped around Oliver's chest. "Nothing is going to go wrong."

"You don't know that. The whole point of a plan is for something to go wrong. That's the way it's been for centuries."

"That's not true. There are hundreds of plans in modern history that have worked out perfectly."

"Oh, yeah? Name one."

"Look, we don't have much time," Oliver interrupted, looking over his shoulder. "The king and his men are not far behind. Corpus, we're ready."

After a brief look of pain on our friend's face, the alien appeared in front of us, and despite our differences, I was glad to see him. I could not spend another minute in this place. I had come far too close to spending the rest of my life in a dungeon.

"All right," Corpus said, casting me a curious glance. "I'm going to return the three of you to your original human forms. I will return the centaur, the mermaid, and the faun back to the river where we first encountered them; they will have no memory of this. Then, I will remove Jason and Jessica from this world. That leaves the rest up to you, Oliver."

"Okay." He nodded, his face expressionless.

The alien closed his eyes and, after a slight tingling sensation, I was myself once again. No more goat legs or goatee. My ears were back to normal and I was wearing clothes once again. Running my hands through my hair just to be sure, I was relieved to feel the absence of horns.

"Yes!" I cried, feeling my now smooth chin. "I'm back!"

"I think we looked better before," Jessica murmured solemnly, standing beside Oliver, her hair now looking dull compared to the golden blond it had once been. "I liked being a mermaid."

"There's no time for mourning," I said, stepping up beside the two of them. "Let's get out of here. I don't want to be in another situation where we get caught because we spent too long talking."

"If memory serves, that was your fault," Jessica said darkly. "You're the one who was wasting our time with false tales about Quaymius the Almighty."

"Whatever, I just didn't—" Before I could finish, Corpus grabbed my wrist and started examining my watch.

"Wait a moment," he said, looking puzzled. "How long have you guys been in here?"

"About two days, why?" I wasn't sure why he'd chosen a moment like this to show an interest in time.

"That's weird," the alien mused, releasing my arm. "Since I left the centaur world only a day has gone by."

"What do you mean?" Jessica asked as Oliver and I both looked at our watches.

"I'm surprised I didn't noticed this before," Corpus continued as if he hadn't heard her. "It would appear that time within your world and the centaur world are not parallel. Here it seems to be progressing at a different rate entirely."

"How will that affect us?" I asked nervously as a wave of horrific possibilities flooded my mind. Would we start aging at an unnatural rate? What if we returned to a world hundreds of years in the future? Or worse cause scenario; we disappeared entirely, erased from existence!

"There probably won't be any side effects," Corpus replied, seeming to snap out of his daze.

I raised a skeptical eyebrow. "Are you sure? Because I don't want—"

"Corpus, get them out of here!" Oliver cut me off as the sound of hoof beats could be heard in the distance.

The alien closed his eyes. "All right. Here we go."

"See you on the other side," Jessica whispered, turning to face Oliver and a nanosecond later she was kissing him on the lips.

Before I had a chance to say anything or even react, I was swept away, the pain and hunger disappearing as my mind left the centaur world. When I opened my eyes I was back in my bedroom. Getting to my feet, I noticed that it took an extra amount of effort to move my body. Like I was out of practice or something.

"What's going on?" Jessica said from my bed, slowly sitting up and looking around. "Corpus, why is everything so hard to move? I feel like a physical therapy patient."

"You've been disconnected from your bodies for a long time," the alien said, once again giving me that curious look as if I were some sort of fascinating science project. "It will take a few minutes for you to get used to being in control again."

Jessica nodded then looked at Oliver who was still lying motionless on the bed beside her. "I hope he'll be all right." She brushed a strand of hair out of his face. "I wish we didn't have to leave him like that."

"It was the only way," Corpus reminded her, getting up from the floor and coming over to the other side of the bed opposite me. "Don't worry, he'll make it. The cave was only a few yards away. Assuming that it can, in fact, act as a back door out of that place, he should be waking up any second."

"Why did you kiss him?" I asked, watching Jessica closely. In all the long years we'd been friends, I never once remembered her showing any interest in anyone, much less Oliver.

"What?" Jessica said as if she hadn't heard me, twirling a lock of hair around her index finger.

"Why did you kiss Oliver? Do you like him?"

"I just… it doesn't…" she mumbled, looking flustered. "That might be the last time I ever see him. I was just saying goodbye."

"I may never see him again either, but I didn't lay a big wet one on him."

"I just wanted him to know how I felt in case something happens."

"So you do like him?"

"I don't know," Jessica sighed, staring at the floor. "I think so. I know he's very different from other guys, but that's what I like about him."

"You don't have to be embarrassed," I started to say. "You're not the first one to—Dude, what are you staring at?!" for Corpus had been continuously looking at me the whole time Jessica and I had been talking and it was starting to get on my nerves.

He quickly looked away. "Nothing."

"Are you sure? 'Cause if you take a picture it'll last longer."

"Jason, calm down," Jessica said, putting her hand on my arm. "There's no need to get angry."

"He won't stop gawking at me," I grunted, glancing at the alien who was now kneeling on the floor, his arms folded on the bed as he stared hard at the covers. "I don't like being stared at. It's weird and unnatural."

"Corpus, why were you staring at Jason?" Jessica asked calmly. "Is something wrong?"

"No," he muttered, not looking up. "It's just that…"

Before he could finish, Oliver suddenly sat bolt upright in bed, his eyes wide open.

"Are you okay?" Jessica asked, her voice elevated.

"Yeah, I think so," he replied, running his hand over his chest. "It was a little touch and go for a moment, but here I am."

"Here you are." Jessica smiled happily, taking his hand.

But almost as quickly as Oliver's energy returned to him, it seemed to fade away. He closed his eyes for a moment, then looking tired, sank back down onto the pillow.

"What's the matter?" Jessica asked, looking worried.

For a moment Oliver just stared at her as if he wasn't a hundred percent sure who she was, then muttered something about feeling really dizzy.

"I don't get it," Jessica said, looking at Corpus. "He was just fine a moment ago. What happened?"

"Just because his mind no longer inhabits the centaur world does not mean that he will not continue to have the symptoms he had before entering. He will not get better until I remove that place from his head. The sooner the better."

"How bad could it be?" I said, sitting on the edge of the bed and holding up two fingers in front of Oliver's face. "How many fingers am I holding up?" But when he just stared at my hand blankly, the smirk slowly slid off my face. "Oh, man…"

"Oliver!" Jessica cried, pushing my hand away. "Are you okay?"

"Yes," he muttered, looking slightly annoyed. "I'm fine."

"Oh, thank god!" Jessica gasped, looking relieved. "Don't scare me like that."

"Are you sure he's okay?" I asked, not so easily convinced. "Oliver, do you recognize this room? Where are we?"

His eyes slowly traveled around my bedroom for a moment, looking at all the posters that plastered the walls.

"The theater?"

I shook my head. "No, man! Don't you recognize my room? You've only been here a million times!"

If Oliver understood or even heard me he didn't let on.

"Questioning him won't help," Corpus said, studying him closely. "Your friend's mind is like a computer; the centaur world is overloading his brain, making it a lot harder for him to process new information. The longer it's there, the slower he will get. The only way to cure him is to remove that place entirely."

"How come he was fine while we were in the centaur world?" Jessica asked, gazing anxiously at Oliver.

"I'm not sure," the alien replied. "It might have something to do with the separation between his body and mind."

"If he loses consciousness will he return to the centaur world?"

"No, I don't think so, but it's probably not a good idea to let him go to sleep. The longer he is unconscious the harder it will be to wake him. And the longer he is like this, the harder it will be for him to remain conscious."

"Then what are we waiting for?" I asked, standing up. "Let's fix this."

"It's not that simple," Corpus said, going over to the foot of the bed and pulling a rolled up piece of paper out from underneath. "While you guys were inside, I designed a device that should be able to fix the problem, but there are a few minor glitches I have yet to work out."

"Like what?" Jessica asked.

"Well, like building it for starters," the alien said. "I had the information I needed to make a blueprint, but I had no means of obtaining the material required. I'll need your help to do that."

"How long will it take to make this machine?" I asked, running my hands through my hair.

"It shouldn't take much more than an hour, once I have all the supplies," Corpus replied. "It's actually pretty straightforward. Here's a list of the things I will need," he added, handing me a small piece of paper. "I hope you know where all these things can be found."

"Whoa!" I squinted hard at the lines of near-indecipherable chicken scratch.

"What's wrong?"

"Is this your handwriting?"

The alien shrugged. "I guess."

"What do you mean you guess?"

"I've never written before, not on paper anyway. This will be my first time."

"What do you normally use to write with?"

"Computers," Corpus said, starting to look self-conscious. "Why? Can you not read it?"

"No, I can. It just might take me a while. This is really—"

"*Jason*," Jessica warned.

"This is really… something! Excellent first try!"

"So can you get these things or not?" the alien asked, seeming to buy my feigned enthusiasm.

"Uh, sure." I shrugged, looking over the list. "We'll have to take a few things apart, but sure."

"Good." Corpus looked relieved as he got to his feet. "This might actually work."

I started for the door. "I'll be right back."

"Where are you going?" the alien asked, his relief gone in a heartbeat.

"To ask my dad for some money," I replied, stuffing the list in my pocket. "These things don't come cheap."

"About that…" he said, looking nervous. "There's something I need to tell you."

"What?" I turned to face him.

Corpus hesitated. "After you guys left me at the river, I returned here to try and re-obtain my energy and, well, I'd only been sleeping a short time when your father knocked on the door. When you didn't answer he got worried and threatened to come in. I panicked and decided the only way to make him leave was to have you answer, so…"

"Corpus, what did you do?" I demanded, not sure I liked where this was going.

"I didn't have a choice!" he squeaked. "If he had come in, he would have known something was wrong. He might have called emergency personnel or the authorities. Who knows what he would have done!"

"Corpus, did you possess me?" I asked, looking down at myself as if I might be able to tell.

"I didn't have a choice!" he repeated, a hint of panic in his voice. "He threatened to knock down your door!"

I took a step back, wrapping my arms around myself. "I can't believe this! I feel violated! I've been contaminated!"

"I didn't contaminate you! You didn't even know what was happening."

"Jason, stop being so melodramatic," Jessica said from my bed. "You're fine."

"How do you know?!" I demanded, glaring at her. "Have you ever had an alien in your body?"

"Technically I wasn't in your body," Corpus pointed out timidly. "I just commandeered it using only my mind."

"Yeah," Jessica added. "He did the exact same thing to Oliver."

"Precisely!" I yelled, gesturing to our friend, who was now watching us with a mild look of amusement on his face. Sort of the way the village idiot watches a town meeting; not really understanding what's going on, but enjoying himself all the same. "His mind is completely shot!"

"That wasn't me!" Corpus cried indignantly. "Magnum Opus made him this way!"

"What did you make me do?" I demanded, ignoring him. "I want to know."

"Nothing," the alien insisted. "Your father just wanted you to meet his new girlfriend."

"What?" All my anger disappeared in a heartbeat. "What did you just say?"

168

"Your father wanted you to meet his girlfriend," Corpus repeated, the fear melting from his face.

"Did you guys go out to eat?" I asked, my heart pounding faster.

"Yes," the alien said, now looking expectant. "We had Chinese food."

"Jason!" Jessica gasped, staring at me wide-eyed. "Your dream!"

"I can't believe this." I ran my hands over my face. "I knew there was something off about that dream. It felt too real."

"So it was you!" Corpus exclaimed, that same look of fascination coming back into his eyes. Now I understood why he'd been staring at me earlier. "I didn't know what to think before. It seemed so bizarre."

"So my father really did hear everything I said," I asked, feeling sick to my stomach. "How did he take it?"

"Actually, I don't think he was that surprised," the alien said thoughtfully. "I think he was more upset about what you said to Emily."

"Who's Emily?"

"His girlfriend."

"I don't remember saying anything to her."

"Well, actually you didn't," Corpus confessed, a guilty look creeping across his face. "I sort of told her to leave me alone before you started yelling."

"Why?"

"I was in the middle of designing this device." He held up the tube of paper. "And she kept trying to talk to me."

"What did you order?" I suddenly asked.

"What?"

"At the restaurant. What did you make me eat?"

"Uh, steamed vegetables."

"Steamed vegetables?"

"Yes."

"You go to a Chinese restaurant and you order vegetables?"

"Your father said you weren't allergic."

"So? I don't do rabbit food."

"Rabbit food?" Alarm swept across the alien's face. "Is that why your dad was so surprised?"

"No… never mind."

"I actually found the vegetables to be quite flavorful," Corpus said, looking more guilty by the second. "I'm sure the experience would have been different in my true form, but still it was amazing. Unfortunately, the portions I was given were far too great. I consumed as much as I could, but I didn't finish. And I wasn't the only one. You humans waist a lot of food." When I didn't say anything, the alien seemed to implode. "I'm sorry! If I'd known how you felt, I would have ordered something else. If it's any consolation, anything I made you eat has had plenty of time to digest."

I considered maintaining my angry, but I changed my mind. "Relax, Corpus. I'm not mad. As for what you said to Emily, if it'd been me, I probably would have done the same thing. So, uh, is that all?"

"Your father doesn't want to see you again until you're ready to apologize," he said really fast, as if trying to get the worst over with.

"Why didn't you apologize?"

"I didn't want to get mixed up in your family affairs to begin with," Corpus said, looking as if he expected me to explode at any minute. "I thought you should be the one to work things out."

"Corpus, you can relax. I'm not going to get angry."

"Are you sure?"

"Yes."

"Why not?" Now he looked confused. "You were mad just a second ago."

"I know. I'm sorry," I sighed, scratching my forehead. "I was a little crept out is all."

"I see." Corpus frowned, watching me uncertainly. "So what's the scoop? What changed?"

"I had a moment," I murmured thoughtfully, staring at the floor. "When I was in the dungeon, I found a part of myself I thought I'd lost the day my mother left. I realized that the bad things that happen to us only ruin our lives if we let them. Sitting there alone, on that cold stone floor, it occurred to me how full of regret my life is, and if I died, I would never get the chance to set things right. I never want to feel that way again. When my time comes, I don't want to have any regrets."

"Oh, Jason," Jessica whispered, tears in her eyes. "That was the most…"

"Let's just take it one step at a time," I said, hurrying out my bedroom door before she could finish. This didn't mean I was going to change who I was. I just wanted to do a few things differently.

I descended the stairs to the kitchen where I heard my father eating lunch with a woman I could only assume was Emily. At first I wasn't sure what to expect. For me the name Emily has always represented youth and beauty. I couldn't imagine my father with a younger woman. But on entering the kitchen I saw that I had nothing to worry about. Emily was a very attractive woman, but she and my father were the same age. Not wasting a moment, I sat down opposite the two of them and began to speak.

"I know my behavior last night at the restaurant was inappropriate and, even though I wasn't a hundred percent myself, I still take full responsibly for my actions. Emily, I hope that you will accept my apology. I didn't mean to hurt your feelings, I was just a little preoccupied. I'm not sure what we were talking about last night, but I'd love to get to know you. As I always say, it's not fair to judge a movie by its critic reviews." With that I stood up, leaned forward, and kissed her on the cheek.

"Dad," I continued as Emily smiled happily. "You and I will talk tonight, you know; father and son, but right now I need some money. Something rather urgent has come up and I don't have a second to lose."

"All right," Dad said, looking just as excited as her girlfriend and handing me his credit card. "Just don't go overboard, son."

"Thanks, Dad." I hurried back up to my room. "Corpus, we're set."

"Okay," he replied, getting up as I slipped the credit card into my pocket. "Jessica, you stay here with Oliver. Someone needs to keep an eye on him to make sure he doesn't go to sleep."

"What do you suppose will happen if he does go to sleep?" I asked, standing by the door.

"He might never wake up," Corpus said bluntly. "Also, try and keep him from speaking. His brain needs to stay as inactive as possible. It doesn't matter how you do it, chances are he won't remember any of this. Jason and I should be back before too long."

Getting in my car, we visited the first electronic store we came across. While the alien collected an assortment of devices from the shelves, I casually perused the speakers. A particularly cool pair had caught my eye when the front door opened, ringing the bell overhead. Looking up, I saw a full-figured girl with tousled peroxide blond hair and an eyebrow ring. My heart leapt into my throat and I swiftly ducked behind a 72" TV.

"What's wrong?" Corpus asked as I peered out from behind my hiding place.

"See that girl with the butterfly tattoo?"

He scanned the entrance. "Sorry. Is a butterfly a kind of animal?"

"Yes."

"I covered several of the indigenous species on your planet, but butterfly was not one of them."

I rolled my eyes. "She has really light hair and markings on her upper arm."

"Yes, I see her."

"Did she see me?"

"I don't think so." Now Corpus looked thoroughly confused. "Jason, what's going on? Why are you hiding from her?"

"Her name is Katelyn. I, uh, kinda slept with her and never called her back."

"I'm not sure what that means."

"I gotta get out of here."

"I can't purchase these things myself." Corpus indicated the armful of stuff he was currently holding. "I need your help."

"Crap." I took another peek at the blond. "Okay, let's do this." Stepping out from behind the TV, I guided the alien over to the register, all the while keeping a watchful eye on Katelyn. So far she still hadn't noticed me. Her back was turned as she checked out some bright pink headphones.

"How does this work?" Corpus asked as we reached the check-out counter.

"Just put the stuff down. He'll do the rest."

The alien obediently dumped the armful of gadgets in front of the cashier. He was a young white guy with dreadlocks and a tie-dye shirt.

"Did you find everything okay?" he asked, looking over our merchandise.

"Yes," Corpus replied shortly.

"That's a lot of tech," the cashier mused, looking him up and down. "What are you up to, little guy?"

"That is not any of your concern," the alien said bluntly.

"Forgive my little brother," I interjected when Mr. Cashier gave him a hard look. "He doesn't get out much. We're working on a science project. It's for his third grade class. He's eight."

"He's your little brother?" the cashier eyed Corpus uncertainty. "I don't see the resemblance."

"Look harder. It's there."

"Jason?" I froze. "Jason, is that you?" Slowly turning around I found myself face to face with Katelyn. Her light brown eyes started on the alien then shifted to me. "You never called. I waited for weeks."

"Really?" I scratched my head with feigned puzzlement. "I could have sworn I had. Isn't your number 555-4385?"

"No, it's 555-1721."

"Wow! I wasn't even close. No wonder I couldn't get a hold of you."

Katelyn whipped out her phone. "How about I get your number this time."

"Okay, it's 555-0128."

"Great!" Her face glowed as she typed it in. "I'm calling you now to verify."

"I actually don't have my phone with me." I said, patting my pockets. "I think I left it at the house. But don't worry. As soon as I get home, I'll call you."

"Promise?"

"I promise."

The moment Corpus and I were in my car, I started the engine and pulled out of the parking lot, breathing a sigh of relief. "That was close. Imagine running into her here of all places."

"Well, now she has your number so she can call you."

"I didn't give her my real number."

"You didn't? Who's number did you give her?"

"It doesn't matter."

Corpus studied me for a moment, but he didn't say anything.

"What?"

"Why sleep with her only to ignore and avoid her?"

"Do you even know what sleeping with someone means?"

"Isn't that what you and Jessica did on your living room floor?"

"What? God, no!"

"Then I don't understand, but I'm guessing it's some kind of human ritual. Something that means a lot to Katelyn… but apparently not to you."

"Hey, don't judge me. Just because you spent a few hours in my body doesn't mean you know me, *alien*. Oliver and Jessica don't know about this and that's how it's gonna be, understand?"

"I understand," Corpus muttered, his gaze shifting to the floor. "And just so you know, I was not judging you. I am not a native to your planet as you so eloquently put it, thus it is not my place to pass judgment. I was just curious."

"Tell me something about you and maybe I'll tell you something about me."

"You know a lot about me. Mind-control, mind penetration, interstellar space travel…"

"I mean something real. Something about you, personally."

"Like?"

"Like what do you look like, what are you called, where are you from?" When Corpus remained silent I turned my attention to the road. "That's what I thought."

The rest of our shopping was in silence. Along with the electronics, Corpus also bought an oversized bicycle helmet. When we returned to the house, we went to the garage and, using my father's welding equipment, he got started. Once the alien got to work, he would occasionally ask me to pass him something or hold something in place as he carefully pieced together the device that would hopefully save Oliver's life. After a while it became apparent what the bicycle helmet was for. From the looks of it, the finished product was supposed to be placed on Oliver's head, sort of like a headset; all the electrical stuff running along the inside, surrounding the top of his head.

"I get it," I murmured, examining the device more closely. "You put that on his head like a regular bicycle helmet, only this contraption has all this stuff on the inside."

"Very good," Corpus said, putting some finishing touches on his creation. "You're smarter than you look." I might have thought he was taking a stab at me, but there was a genuine quality to his voice. He might have been frustratingly secretive, but when it really matter he was there.

"So how exactly does it work?"

"The wires along the inside of the bicycle helmet will send electrical waves into Oliver's brain, removing the centaur world and relocating it to a place of our choosing."

"We won't have to shave his head or anything, will we?"

"No." Corpus shook his head, a slight smile on his face. "We won't have to shave his head."

Chapter 25

JESSICA

After Jason and Corpus left, it was just me and Oliver. I sat on the bed, his head in my lap. For several minutes he stared up at me in silence, a pained look in his light grey eyes. It was obvious he wanted to go to sleep. He definitely had the air of someone who had been through enough, but I couldn't let that happen. If Corpus was right and Oliver shut his eyes for too long, he may never open them again. So, despite how miserable he looked, the thought of him falling into a never-ending sleep drove me to be strict.

"Just let me close my eyes for a moment," Oliver pleaded softly, his eyes rolled back in their sockets. "My head hurts so bad."

"Shh." I gave him a gentle shake, forcing him to look at me. "Try to stay awake a little longer. This will all be over soon."

I didn't know if that was true, but I had to tell him something, anything to make him feel better. I had to make him believe everything would be okay. In the meantime, I tried to think of something to keep him preoccupied. If he wouldn't remember any of this, then I could be honest about how I felt.

"You know what?" I said, running my fingers through his sandy blond hair. "I've always liked you… since the day we first met. It's true. Of course, under different circumstances, I would never admit this to you, but growing up I was drawn to you. I was always too shy to say anything… in many ways I still am. But now, after everything that's happened, I don't want to leave anything unsaid. I don't know what it is exactly, but you're different. I like that. I know, I know, we've been friends since kindergarten, but I still feel like there's so much I don't know about you. It sounds crazy, of course, but I don't know what I'd do without you. You're so smart and creative. Some people express themselves through music, some through dance. You do it through literature. I know I have yet to read an ending to any of your stories, but what I have seen is like getting a glimpse into your soul. You're a guy of few words and while that can be frustrating at times, it is also fascinating. As much as I want to unlock the mystery that resides behind those eyes, I also want to keep that mystery alive. Please, Oliver, don't go. I still need you."

I was so caught up in the moment, listening to the sound of my own voice, I jumped when he suddenly spoke.

"Don't worry. I'm still here."

Chapter 26

MANDAYUS-CORPUS

The more I learned about human interactions, the more it puzzled me. After my first day on Earth, I thought I'd acquired a reasonable understanding of their connections. Sure, I was still lacking a lot of the terminology, but I believed I had grasped the basics. Jason changed that. After the encounter in the electronics store, I didn't know what to think. I had so many questions, but unless I was willing to further break the Spacing Program's rules on alien contact, I had to keep quiet. I was already in enough trouble as it was. Despite Jessica's blatant excitement, I didn't think the humans were ready to meet my kind. Still, I knew I would have to tell them something. If I didn't, I feared Jason would never trust me. But for now that would have to wait. Oliver's life was in the balance. So, swallowing my curiosity, I got to work building the extraction device. It didn't take as long as I thought it would. When was finished, Jason and I returned upstairs to his room where Jessica and Oliver were waiting. I put the machine in my duffle bag and slung it over my shoulder, before the four of us left the room. Mr. Garrett had left a note saying that he and Emily had gone to see a movie and they wouldn't be back for a couple of hours.

"Because of the manner in which this device is supposed to function, we need to find a secluded area with some form of power to relocate the centaur world," I said as we headed out the front door. "We don't want anyone accidentally stumbling across it."

"What exactly did you have in mind?" Jason asked as we arrived at his car.

"Well, it's going to take an exceptionally strong source of power to operate this device," replied as he and Jessica helped Oliver into the backseat. "Are either of you familiar with any such place?"

"An exceptionally strong source of power in a relatively remote place," Jason mused thoughtfully. "Do we look like the kind of people who would be familiar with something like that?"

"Please, Jason," Jessica said as she fastened Oliver's safety harness, hearing the urgency in my voice. "This is important."

"I'm sorry," Jason grunted, not sounding the least bit apologetic. "But maybe he should have warned us about this before getting our hopes up. What if no such power source exists on this planet?"

"I'm not talking about anything too extreme," I said, attempting to maintain calm. "Every device needs some source of power."

"How big does this power source have to be?" Jessica asked.

"Well, since it will be acting as a battery, it will need to generate at least 10,000 volts."

"Ten thousand volts!" she gasped, her eyebrows shooting up. "That's a lot of power!"

"Yes," I admitted. "But it is necessary. Surely you guys know of something that generates that kind of power."

"I don't know." Jessica looked stumped. "I can't think of anything that big. Jason?"

"What about the power plant outside the city?" he suggested. "Would that work?"

"Good thinking!" she said excitedly, looking impressed. "That could work, right, Corpus?"

"Do a lot of people go there?"

"Not really, no," Jason replied. "The fence surrounding the place is covered in all these big danger signs."

*   *   *

The trip out of town was slow. Just like on the way downtown, there was a traffic light at almost every crossroads, forcing us to stop. On my first night here, all the lights flashed red or yellow. Now they interchanged between red, yellow, and green. For the most part, Jason seemed calm, sitting back in his seat as he drove. In the back, Jessica's posture appeared relaxed as she held Oliver close, but her face was brimming with apprehension. Oliver was still conscious, but as time progressed he was less aware of his surroundings. To the untrained eye he looked exhausted, dark shadows looming under his eyes. When we arrived at the power plant, Jason and Jessica had to help him out of the back seat. He could walk on his own, but he had trouble keeping his balance so Jessica stood beside him, her arm around his waist. I knew we had to hurry. He was looking more and more out of it by the minute.

"Where's the power plant," I asked, grabbing my duffle bag and getting out of the car.

"Through there." Jason pointed to the other side of a large grassy clearing where a solitary tree stood overshadowing a wooden table/bench. It took five to ten minutes to pick our way through the vegetation. When we finally arrived we were met with a ten foot, high wire fence. Just as he'd described there were several danger signs warning people away.

"How do we get in?" In my current form I doubted I'd be able to scale the wire barrier.

"Kids are always trying to break in here," Jason said, calmly surveying the perimeter. "We shouldn't have too much trouble finding a way in."

I strolled over to the wire mesh and squinted in at all the power converters and transformers on the other side. "I thought you said this place was secluded. Now it's the center of attention?"

"It is secluded," Jason insisted, moving along the fence, every now and then pressing on the wire as if looking for something. "People don't come here often. But when they do, they try and get in. But don't worry," he quickly added when he saw the look on my face. "Most people fail in their attempts. They're mainly college students just horsing around."

"Okay, so what makes you think we'll be able to get in?"

"Because…" Jason stopped a few feet away, now standing at the far corner of the fence. Pushing on the mesh, he caused it to slide back, revealing an entryway. "We know where to look."

"Wow!" Jessica exclaimed, leading Oliver over to the hole in the fence. "How did you know that was there?"

Jason hesitated, his gaze shifting momentarily to me. "Not long before she left, my mom liked to take the dog for walks in the park. One day, he slipped out of his collar and came over here. We spent the better part of an hour trying to figure out how he got in. Finally, I found this break in the fence. We liberated him and decided to call it a day." Jason cleared his throat, a far-off look coming into his eyes. "That was the last real thing I did with my mom before she left. I remember being so mad at that dog for wasting so much of my time. Now it's like he knew she was leaving and was just giving me one last goodbye."

"I'm sorry," Jessica murmured, looking as if she wished she hadn't said anything.

"Forget it." Jason cleared his throat a second time and shook his head as if snapping himself out of a daze. "That was a long time ago."

"We must hurry," I urged, clutching my bag to my chest and sliding through the break in the fence. "We don't have much time."

Jason held the fence back while Jessica helped Oliver through, then the four of us made our way deep into the heart of the power plant. We didn't stop until we were so far inside the mass of wires and cables that the surrounding forest was no longer visible.

"We'll set up here." I started hooking up the extraction device to one of the power boxes while Jessica helped Oliver into a sitting position and knelt down behind him, resting his head in her lap.

"How long will this take?" she asked, brushing a lock of hair out of her face.

"Once I get everything set up, it shouldn't take too long," I replied, making sure everything was hooked up properly. "Five, ten minutes tops."

"Just out of curiosity," Jason ventured, standing a few feet away, his arms folded across his chest. "Will people be able to enter the centaur world after you transfer it out of Oliver's head?"

I thought that over for a second. "Theoretically, I suppose it's possible. If this process works the way it should, the centaur world will be transferred within the confines of this place, away from prying eyes. But if someone penetrated the barrier, with the proper elements, he or she might be able to find a way in. Mind you, the odds of that happening are millions to one."

"And if someone passed by, would they be able to see it?"

"No, just like we couldn't see it when it was in Oliver's head, it will not be visible to the naked eye. But hopefully no one will stumble across it accidentally. Since there was a specific way to getting out, that may also apply in trying to get in. Fortunately, we don't know what that is and based on the location, that will minimize the chance of someone else finding it. I'd hate for someone to get trapped in there."

"Yeah," Jason agreed. "No one deserves to endure what we went through."

"All right," I said, first taking the cerebral scrutinizer out of my bag and setting it down beside Oliver's head, then picking up the bicycle helmet. "Before I put this on, Oliver must be unconscious. That will help ensure minimal brain damage."

"Assuming, of course, this while process doesn't kill him," Jason mumbled, examining a nearby power converter.

"We must stay positive," Jessica said, then, speaking to Oliver, whispered. "You can go to sleep now."

As soon as the words were out of her mouth, his eyes slid shut. It was as if he had been waiting for her permission and now that he had it he could finally relax. I pulled back Oliver's eyelid to make sure he was asleep, then slid the helmet onto his head and fasten the chin strap. After the device was securely in place, I switched the machine on. At once it started making a whirring sound and, although Oliver did not open his eyes, his face scrunched up slightly in distress.

"Is he okay?" Jessica asked as he slowly started shaking his head back and forth, his eyes still shut.

"I think so." I observed the cerebral scrutinizer closely. "So long as the waves do not go into the danger zone he should be fine."

We waited in silence as the machine proceeded to remove the centaur world from Oliver's mind. At least I hope that's what it was doing. But after a few minutes, when Oliver's brain activity hadn't changed, I started to worry.

"What is it? What's wrong?" Jessica asked when I started casting uneasy looks at her friend.

"I think I might have to increase the power," I said, looking back at the cerebral scrutinizer. "The device isn't getting enough juice."

"Is that safe?" Jessica's eyes were fixed intently on Oliver's face. He had the look of someone who could not wake from a bad dream.

"There's nothing safe about any of this," I said as I slowly turned up the dial. "But the onger the machine stays on, the more damage it will cause. If it's not getting the power it needs to operate, it will have to be left on longer, ultimately causing more damage."

As the power increased, Oliver started gritting his teeth. If he had been trapped in a bad dream before, now he was in a full blown nightmare.

"This will all be over soon," Jessica whispered, her hands on his shoulders.

"Uh, I'll be over here," Jason suddenly said, casting Oliver a nervous glance before hurrying out of sight.

"Tell me this is almost over!" Jessica was starting to look desperate.

"Just a little longer," I murmured, still watching the screen closely. "The centaur world has almost completely been removed." The instant Oliver's brain activity hit normal, I switched off the machine. As I did so what appeared to be a wave of energy rippled out around us.

"What was that?" Jessica asked as the wave ruffled her hair on its way by.

I scanned our surroundings. "I'm not sure, but whatever it was, it's gone now. Oliver's brain activity is back to normal, his vitals are stable. He should be fine."

Jessica opened her mouth to say something when Jason came hurrying back, his eyes wide. "You guys aren't going to believe this, but the weirdest thing just happened!"

"In case you were wondering, Oliver will be fine," Jessica informed him, not looking up as I removed the bicycle helmet.

"That's great," Jason said, glancing at him, but I don't think he heard a word she'd said. "I think we just went back in time!"

"What are you talking about?" Jessica asked, reluctantly tearing her eyes away from Oliver to give him a puzzled look.

"I know it sounds crazy, but when I was standing by the fence just now, this wave of white light passed by and everything beyond the power plant changed. The trees melted away and suddenly we were sitting in the middle of what looked like a swamp. It was filled with these weird plants that looked like they might have gone extinct a long time ago. Then a second later everything went back to normal as if nothing happened!"

"You're right, you do sound crazy," Jessica said, turning her attention back to Oliver who still appeared to be unconscious. "How long before he wakes up?"

"I don't know," I replied, putting everything back into my duffle bag. "It will take some time for him to fully recover."

"Come on guys, I'm serious!" Jason yelled, his eyes wide. "I'm telling you, something really weird just happened. I'm not making this up. I swear!"

"What you're describing is highly unlikely," I said, standing up and swinging my bag over my shoulder. "Although many races have dreamed about it, time travel has not yet been achieved. There must be hundreds of much more logical explanations for what you think you experienced."

"I'm not crazy," Jason insisted, sounding determined. "I know what I saw."

"Whether you're crazy or not, I think we have more pressing matters to think about," Jessica said, gesturing at Oliver. "I don't know if you noticed, but your friend just underwent a rather dangerous procedure, and we still don't know what the full effects of it are. For all we know, he could wake up not knowing who he is. I think you should spend a little more time worrying about Oliver and a little less thinking about what century we're in. Now I'd appreciate it if you gave me a hand getting him back to the car."

"I'm sorry," Jason muttered, seeing how upset Jessica was and the two of them sort of half carried, half dragged their friend back to the vehicle.

Once we were back at Jason's house and Oliver was once again on the couch, his head propped up on a pillow, everyone seemed to relax a little. Jessica knelt in front of the couch, Oliver's hand in hers, an affectionate look on her face. Jason was in the armchair, picking at some dirt under his fingernail and I sat by the arm of the couch, making sure there were no unusual changes to Oliver's brain activity.

"I was thinking," Jason suddenly said, after a few minutes of silence. "Shouldn't we have stayed at the power plant to make sure this device of yours worked before bringing Oliver here? What if he needs more work?"

"If things did not go according to all my careful calculations, we would have had to come back here anyway so I could fix my mistakes."

"So if this device does work, what are you going to call it?"

"I can't imagine how it might come to use on my home planet, but when naming an invention, there is a specific way one goes about it; the maker uses the device's power range, his or her initials, and age to title the invention. So I guess this gadget would be called the Mega MC 5,000."

"You're 5,000 years old?!" Jason looked thunderstruck. "Are you serious?"

I didn't respond. Caught off guard, I had divulged more than I should have. For a moment I forgot that humans only live a fraction of our lifespan. When I maintained my silence, the shock slipped from Jason's face, leaving him expressionless. For several seconds we stared at each other. At first not being able to sense human emotions was an intriguing oddity. Now it was annoying. The look in his eyes said something, I just wasn't sure what.

I was given this measly form to blend in, but these guys already knew that I wasn't of this world. The Spacing Program is very touchy about what undeveloped civilizations know about us. So far Oliver, Jason, and Jessica were handling my encounter pretty well. Granted, they knew very little about my people, but of what they have learned they accepted. If anything, keeping secrets was becoming the issue.

"Yes, I am 5,000 of your Earth years old. But on my home planet we do not measure our age in revolutions. Instead we use total eclipses. Interestingly one of these occur once every 365 days and our days are equal to yours. If we were to measure our age in revolutions, I would actually be 500 years old."

Jason looked perplexed. "How come you never mentioned this before?"

"It never came up."

"Seriously? That's your answer?"

"It's nothing. For my people I'm still very young." *Shoot!* He knew I was holding back. I couldn't delay any longer. Taking a deep breath and letting it out, I began to speak. "In my universe, we are known as the Vongarians. Over the ages we have built a powerful empire. Our territory includes the planet Vongar which is roughly the size of Jupiter. We don't have countries as you do here. Instead, Vongar is divided into nine regions. Each one represents one of nine orbiting moons, though their gravitational pull has been altered to match Vongar. Millennia ago, people found the change too disruptive; prolonged stays would result in muscle atrophy as well as other health problems. Equalizing the gravity led to people referring to these moons as sub-level planets. It also helped that one of the moons has moons of its own. Not including us, there are seventeen inhabited moons and planets in our solar system and many more scattered across our galaxy. It's nothing like here. Not only are you isolated on your planet, according to my observations, there doesn't appear to be any intelligent interaction between species. In my universe, that is not the case. We have continued contact with at least 100,000 different civilizations everyday. In Vongaria alone there are a multitude of high-functioning beings."

"Is that it?" Jason asked when I fell silent.

"That's as much as I can say."

"Can you at least clarify a few things?" Jessica asked. She had released Oliver's hand and was now giving me her full attention, her pupils dilated.

"That depends. What needs clarification?"

"You mentioned a solar system? I thought you said your universe didn't have stars."

"Not like here, no. I was simply using a term you would understand. We have massive balls of energy that provide us with light and heat. We call them light sources."

"Why do your people have control of so many planets?"

"Wars, mainly. We are currently in a state of harmony, but there have been many battles in our past."

Jason started to look uneasy. "So you do go around overthrowing other races?"

"Once upon a time, perhaps, but now we are a peace seeking people. It is our goal to achieve total tranquility. We're the ones who started the Consortium."

"The Consortium?"

"An organization dedicated to the protection and preservation of alien life. We help those who cannot help themselves."

"Do your people have a lot of enemies?" Jason suddenly asked.

"Excuse me?"

"Are there a lot of people out there who hate you?"

"You can't become the most powerful civilization in the galaxy without making a few enemies. And yes, there has been the occasional group who has tried to overthrow us, but, like I said, we are currently in a state of harmony. We haven't been to war in over two hundred thousands years."

"Really? Who with?"

I didn't respond for several seconds, causing Jason to raise an eyebrow. "Please don't miss-understand my hesitation. It is not to deceive you. There are things about my world I do not believe you are ready for."

"Let us be the judge of that."

"The truth we seek is not always the one we find."

Jason studied me for a moment. "Okay, fine. Riddle me this. How does anyone attempt to not only overthrow the most powerful nation in their galaxy, but also a civilization with your mental capabilities? Couldn't you guys just get in their heads? The invasion would be over before it began."

"We cannot commandeer the body of any living organism we choose. Some beings are impervious to our mind tricks."

"Like Jabba the Hutt."

"Who?"

"From *Star Wars*," Jason said, looking more at ease.

"Never mind that," Jessica said impatiently. "If your world is comprised of not just one, but several planets, how is it governed? How do you guys keep track of what's happening?"

"Each region has several leaders who oversee the activity in their area and their planet. As I'm sure you've noticed, we've pretty much mastered space travel so getting around is easy. But if there is any problem, everything is monitored by the High Court, which is comprised of one representative from each region and a judge."

"Who's the judge?" Jason asked.

"Does it matter?"

"Uh, no?"

Jessica looked uncharacteristically suspicious. "Why don't you want to tell us?"

"Because it's not important."

"Well, you've just made it important."

"It's my father," I blurted out. "My father is the judge."

Jason let out a sharp whistle. "So are you like royalty or something?"

"No," I stated flatly. "There are no kings or queens in Vongaria. The judge there operates pretty much the same way one does here."

"Is he the one who decides what happens when you are tried for all your crimes against humanity?" Jason inquired.

"Yes."

"You caught a break, man. Lucky you."

"Being his son does not give me any advantages," I snapped, my heart rate quickening. "I get the same treatment as everyone else. If brought to trial, I will get the exact same ruling as anyone else in my place."

"Sorry," Jason muttered, eyeing me uncertainly. "Didn't mean to offend."

Searching for an excuse to look away, I glanced at the cerebral scrutinizer only to realize that Oliver's eyes were open and that he'd been silently watching us.

"Are you okay?" I asked, coming around to the front of the couch, grateful for a reason to terminate the conversation. When he didn't answer, Jessica leaned over, the all-too-familiar look of worry in her eyes.

"What's going on? Why isn't he saying anything?"

"Maybe the Mega MC 5,000 turned him into a vegetable," Jason suggested, getting up so he too could stare into their friend's expressionless face.

"A vegetable?" His terminology was perplexing. I was fairly certain he wasn't using the word in its literal sense.

"He's probably brain dead." Jason clarified.

"His brain is not dead," I said, holding up a finger and slowly moving it back and forth. "See, his eyes are responding to visual stimuli."

"So?" Jason grunted as Oliver's eyes continued to follow my index finger. "If he can't move or speak, what difference does it make?"

What was going on? According to my machines, Oliver had not suffered any complications during the procedure. It was highly doubtful he was 'brain dead' as Jason put it. Still, I was stumped. There was no reason he should be experiencing any kind of paralysis. It didn't make any sense. I could only hope that whatever was happening would resolve itself quickly. The crew would be returning soon. I didn't want there to be any evidence that I'd had direct contract with the humans. My future depended on it.

Chapter 27

OLIVER

When Corpus and my friends vanished, I waited until I could see King Mytus and his men through the trees before making a mad dash for the cave. It was roughly thirty feet away. I had plenty of time... or so I thought. I was only half way across the grass when the king breached the clearing. When his hooves thundered to a halt, I looked over my shoulder. He was watching me, his face twisted in bewilderment. It was only then that I remembered I no longer looked like Quaymius. Not sure what to do, I slowed to a stop. Without the king's pursuit, the cave wouldn't open. Behind him Kobalt, Arsenic, Almaeon, Norus, Clydon, and the youngest of the guards all came to a stop. For a several seconds the seven of them stood there, looking me up and down, clearly not sure what I was. Then a look of realization came across King Mytus's face.

"Human!" he declared, his eyes wide. Rearing slightly, he lunged forward, a look of determination on his face. Pivoting on the spot, I took off running, now an equal distance between both the king and the cave. My heart pounded like a hammer as the lord of centaurs closed in on me. Just when I thought I could feel his breath on the back of my neck, I slipped through the entrance. I wasn't sure what to expect. Only a few feet in everything suddenly went black. Seconds later, I found myself in Jason's bedroom. Relief filled my chest, unfortunately, it didn't last long. Very quickly I started feeling lightheaded. The room was spinning and there was nothing I could do about it. I remember hearing voices, but I couldn't understand them. Everything was moving too fast. Before I could process what was happening I was plunged back into darkness. What was happening? Was I being dragged back to the centaur world?

After what could have been minutes or hours things gradually slid into focus. I expected to wake up back in the Brambee Forest, but instead I was lying on the couch in Jason's living room and he, Jessica, and Corpus were talking about something called Vongar. How much time had passed? Listening closely, I quickly realized there was something off about their voices. I was only lying a foot or two away, but they sounded distant. I tried to say something, but I couldn't open my mouth. In fact, I couldn't move any part of my body!

186

The only thing that still functioned were my eyes. Panic instantly set in. Over and over again tried to say something, move anything, but I couldn't. I was trapped! All I could do was lie here and hope that someone noticed. After what felt like forever, Corpus turned to look at he cerebral scrutinizer and caught my eye.

"Are you okay?" he asked, but since I couldn't move, all I could do was stare at him and hope he realized something was wrong.

"What's going on?" Jessica asked, also leaning in to look at me. "Why isn't he saying nything?"

"Maybe the Mega MC 5,000 turned him into a vegetable," Jason said, appearing behind hem, his arms folded across his chest. His laid-back manner bothered me. How could they ll be so calm? Couldn't they see the terror in my eyes? Maybe not. As fear clouded my mind, heir voices became white noise. What if I was stuck like this forever? Could I live the rest of my life as a quadriplegic? In the midst of my internal melt down, I felt Jessica grip my hand. It was the only thing that rescued me from the brink. Her warm fingers cocooned my palm, reassuring me. Looking over, I saw that she was kneeling over me, her light blue eyes full of compassion. She could see passed the paralytic wall.

"Don't worry," she whispered, squeezing my hand encouragingly. "Everything's going to be okay."

"Are you sure you should be giving him false hope?" Jason asked.

"The hope I provide is never false."

"What the hell is—"

"Corpus?" Jessica said, overriding him. "Is this the same thing that happened to Jason nd I when we left the centaur world? Doesn't this mean his brain is still getting used to being in control?"

"That was different," Jason said, sounding impatient. "It was difficult to move. We weren't paralyzed."

"Paralyzed?!" Clearly that thought hadn't occurred to Jessica. Placing her free hand on ny chest, she leaned in so close our noses were practically touching. "Corpus, he isn't paralyzed, is he?"

"I don't know," he said, gently pushing her back a few inches. "According to the cerebral crutinizer, his brain activity is still normal. Hopefully whatever is wrong is only temporary."

"How can we know for sure?"

"Unfortunately in medicine there is no certitude."

"You guys are making this way more complicated than it has to be," Jason sighed, tarting to sound annoyed, then to me said. "Oliver, if you can understand us, blink twice."

"Thank god!" Jessica gasped when I blinked two times in rapid succession. "You had ne scared for a second."

"What? It's a good thing he's paralyzed?" Jason demanded, his left eyebrow skyrocketing.

"No, it's a good thing his mind isn't jumbled. Or something much worse."

"What's worse than being paralyzed?"

"Loads of things."

"Like?"

"Guys," Corpus intervened. "This really isn't the time."

"Will he be stuck like this forever?" Jason asked, voicing my fears.

"How can you even say that?" Jessica hissed. "Of course he won't... right?"

"It's very doubtful," the alien said. "But the real question is how long will it take for him to recover."

"Isn't there anything you can do to help?"

"Actually there is." Corpus pulled the IRD out of his duffle bag. "This should fix any major damage. But I can't guarantee it will have any immediate results seeing as we don't know the exact problem."

After running the beam of green light over my entire body a few times, Corpus put it back in his bag and sat back. "Now all we can do is wait."

About five minutes later I could move the fingers on my right hand. Seeing that my paralysis was starting to wear off, I tried to speak. "Is it over?" It took every ounce of energy just to make the words coherent.

"Yes," Jessica whispered comfortingly. "It's over."

"How long have I been out?"

"Thirty minutes."

"I mean how long since I exited the centaur world?"

"You came out about three hours ago," Jessica said, squeezing my hand, then she added somewhat casually. "Do you remember anything after entering the cave?"

"I wasn't unconscious?"

"No. You were pretty out of it, but you were awake."

"It's all a blur. Why? Did something happen?"

"No," Jessica replied shortly.

"Do you remember what happened before you entered the cave?" Jason asked, smiling as her cheeks turned pink.

"No," I lied, not sure what to say. I did remember the kiss. How could I forget? When our lips met, the most amazing feeling washed over me. It felt like a surge of electricity passed through me, charging every cell in my body. But before I could react, Jessica was gone, taking that incredible sensation with her. And as much as I enjoyed that moment, I wasn't sure what to think of it. Did she kiss me because she liked me, or was it just a spur of he moment thing? Unlike me, Jessica was always very outgoing. If she had been harboring feelings for me, surely she would have said something. And even if this was her way of doing that, I didn't know if I should do anything about it. I've never been very good at talking to people, much less girls. On the few occasions I've tried, I usually end up making a fool of myself. On the other hand, I could be over-thinking the whole thing. If that kiss was just a spur of the moment thing and it turned out Jessica didn't really like me, I didn't want to say something and end up embarrassing myself. I'd probably be better off forgetting the whole thing.

"There are a lot of blank spots," I said, trying to move my hand.

"Oh." Jason looked a little disappointed. "That's too bad."

After ten minutes, it was still very difficult to move, but I was able to get into a sitting position. During that time, Jason and Jessica continued to watch me closely. They didn't completely relax until, satisfied that I would be okay, Corpus put the cerebral scrutinizer back in his duffle bag.

"Now that you're alive and well," Jason said, sitting down in the armchair, "Perhaps you can shed some light on some of the events that took place before our escape from the king's dungeon."

"Yeah," Jessica joined in, sitting down on the couch beside me. "How is it that the old librarian knew who we were? That completely took me off guard."

"I don't know," I said thoughtfully. "I never mention our real names in any of my stories. That surprised me too."

"He said something about others who were also invested in ensuring Quaymius's escape."

"He might have been referring to the mermaids," I said thoughtfully.

"The mermaids?"

"Yeah. I didn't have any names in mind, but there are mermaids living undercover in the centaur kingdom, keeping an eye on the king and his operations. Usually the centaurs and mermaids don't take part in each other's affairs, but I guess, deciding that the king was going too far in his battle against Quaymius, they decided to intervene."

"But why now?"

I shrugged.

"So," Jason said, glancing casually at Jessica. "What did that old centaur mean when he said, 'she still loves you'?"

"What?"

"Right before we left the dungeon, he looked right at me and said verbatim, 'Oh and Jason, she still loves you.'"

"I don't know."

"Great!" he said, clapping his hands together with false enthusiasm. "Now that we've established just how little Oliver knows about the world he created, let's move on." He turned his attention to the alien. "There's something I gotta ask…. if you're game, that is."

"What exactly did you have in mind?" Corpus asked, eyeing Jason warily.

"Well, you seem moderately familiar with humans and life on this planet. I was hoping you could shed some light on the myths surrounding human abductions and aliens living among us."

"I'm sorry, what is the question?"

"Does that happen?"

"Does what happen?"

"Do people get abducted by aliens and are there aliens living among us?"

Corpus's muscles promptly relaxed. "In my universe, there are groups of beings who devote their entire existence to observing and studying species on other planets. But that is not my field of expertise. I do know, however, that there are organizations who try to monitor the activity of the slightly shadier civilizations. The ones who conduct unusual experiments on unsuspecting creatures. Sadly some of them do manage to slip through the cracks. I wouldn't be surprised if there are groups out there who are more familiar with your race. As for aliens living among you, I suppose that is also possible. Visiting foreign worlds and galaxies is popular where I come from. People like to experience new and different things. But like I said before, my people weren't even aware of your existence until a few days ago. I don't know if there are any alien species living among you, but given more time, I could definitely find out."

"Speaking of which," Jessica said as if she couldn't believe it hadn't occurred to her before. "How long are you staying?"

"The fleet should be back tonight," Corpus said, looking slightly nervous.

Jason shook his head. "Man, you must be freaking out."

The alien looked at him, but otherwise didn't respond. Silence followed. Jason was clearly reevaluating his comment. The alien was staring at the floor, his right pinky finger noticeably trembling. Meanwhile Jessica was practically bursting with questions that she was too afraid to ask. Finally, sitting hunched over, her shoulders caving inward, she spoke. "Earlier when you said 200,000 years did you mean eclipses or revolutions…? Just to clarify."

"Whenever possible, I will use terminology that you understand. We do measure our history in years, but for your sake I converted it to eclipses. In our world it would actually be 20,000 years."

Jason's brow furrowed. "Doesn't that get confusing?"

"Not really. I just multiply or divide by ten."

"I mean in your world. You said you're 5,000 eclipses old, but that you're also 500? I don't get it."

"That's because you're confusing our years with yours. From your perspective it's like years verses decades. Just like you, we have different means of keeping track of time. Traditionally, eclipses are used for age as well as recent events while years are applied to history and other long lasting episodes." Corpus paused for a moment. "One other thing. We don't say 'I am 5,000 eclipses old.' It's either 'I am 5,000' or 'I have witnessed 5,000 eclipses.'"

Jessica looked like she was about to say something, but the alien held up his hand. "Please, I've already said too much."

*   *   *

A few hours later, I was able to walk around without too much trouble. Jessica had stopped looking at me like I was made of glass and Jason was in the kitchen talking to his father. But the more we relaxed, the more tense Corpus became. It got to the point he just sat on the floor, staring out the window as the sun gradually made its descent toward the horizon.

"What exactly will they do?" Jessica inquired softly as the room began to dim.

The alien's pale blue eyes remained fixed on the sky. "If I am unable to provide a logical explanation for being in possession of Magnum Opus, I will be sent to the brig, where I will remain for the journey back. The moment we arrive, I will be reprimanded and taken to a detention center to await trial."

"Why not make a break for it?" Jason asked, appearing in the doorway. The heart to heart with his father appeared to have done him some good. "Don't let them bring you in."

"That is out of the question," Corpus said, glancing at him before returning his gaze to the window. "All prisoners are brought in by Mind-Control Masters. I could not escape even if I wanted to."

"How many years will you get?" I asked.

"It depends. Anywhere from fifty to a hundred."

"A hundred years!" Jason's jaw dropped. "Why so long?"

"Are you kidding?" Corpus gave him a bored look. "A hundred years is nothing to my people. I'm 5,000, remember? The real punishment will be when they take away my navigation license."

Jason held up a hand. "You talking your years or ours?"

"Yours."

"That's not too bad… for you."

"Jason," Jessica signed indignantly, then turning her attention to Corpus added, "There must be some way you can prove your innocence."

"Walmus-Marcus must have put it in my bag while I was in the captain's chambers.

That's the only logical explanation I have been able to come up with. The only problem is I have no idea how he gained access to the security room. I don't recall seeing any guards on the security level when passing by, but they keep the room locked at all times. And if an unauthorized person so much as asks to see a security key, they get thrown in the brig, no questions asked."

"I'm really sorry," Jessica said, shaking her head sadly. "If there was anything we could do to help…"

"Thank you, but there is not." Corpus slowly got to his feet as the sun disappeared beyond the horizon. "The less the crew knows about what happened here the better."

"Are you leaving now?" I asked, feeling a sudden wave of sadness.

"Yes," he said, picking up his duffle bag and swinging it over his shoulder. "It is a long walk out of town. I might as well get it over with."

"I could give you a ride," Jason offered, his hands in his pockets as he stared at the floor.

Corpus didn't respond immediately. Clearly he didn't think Jason was being serious, but seeing the look on his face, the alien smiled. "Thank you."

The trip out of town was in silence. Corpus stared intently out the passenger side window as if trying to commit everything to memory. Jason's traditionally relaxed posture was looking kind of stiff. Every few minutes he would cast the alien a thoughtful look before returning his gaze to the road. I could only guess what he was thinking. On the other hand, Jessica's face was like an open book, the tears in her eyes illustrating her grief. Personally, I was torn. After everything we'd been through, I definitely felt a connection to Corpus, but the circumstances were hardly ideal.

When we finally pulled into the park outside of town, Jason turned off the engine and the four of us climbed out. After retrieving his bag, the alien turned to face us. "I can walk the rest of the way from here." His gaze shifted to Jessica. By now her tears threatened to burst forth. "I am sorry my departure brings you pain."

"I'm just thankful to have met you."

"It was a privilege meeting you too, Jessica."

"Is there any chance we could see your spaceship?" Jason asked, coming around the front of his car to join the three of us.

"If only that were possible," Corpus said regretfully. "But I cannot risk the others finding out I made human contact. This is goodbye."

"Will we ever see you again?" Jessica crocked, her voice succumbing to grief.

"I do not know," the alien replied, empathy haunting his young face. "I will be lucky if I ever see the light of day again. This was supposed to be the last mission for several millennia."

"Well, if our paths ever do cross again, I hope it's under completely different circumstances," Jason said, his hands in his coat pockets. "This whole adventure was a little much for me."

"Yeah," I agreed. "My mind has been through enough to last a lifetime."

"Maybe this isn't the end," Jessica whispered, bending down and wrapping Corpus in a tight hug. "Maybe this is just the beginning."

After she released him, the alien cast us all one last look before turning and heading up the road. After everything that had happened in the last few days, it was weird watching him walk away, knowing that we might never see him again.